Sin and Zen

By S. W. Stribling

1

I walked into a bar. Two and a half minutes later, another guy walked in.

'What's that you're drinking?' the guy said.

'Life with a bit of juice.' I said. 'I try to start my day with both.'

'Smart,' he said, 'haven't seen you around here until this morning's formation, noticed you were a 2°REP anglophone.'

'Ah yeah,' I said pointing to where my name tag usually is, 'must be the clever name they gave me: Slater. Or as the French say it, 'Slaughter.''

'Murphy,' he said right before he put his newly arrived Carlsberg to his lips for the first sip of the day.

'Pleasure.'

'Likewise.'

It was beautiful out. It usually was in this little part of sunny Marseille called Malmousque, a place that both the rich French and poor, broken foreigners called home.

'Smoke?' I said.

'Yeah, go on.' He said. He grabbed the cigarette and hopped off his barstool. 'So what brought you to the Legion?' Murphy said as he lit up.

'Long story best told when drunk,' I said, 'but the short answer is boredom. You?'

'I think I always knew I wanted to join.' He said. 'Can't do much in the Irish

army and thought the Legion seemed like a
good idea.'
'Past tense,' I said. 'What did you
break to end up in Malmousque?'
'Back and foot. You?'
'Femur.' I said.
Another moment of silence as we let
the chilly sea breeze run through our short
shorts and broken bones.
'I met an English guy in Aubagne that
warned me about going to REP.' I said. 'He
broke his ankle on his first jump. I didn't
believe him, so I had to find out for
myself. I guess he was right.'
'Yep.' Murphy said. 'Lot of
anglophones in the REP. I was there for
four years before my accident, so I got a
few jumps in.'
I hadn't been so lucky. A veteran of
two armies, two countries and I ended up
injured off a training exercise.
'Lost the air to my chute,' I said,
'événement avec un autre parachutiste.'
'Same story.' He said.
'And it's supposed to be a one in a
thousand chance of happening?'
'Something like that.' He said.
'They're supposed to be switching over to
the bigger chutes next year. The ones you
Americans use over there. The regulars have
already switched over, but you know, we're
at the bottom of the list for new
equipment. Expendable is the way most of
the French see us.'
'Well, I guess I shouldn't complain,'
I said. 'I get paid to sit here in the sun

and drink and it's not even nine in the morning yet.'

'Yep,' Murphy said, 'Living the dream in the south of France.'

We dragged on our cigarettes while Murphy's last words lingered in our minds. Contemplating what we have lost and what we have gained in just a short time. Almost as quick as the fall that left us both in hospital beds and now hobbling around on crutches.

I always felt lucky when I stepped outside here. The white refracting light glistened off the small, choppy blue-green waves of the Mediterranean. The wind always present, but welcome in the late summer heat, blew gently over us and kept us cool while we sat in the morning sun. It really wasn't so bad here once you got past the normal nitpicking and *angoisse* any military gives you; the cleaning, the uniforms, the standing in formations three or four times a day for no apparent reason, and the sharing of rooms with people that always seem to be the most inconsiderate bastards you've ever met.

With two drags left, Murphy said, 'Have you met many other guys, yet?'

'In Malmousque?' I said. 'No. I made a few friends in Laveran while I was there. But I just got here yesterday evening.'

'Right.' Murphy said. 'Well, there are a few anglophones around; two South Africans, a few Englishmen, and a Kiwi. We usually grab a drink together in town from time to time. We will see off one of the

Safas who's deserting tomorrow. Probably
get shitfaced tonight and head to Paris
first thing in the morning.'
    'Why not?' I said. 'I've only seen
Paris by plane. I guess I should probably
go visit and see what's so fascinating.'
    'Beer?' He said.
    'Yeah, go on.'

#

    I can barely remember getting on the
train to Paris, and I can barely remember
seeing the young man off that was heading
home to South Africa. I definitely didn't
remember heading back to the pub afterward.
I remember meeting Murphy's girlfriend who
lives in Paris. Nisrine her name, a giant
of a woman. He had told me she was tall.
Everybody is tall to me. I'm five-six with
my shoes on. But she was fucking tall.
Sweet though, a gentle giant. Nothing like
the Amazonians you hear stories about with
spears, nets, and horses.
    Murphy and Niz were back at McBride's
for lunch and a pint. I was sitting across
from the girl I woke up next to at a quaint
little brasserie that probably looked like
something many Americans have paintings of
at home.
    We ordered a bottle of wine and I let
myself feel the sun soak into my skin.
There isn't a better way to drink than
sitting outside at a small table, cigarette
in hand, and a good-looking woman on the
other side.

'So…' she said, 'Tell me about yourself.' Luckily, she spoke English fluently. It makes me self-conscious being a small-town American when I see these Europeans have spent just as much time learning English as I have and most of them speak it better. Though, I'm sure it was my broken French coupled with an American accent that got me past the first drink with her last night.

'Tell me about yourself, pretend it's a date, the first, and we never had sex before you knew my name.' she said.

I wasn't sure I could remember her name now or if it just didn't register because I had never heard a name like it.

'A date, eh? Never been good at those.' I said. 'So profession and pastime questions?'

'Yea,' she said, 'cause I'm still not sold on you being a penguin trainer. Though it was pretty cute you trying to convince me of it last night.'

'No.' I said.

'No, you're not a penguin trainer, or no you won't tell me your life story?'

'Both.'

'Why not? Because I've already slept with you? You don't have to work for it anymore?'

'No,' I said, 'it's definitely not that. I'm sure you'll make me work for it again.'

'So, why not?' she said, 'You plan on walking away from here and never speaking again?'

'No,' I said. 'Not that either. After
this morning, I would like to see you a few
more times. I'm hoping it was good for you
last night.'

She smiled. 'Yea, all three and a half
times. I'm sure you even started to propose
to me. Albeit a half-assed attempt at
declaring your love and future plans with
me if I promise to see you again.'

'Damn,' I said. 'That bad, eh? Well, I
guess I better confess that it's been a
while since I've been with a woman until
last night. Congratulations on being the
first French one, and the first one this
year.'

It's September.

'I'm honored.' she said, 'So who are
you?'

'I don't know. Somebody new.'

'Ah-ha, with me?' she said. 'Why me?'
She paused for a moment and stared at me,
looking for an answer, or just waiting for
one. 'You let your guard down with me. I
left you feeling… Comfortable? Vulnerable?
Accepted?'

'Jesus. You always analyze guys like
this on the first date?'

'Only interesting ones.'

So I told her my story, briefly. She
told me hers. We were as equally impressed
as we were different. A few times I
repeated a few things that I had said the
night before and couldn't remember telling
her. She was a sweet girl; fed me and made
sure I never had an empty glass. A rare
quality I would come to appreciate in my

future time in this country. And then she
wanted to pay for it all herself, a quality
I appreciate about French women that is
rare back home. I really tried not to let
her pay the whole bill, but she wouldn't
have any of my hard-earned cash. I'm not
sure if she felt sorry for me as the
shaved-head, crippled monkey that I was or
if she really found something entertaining
about my company.

'Are you staying in Paris again
tonight?'

'If you'll have me.' I said.

'Of course,' she said. 'Though this
time we'll try to spend a little more time
together before you stick your hand between
my legs, okay?'

'No promises, but I'll try.'

'I know you took a shower earlier, but
do you have any clean clothes? You got a
beer stain on that shirt and those socks
look like something you pulled out of your
military sack.'

'Well, I wasn't sure how long I'd be
staying and these are the only civvies I
have. So you knew last night I was in the
military?'

'Well, I'm not an idiot. Between you
and your friend, you didn't look like much
else. Besides, the shaved head and heavy
drinking kind of helped.'

'So you have a thing for military
guys?'

'Not at all. But you seemed innocent.
You have nice eyes.'

'Innocent enough, I suppose, but

probably not as much as you think.' I said.

'*Ecoute*, I got two hours before I have to go to work. I'll take you shopping for a shirt and some socks, and if we have time, we can go back to mine before I have to leave.'

'You're sweet.'

She smiled.

We left the brasserie and walked around one of the main shopping streets. I think she had more fun dressing me than I did. Being in one of the fashion capitals of the world, I was sure anything would have left me better dressed than the top of the line Wal-Mart clothing that I was wearing back in Arkansas. I would probably even get gay-bashed for looking this stylish. I'd have to keep an old shirt and ball cap lying around just in case I ever went back home.

So I let her lead me along and do the shopping. She found me some clothes that got her more excited about me than she had been the previous night. So we made the time to swing by her place and see what they looked like on the floor. I then walked her to work and was getting ready for the kiss goodbye and to find my way back; back to wherever I was before to grab a drink and see how Murphy's night ended.

'Have fun at work.' I said.

'Wait,' she said, 'Shouldn't you take my number, first?'

'Well, I was planning to play Marco Polo, but if you insist.'

I gave her my phone and let her put it

in. I still couldn't remember her name.
Within five seconds she'd typed in the
number and her name and then call her phone
so she had mine.

'Voila,' she said. 'I'll call you
later.'

'Okie doke. See you later.'

A little kiss and I was off in the
general direction she pointed me in. Her
name was Margot, pronounced 'Mar-go',
without the 't' as is standard in the
French language.

#

Later that night, Margot came back and
joined the three of us for drinks. I went
home with her that night too. The next day
we met up back at the bar for lunch and a
few drinks. Then Murphy and I were on the
train back to Marseille. I kept in touch
with Margot, not the Facebook way, but we
texted each other a lot over the following
days. She really was a clever girl. I would
see her again two weeks later when she and
a friend would come down to visit, but
after that, we would slowly lose touch. She
would find herself a real boyfriend and I
would continue moving forward in a way that
I never had before in my life.

2

After Margot, I had gotten lucky a few more times, but nothing that ever really stuck. Not that the sex was bad; I just didn't seem to like the person the next morning as much as I did her body the night before.

Once was with a middle-aged woman who took good care of herself. An artist she was. Met her at the Vieux Port pub that I started to frequent. She took me and had her way with me after the first two glasses of wine and a block of cheese at her place. It was good. It was everywhere. There was once she even said, 'I'm not done with you yet.' We danced naked, literally. We climbed the sink. And whenever I would pass out either from exhaustion or booze, she would go down on me until the little man was singing. And whether I gave consent, she was already on top. She had some built-up pressure to release, and she kissed me as I imagined a lonely woman would.

She must have had a bedroom full of her abstract paintings. She slept on a mattress on the floor of her living room.

'Why don't you hang 'em up?' I asked.

'I hate them.'

Right. Art. I'm not cultured enough to understand. She complained a lot about how difficult it was to sell them. I thought that was obvious. I mean the only people that buy that shit are people with money to waste, right? How many of those are there

in relation to starving artists? But I
heard her woes. I wasn't an artist myself,
but she had spirit. A twisted one, but I
suppose it's better to lose your mind and
keep your spirit rather than to lose both
and become normal. I would've seen her
again, but the next morning when I was
trying to leave to get to base on time for
formation, she literally stood in front of
the door and wouldn't let me, not until I
promised I would call and see her again. So
I did. And I left. And I never called her
again. I even avoided the pub for the next
few nights just in case she came looking
for me.

#

One day in the fall, I got chatty with
a girl on the metro leaving the hospital
where I do my physical therapy. She was
Italian-Spanish-French. I'm not sure how
you divide that up, but she was dark-
complected and seemed more proud of her
out-of-country heritage than her live-in
country one. We were getting off at the
same stop and so I asked her if she'd like
to have a drink. She seemed hesitant, so I
showed indifference and then she said sure.
We had a few drinks and then went for a
walk around the port. Not too much of one,
she felt sorry for me with my crutches. But
far enough away from the noise and onto a
bench overlooking the boats. It was nice.
We talked, and I tried to understand what
she was saying as I was thinking about how

to kiss her. Confidence not being high to
make a smooth move I went for pity, 'Have
you ever kissed an American before?... Do
you want to?' It's sleazy, but it worked
with my timid boyish charm.

Eventually, it was late, past ten in
the evening, and there were no more buses
to take me back to base. With crutches,
it's an hour and fifteen-minute walk from
the wrong side of the harbor. I played my
sympathy card again, and she said I could
stay with her, but that we weren't going to
have sex. In all genuineness, I said okay.
At hers we watched a movie, cuddled, made
out and went to bed. The bed led to touchy-
feely, rubbing, and eventually me in her
mouth.

I was pleasantly surprised and
enjoying it, but I can rarely finish that
way. It's not that I don't enjoy getting
head. I can just never seem to get past the
idea of cumming in a girl's mouth. It
seemed pretty fucking disgusting and
disrespectful, even in a giving sense. She
must have noticed that I didn't finish that
easily because she gave it a good go and it
was one of the best I've ever had. No doubt
if I had put my mind to it, I could've
finished, but the girl deserves some reward
for her efforts and I would not go down on
her. Not on a first date. She ran off,
handed me a glass of water and then threw a
handful of condoms on the bed. I was
thinking one round ought to do it; I was
pretty tired, but maybe I could make it
twice.

The first time I proved more mobile and flexible than I thought I could with my leg.

The second time I let her do the work. She mounted and showed me how lovely the southern European women looked with the dim streetlight creeping through the windows. It was exciting. I was enjoying this young woman.

Then, she slapped the shit out of me. I wasn't sure why, but it seemed to be a positive thing for her. It definitely put my percentage of finishing back down to zero. She slapped me again and started moaning. I wasn't sure if she was doing it for her pleasure or to take away mine. It fucking shocked me and I was back in the war just thinking about survival. The third time I tried to catch her arm. Eventually, I had to grab both arms and power through until I heard it was time to finish.

I slept.

I took a shower the next morning. Kissed her and left. I responded to her text out of courtesy for two days then fell off the map. She'll find somebody better for her.

#

It was the winter holidays now, and I was walking with one crutch rather than two. I spent actual Christmas back in my original regiment in Calvi; the colonel wanted all his injured boys to be there for the holidays so he flew us in. I could have cared less, but it gave me a chance to grab all my stuff I had left behind. What was left of it after the scavengers had had their way. It was boring and left me feeling deprived of feminine affection so much that I ended up reconnecting and losing touch again with my ex-wife back in Virginia. I survived thanks again to the amount of alcohol they shoved in front of us.

#

Claudia was beautiful, intelligent, and cocky to the point it could be hostile. But she was mature and knew what she wanted and knew she could get it from whoever and whenever she wanted. However, she was polite and conservative when I had met her, even though I could see she had a hidden side. Ms. Claudia was like a schoolteacher you wanted to bang but intimidated you, calculated and indifferent to anybody else but herself, one woman taking on the world alone. So when she asked me to go out for New Year's Eve, I said yes.

It surprised me as there seemed to be no connection between us when we first met. I had only met her twice before, both times at dinner with Eeva, a mutual friend of ours. They were both neighbors and just down the street from where I was sleeping. Working as *fille-au-pairs* for two different French families. Taking care of the family and the house for a bed to sleep in and the opportunity to learn French.

At the time, I thought Eeva was introducing me to Claudia to 'pass the friend test.' As Eeva and I had been spending some intimate months together walking and talking but barely made it to a drunken kiss. Maybe it was the dog and pony show for her friend's approval, but apparently, I didn't pass, or Eeva just wasn't bold enough to take a chance with the likes of me. It wasn't long before that she finally admitted she still had a boyfriend back in Estonia, and I backed off after that. I had known since the day I met her she wasn't the girl to sleep around on her lover, even if he was thousands of miles away. And despite my faults, I'm not much of a home-wrecker and she seemed too good for me. But despite this revelation and split between our false connection, she still occasionally invited me out afterward and seemed to show interest in a very timid and endearing way, innocent and pure as the snow she was probably born in. And I continued to see her and have dinner with her because I enjoyed the female company. It was a hell of a lot better than sitting at a bar of testosterone that was always waiting for me at the Legion bar.

It had been a year since I had really been on the make despite being lucky from time to time at the bar and chasing a young girl that was unavailable and only seeking friendship. So on New Year's, I was nervous about my date or non-date. I wasn't the same young man when I used to think I woke up in the morning and pissed excellence. A

blessing and a curse to the opposite sex.
Even back then it was just an inflated ego
the army brainwashed me into believing. But
now I was broken, alone, and in an
unfamiliar world where the language was
alien, the culture made little sense, and I
left my confidence on the ground with the
rock that shattered my femur.

Claudia had a friend that came to pick
us up. I assumed it was her date, and I had
just become a third wheel, another point of
sympathy for me. Well, shit. It's a free
ride to a town outside of Marseille that I
hadn't visited yet and a chance to sit and
drink in a different hole.

I kept mostly quiet since she didn't
speak English and I didn't speak French or
Romanian. She spoke French fluently, or at
least well enough to piss on my French. She
would giggle and smile every time I would
say something, which wasn't much. I
expended all the vocabulary I knew just to
make the effort; her favorite word that she
teased me about all night was *brosse à
dents*.

The bar we went to wasn't so much a
bar as a student recreation center set up
like prom for a small town. And it seemed
to be primarily Asian in ethnicity. The
music was playing but nobody was dancing.
The drinks were there but not being drunk.
I was in New Year's Eve hell. Luckily the
drinks were cheap and I, therefore, headed
straight to the minibar to keep my buzz
going.

Claudia and her friend, Olivier,

walked in slowly as if absorbing the
overwhelming grandiosity of the place. I
was still unsure by the conversation in the
car if they were together or not and
therefore unsure of my role to play in the
night's events. They hadn't made any
physical contact yet but had been talking
friendly in the car ride over. I didn't
understand most of it and didn't pay
attention to the rest.

I had my drink by the time they
arrived at the bar and Olivier ordered a
drink for both of them. I sat there and
took a drink every time I tried to think of
something to say but couldn't. By the time
we sat down, I was on my third whiskey and
they still had their first punch.

We found some chairs near the music
and around the dancefloor. I was happy to
be sitting down as my leg kills me if I
stand on it for more than a few minutes.

Olivier kept chatting up Claudia, and
I could see a better picture of their
relationship. She would smile and talk, but
despite his best efforts, she wouldn't
budge. I could hear this and I didn't even
know what they were saying. Olivier was
sitting on the other side of Claudia from
me. All three of us knew that he wasn't
getting anywhere with Claudia, but he just
kept talking. And he talked, and he talked.
Thankfully, I couldn't hear him because the
stereo was too loud.

Eventually, he got up and asked her to
dance. There were a few Asians on the floor
at this point. Some 80s pop music bumping

that everybody knows but never said the
correct lyrics. She politely declined and
turned towards me. He looked over at me,
got all pissy and went to play pool with
some girls over at the table.

She tried talking to me, but not as
she had done before. She was more open and
warm now; it wasn't quite the gestapo she
had put me through at Eeva's dinner.
Unfortunately, we had already gone past my
level of French and I proved to be the
opposite of her French friend in talking
capacity.

We sat rather quiet, and I got up to
get us both a drink. She took a sip but
said she doesn't drink too much. I wasn't
sure if I liked her.

I got up to go see how Olivier was
doing with the young coeds. They were cute,
but almost annoyingly so. He seemed to have
a laugh and showed them a thing or two
about pool. I watched, and if they were
learning something, it wasn't about pool.
We chatted for a minute and he either
wasn't too interested in them or was
getting nowhere. He seemed to have given up
for the night. I looked over at the girls
and said a few hellos and made a few bad
jokes. They were young, too young. I'm only
a few years older, but they just felt
young. It must be the school mentality. I
left the student life behind when I was
seventeen. They were twenty and still
living it. At twenty-four I must be six or
seven post-school years older than them. No
thanks. I prefer them older and showing me

a thing or two.

I looked back over to the dance floor
and saw that Claudia had gotten up and
started dancing, moving around the middle
of the floor. A few guys tried to get
close, and she would keep them at arm's
length and then move on after a few
seconds. I watched her, and she would
glance over at me watching her.

She waved me in. And I just pointed to
my drink in one hand and crutch in the
other. But she had a gaze. Eyes that seemed
dangerous like a wild animal staring at you
from a forest fire. She was daring me to
come over and dance with her. I probably
looked excited and confused. Why I thought
is it scary to come closer, I couldn't
really tell you. To touch her? Talk to her?
Bring her a drink like a good little boy?
Or just to make the other guys jealous? She
looked at me as if it scared me. Maybe it
did. So like the abandoned house at the end
of the street your friends dare you to go
into, I did.

She danced. I tried. We were closer
than an arm's length. I leaned in for a
kiss and she leaned in to put her forehead
against mine and gracefully avoided the
kiss. We danced like that until the end of
the song. Then we danced again.

We talked a little, and I tried being
flirty. My spirit was up and for the first
time in a long time, I really felt alive
with a woman.

We didn't stay too long at the *soirée*
and my midnight kiss was nothing more than

the French bisous which I shared with every
girl within stepping distance.

#

Olivier dropped us off where he had
picked us up on la corniche John F.
Kennedy. It was a small walk to Claudia's
house from there. I was buzzing but not
drunk, so when I walked her to the door, I
said goodnight there and walked off back
towards mine.

It was chilly and misty out, but I
didn't walk home. I could hear the waves
crashing against the rocks down the street
from Claudia's and just before the turn to
mine. I sat down over a ledge and let my
feet hang over the twenty-meter drop to the
water. I wanted to kiss her and now it was
driving me insane that I hadn't tried
harder.

I sat there for twenty minutes until
the cold finally forced me to act. I texted
her asking if she would like to go grab
another drink.

She said no.

I sat there for a few more minutes to
allow my defeat to settle in before I went
home to sleep and start a new day.

'I don't want to go out, but you can
come over.' she texted.

I replied okay and started to feel
warm again.

I limped as fast as I could over there
and sounded her buzzer. I walked up the
stairs past the garage and towards the

house itself. She opened up, smiled, and let me in.

I was wetter than I had thought and took off my shoes and jacket at the door.

She had been watching a movie and so we settled on the couch and continued it. I was braver now. I was in the lion's den and here to act or be eaten. I played my role as smoothly as possible to get closer to her.

Before I made it too obvious, she helped me out and quickly found her place under my arm and her head against my chest. With the momentum in my favor, I lifted her chin and kissed her.

She kissed back and then pulled back.

We watched a few more minutes of the movie.

I tried again. This time it was more than a kiss. She pushed her tongue into my mouth and wrapped her leg around mine, moving it up and down between my legs. It didn't take long for her to have something to rub up against. I had my hands everywhere. The back of her neck, under her shirt, my fingers sliding across the top of her ass and down her crack.

She put her hand down my pants and started rubbing me off. I tried arranging myself to do the same for her when she said, 'I can't.'

Fuck. Too soon, I thought.

'I've got my period.'

'Ah. Okay....' I said.

'You can sleep here though.'

It was the holidays so no formation

the next morning, not that I would have cared at this point. She wanted me to stay. Even if we didn't have sex, I may get a handjob out of it. As unfair to her as that might be.

Then the liquor started talking.

'You know it doesn't bother me.' I said, 'We could take a 'shower.''

She just kind of smiled and didn't reply.

After the movie, I followed her downstairs to the little hole she called a bedroom. It was barely a single bed, smaller I think than the bed I had back at the barracks. Luckily, she was fifteen kilos less than I was and I barely weighed sixty kilos now after my injury. We would fit.

I got undressed, and she headed towards the bathroom that's just right across the hall. Laying down, I thought about how foreign and exciting it is to lie in somebody else's sleeping place. The feel of their sheets and the smell of their pillow. Just how comfortable it is, despite not being your own. Maybe part of that comfort was knowing I could leave.

I could hear her spitting as she finished brushing her teeth with her *brosse à dents*.

'Are you coming or what?' she said.

What the fuck would I be coming for? Then I realized she was in the bathroom.

'Yep.' I said and hopped out of bed and into the bathroom without a thought to my crutch, only my crotch.

I saw her standing up in the tub, naked. She was skinny, not skeleton-like or anorexic; she had the body of a model. Everything directly proportional to her size. Perfectly shaped breasts that only seemed to exist on sculptures. I thought small tits must be a blessing as you get older because they still look so young. She was thirty then, but I bet they didn't look much different when she was twenty, and probably wouldn't change much when she was forty.

I stepped in and had a hard-on by the time the second foot touched the bottom of the tub. We started kissing again. My hands on her ass, hers on my little soldier, using a nice twisting motion that sent my body shivering.

'*Assieds-toi*' she said.

I sat.

She climbed on top of me. Just the tip, then a little more, and then she slid me halfway into her. She was definitely on her period. Up again and back down, this time all the way. Slowly then quickly. Rocking back and forth, then back to up and down. This was good and I may have just found somebody to see more than once. I've got to hold out. I've got to last.

And I did.

I came inside with no thought but 'I did it'. Like a boy who just hit his first home run. It wasn't my first time; it wasn't my best time. But my blood-stained cock was my weapon of choice in this murder. This stabbing that led me straight

through her body to her soul. I was the
prey who had become the predator. I had
won.

She laid her sweaty chest against mine
and I could feel her heavy breathing. She
kissed me just above my left nipple. Then
kissed me a few more times in rapid-fire
succession all over my chest. She laid her
head back down. I was still inside of her
at the bottom of that bathtub. A tub
without water. Just us. I put my hand on
her head and lightly caressed the back of
her neck where the hairline started.

We both had won.

3

The first week Claudia and I spent together, she always told me that 'this was the last time.' I said okay and thought 'this was just this time.' Why spell it out? Why limit it? After that first week though, she gave up on telling me and without words admitted she enjoyed my company too.

About a month later, we were having a get-together at her place. The parents were out-of-town, so she invited some of her Romanian friends, Eeva, and a few other fille-au-pairs she knew from her French class. We had a good time and since supposedly nobody knew that her and I were sleeping together, so we kept to ourselves, drank, and had a good time until it was bedtime.

When things started to wind down, I pretended to leave and went to her room to wait. She told her goodbyes to some and gave blankets to those who crashed. One of those who stayed was a friend of hers from when she first moved here. A Romanian guy who helped new arrivals, particularly girls, find their way around Marseille and get settled. Claudia had been one of those girls. I guess they slept together a few times in the first few weeks after she arrived. He got attached, and she said get over it. That was months ago, but the guy was obviously still in love with her.

Claudia came to bed, and we started

doing what we had been doing all month. She was flexible, and I had her above me in a back to stomach fashion, only her arms were outstretched, so it was more like her holding a crab walking position over me.

She was a squirter and after it happened the first time, it usually happened again two or three more times within the following minutes. It was amazing and messy. Sometimes it was like fucking a glass of water, but sticky and kind of smelled like piss.

I was taking my time. I was enjoying watching her shake as I held her up and held her together when her friend walked in.

'Claudia,' Vasile said. He opened the door and saw his Romanian sweetheart being pounded by some American douchebag. Poor bastard.

She moaned.

He was drunk and emotional and ran out of the room crying. I like the idea of crying sometimes too, but Jesus, man, you're thirty-six years old and you barely know the girl. I still felt sorry for him though.

'It's okay,' Claudia said. 'Just finish.'

So I did.

'What the fuck was that about?' I asked. Referring to the interruption by a crying, middle-aged man.

'Uff.'

'Should you go talk to him?' I asked.

'Yeah,' she said, 'He and I used to be

together. It was a few months after I had
arrived and he was always helping me out
with papers and stuff. I slept with him
once one weekend. Just sex. I thought he
understood, and so sometimes after a party
on the weekend, I would stay with him. He
was nice.'

'Damn.'

'But after about a month he told me he
loved me.' she said. 'I told him it wasn't
like that. That I had a boyfriend I loved
and that I only wanted sex.'

I had just found out she had a
boyfriend, too. When the question came up
on feelings, I told her it was just a good
time. She saw me every night, not just on
weekends. This could be because of
proximity convenience.

'I think you should go talk to him.' I
said.

'Yeah,' she said.

She got up and put on some clothes.

'You aren't going to fuck him though,
are you?'

She gave me a quick laugh and look.
'No.'

She disappeared for a good hour; it
felt like four. I stayed up. I couldn't
sleep as I was waiting to hear fucking
noises.

Eventually, she came back in the room,
tense and frustrated. Well, if she fucked
him, I doubt she'll do it again.

She told me a bit, but not the whole
thing about what had transpired. He was
still madly in love with her and wanted her

back despite the infidel American semen
inside of her. She reiterated that she
never saw him as more than a friend. And I
imagined that five-minute conversation with
a person in love and that drunk going in
loops for a very long time.
 I still felt bad for the guy and told
her she should stay and sleep with him
tonight. She just looked at me as if I was
crazy and I said, 'Okay, let's just go to
sleep.'

#

 The next few days the shit hit the
fan. Eeva was asking me if I thought it was
right how Claudia was treating me and
Vasile and her boyfriend. Eeva then
confessed she had feelings for me and
Claudia had known. That in fact, it was a
dog and pony show those nights ago before
Christmas. That she can't believe her 'best
friend' from here could fuck me in the one
week she went home to visit for the
holidays. Claudia politely told her to fuck
off.
 Even more so my overly intrusive South
African friend, the great Mr. Easterhouse,
forced his way into the middle and
confronted her as well about what her
intentions were with me. She impolitely
told him to fuck off.
 All these people fighting over my
well-being and interest, I felt so loved,
so special, almost a charity case.
 Claudia ended things with me there. I

said fuck off to everybody.

4

A girl I had met in Lyon was having a birthday party and invited me to come up. I had met her on a drinking weekend playing pub quiz when I came to visit the previous fall. She was English and taught English to Chinese people over the Internet. She was fun to talk to, and she liked a lot of the same things I did. I also loved hearing her rap 'Gangster's Paradise' with her thick southern English accent.

So I said I'd go if I could bring a friend and stay at her place. She said sure. I think she thought we were becoming something. We weren't. And I hoped that Murphy might cock block us over the weekend. We had slept together before, but it didn't leave me excited enough to want to do it again. The first time I understood why it was dull: she said it had been a while. The second time just felt like a burden. Also, Claudia and I kissed and made up the day after she broke us up. Though, we still weren't 'together.' Despite not being officially an item though, I still didn't feel right about sleeping around and it made a good excuse for why I couldn't sleep with Louise while we were there.

The food she cooked was lacking any flavor and I'm not sure if the stomach was the way to a man's heart, but it was definitely important to have something to eat in the house. She was sensitive physically in every way. In bed, it had to

be slow, and it almost seemed painful for
her. With food, she could only eat raw
vegetables. Or cooked. Something strange
like that.

But she was a great laugh and easy to
get along with. I just wouldn't marry the
girl.

Murphy jumped on board to the idea. He
had family friends in Lyon due for a visit
and we never needed a reason to go piss it
up somewhere new.

#

The weekend in Lyon was brilliant.
Murphy and I stayed in a drunken stupor the
entire weekend. We made friends, we
laughed, and I got behind a bar and served
drinks. The girl behind the bar, and owner
of the place, was patient with me trying to
give free bottles of whiskey away and even
let me play the music.

Photos of shitfaced grins were taken,
and I learned to really love the magic of
booze. Friends, girls, and an absence of
thought to the rest of the world.

We went as visitors; we left as
conquerors. I bet my green Legionnaire
beret is still hanging up behind that bar.

#

My phone had died after the first day
I was there. We were supposed to stay just
for the weekend but ended up staying until
Thursday. Alcohol, it frees you of all

sense of time and responsibility.

I charged my phone and noticed I had a few missed text, calls, and emails, mostly from Claudia. The email was serious.

'I think we should stop seeing each other.' She wasn't much for words. She wrote it in English though. She'd been speaking to me in English since I found out that she could, or at least some variation of French and English known as Franglais.

In my mind, I was thinking 'Jesus, what now? We aren't together but you want to stop fucking each other. Is there another? Are you bored?' Maybe she's just falling in love and wants to stop before she does. I thought I was, but if she asked I would lie.

I texted her and asked if we could talk about it in person. I'm not much of a phone person.

She said no, but after a few convincing words, she agreed.

#

I met her later that night after she had put Léa and Emma, the two little girls she was au-pairing, to bed. The parents were still home and awake so I couldn't go in, even though they lived on the second and third floors of the house. Claudia lived on the 1st floor where the guest room and pool storage was. They didn't know I existed yet and Claudia didn't want them to. I really didn't either. So I just met her outside at the gate.

We talked. She stood her ground.

'So, why this sudden change?' I asked.

'I don't know. I was just thinking while you were away.' she said, 'This has been going on for a while now, it's been great, but I just don't want it to get confusing for you.'

I knew this was about her too. She was in a committed relationship with a man back home. A rock star of sorts. They had some understanding that when they were together; they were together. When they were apart; they could sleep around. Too mature for me to understand, but it seemed to work for them. Either that, or she didn't think she had a choice. I knew she liked me. I had seen it on rare occasions when the walls were down and her eyes said, 'Hold me.' I wanted to tell her she was the kind of woman that needed a good lover. That she shouldn't hide from her feelings.

'I won't fall for you.' I said.

'I don't know. I've been thinking about this for a while, actually. I mean to do it every week.'

'Yeah, but every week you call me to come over.'

'I know.'

'The day I tell you I love you, you have all permission to leave me and say 'I told you so.''

'You say that now.' she said.

I knew this would not work out between us. I knew that the day I woke up, fucked her, and then she pulled out her computer to Skype her boyfriend. I told myself every

week that I should end this too. But it was
good. We were good. And I wanted it to last
as long as possible. I wanted to know that
I got to her the way she was getting to me.
Valentine's day was around the corner and I
was telling myself not to do anything
stupid.

#

The week leading up to Valentine's
Day, I was so full of charm and romantic
thoughts. I planned to shower her with them
and expect nothing in return.
The family was away yet again and so
we had the house to ourselves for a long
weekend. I made her something to eat with
candles and soft music. I have always
enjoyed cooking. Especially for someone
else. She hated cooking and did the bare
minimum for survival it seemed, so she
enjoyed watching me work.
She showed me around the house as the
meal cooked and we looked at the family
pictures on the walls and end tables. They
looked happy.
'So, are they really that happy?' I
said.
'They are,' she said, 'but separately
most of the time.'
I laughed.
'I heard them arguing once over me.'
She said.
'Because you're a young, attractive
woman living in the same house.'
'Yeah.'

'Has he ever tried anything?'
'No.' She said. 'Not really.'
That disappointed me.

'Well,' she said, 'he seems to
purposely take a shower when I am here and
his wife isn't and struts around in just a
towel until I see him.'

Then I laughed again, imagining the
man in the picture doing just that. He
wasn't ugly, but his wife was definitely
better looking than him. French men. Every
woman thinks they are the most romantic
breed of man and the French men even
believe it themselves. I wonder why all
these French women are running to me and my
foreign friends if they are. Stereotypes
are usually disappoints I thought. That and
having such expectations is usually a
recipe for disappointment. A double-edged
sword. It cuts both ways.

We did our Valentine's dinner, and we
did it all with a laugh. Poking fun at
Valentine's, but secretly enjoying it. She
accepted it and just her smile was more
than the reward I was looking for.

We later made love around the house -
in the kitchen, on the sofa, even on the
balcony overlooking the pool below. There
was romantic music playing in the
background, and we pretended we were really
a couple in love.

The whole weekend was full of little
surprises to follow it up. Chocolates.
Flowers. All the shit I hand never done
before; I was doing it now. I didn't know
why, really. It wasn't me. And it was

cheesy and probably disgusting to anybody
watching from the outside, and after a few
days, I pulled myself together and told
myself to cut it out before she saw the
truth behind my playful romantic gestures
and ran away.

It wasn't me to be like that. And it
wasn't her to accept it like that. But we
did, and it made sense and it made us
happy, at least for a moment.

The weekend ended, and I didn't stop
the cheesy storybook romance I pushed on to
our 'just friends' relationship. I had
figured she deserved to be treated special.
For a month and a half, I had been laying
her down, most of the time coming home to
her drunk, and she would always take me in.
So I felt she deserved more than just a
special Valentine's. I had made it sexy. I
had made it sweet. But I also told her I
had feelings for her. Then I told her I
needed space, or I'd fall in love.

It was another scholastic break for
the kids in France as it always seemed to
be, and when the kids don't school, the
parents don't work. I was not sure how
anything ever got done in this country. So
Claudia had the week off; she was going on
her own vacation for a week to visit a
family she stayed with before in Perpignan.
We decided it was a good thing.

5

Claudia left, and I was exhausted from it all. The week off from regular sex would allow me to screw my head back on. Only it didn't.

She thought she was pregnant.

Great.

Now, I was broken foreigner, knocking up a different foreigner. I was too young for this. I could barely take care of myself. What was I supposed to do? The only job I ever had as an adult was soldiering and continuing that career seemed less and less likely. I worked in a garage in high school. I also spent two years working at a Subway. I was more of a sandwich-thief than a sandwich-artist though.

But hell, maybe it would be a good thing for me. Sex hadn't made me feel like any more of a man. Neither had going to war. Both made me feel even more infantile. What would happen to me as a father? Is that what I needed to grow up? To take life seriously, you must create life? Or would another cliché step towards manhood bring me so far up my mother's uterus that I would just regress to the point I'd divide into two small microscopic puddles of my mother's egg and daddy's fastest swimmer?

I wasn't sure what would happen. It was an overload and the whole system of thoughts just crashed and broke me down. I would just mirror Claudia and hope for strength from her. Through her.

We talked every night on the phone. We hardly talked about the potential new life growing inside her. It was a relief. I had no idea about her passions before. Yeah, she was smart. She was ambitious. But I never really knew about her until these late-night talks. Talking was not something we did a lot of before.

She wanted to get into movies and more involved with all aspects of the big screen and small screen. She wanted to maintain her small puppet shows and one woman acts for kids. She introduced me to some music videos she acted in and the modeling she had done and gave me a lot of the behind-the-scenes information about that world.

She wanted to go back to school to get her masters in audio-visual. And do it in French at a French university, the *Aix-Marseille Université* in Aix-en-Provence. I couldn't even imagine surviving sitting in a classroom in my language. It was well beyond my capacity to do it in a foreign language.

And now, if she was pregnant, she was thinking of keeping the baby. She was already thirty and didn't know if she would have another chance. I was afraid. The hormones were obviously doing something to her. We were talking, and we never talked much before.

She said she would keep it herself and expected nothing from me, but her tone was loving. The only time I heard feelings like this before was after my trip to Lyon. She showed a few signs of jealousy at the thought of me sleeping with somebody else despite us not being together. And when my phone died and she couldn't contact me for three days, she showed real concern.

I knew she felt something but wouldn't show it. Once you say it, everything changes.

So I said it.

I wrote her a poem for her Romanian valentine, *Dragobete*. I enjoyed writing bad poems that I would send right away and then feel ashamed about a week later. In it, I dropped the dreaded 'L' word. She said she 'likes me very much and passing time with me.' I think that's the worst thing you can say about a man. If that's all you can say about him, then you may as well just be alone.

I guess I didn't have much choice now though; she was carrying my little vampire baby in her belly.

#

Claudia came back. She got her period. The world was back to normal. Though it wasn't. The scare and the late-night conversations changed her. Now she wanted me to sleep over after our rodeos and I would wake up to breakfast. Usually leftovers from the kids' dinner the night before. Still better than the chow hall on base.

It was usually fairly easy to sneak in at night. The front gate was a bit of a walk from the front door. And her room was

on the ground floor of the house right
beside the front door. It felt so excluded
from the rest of the house, not even a
picture up. Yet, we still always made sure
that I came after the parents were down and
left after a few hours before we fell
asleep.

Now, parents there or not, I would be
in her bed and leave early in the morning
before they got up. We made love, we
cuddled, and we slept together every night.
How fucking romantic.

I was losing myself and started
thinking like an idiot. Thinking about the
fact that she still had a boyfriend.
Thinking about what the fuck that meant for
me. He's back, I'm gone. Why do I care?

So, I stopped caring or tried to.

6

The days of spring rolled by smoothly. Claudia and I were no longer just seeing each other at night. We were hiking, going to parks, and spending time together with clothes on; drinking with the guys, BBQs, and we hadn't had one argument about love or relationships.

It was kind of nice. Talking on the metro or the bus as we went on one adventure to another. Exploring the city and the surrounding nature. I would speak to her in English; she would respond in French. The people would stare and we would just laugh.

After one of our days of visiting *Les Calanques,* we were back at her new place. She was still working for the same family, but she finally realized how strange it was to be a 30-year-old woman living with a family in a small little room for no pay and no privacy. I'd like to think her wanting to spend more time with me was part of the cause.

So she moved out and made arrangements to be paid for her work in money rather than living space. The *fille-au-pair* title got her foot in the door, now she was here and proved irreplaceable enough to be promoted to *la garde d'enfants*. The pay wasn't amazing but considering the work was just glorified babysitting a few hours in the afternoon; it was perfect for her. She could focus on her other things during the

day and make a little survival money in the
afternoon.

Given the difficulty of finding a
place to live in France without having a
traditional work contract with three times
the rent in wages that most people ask for,
nor did she have a co-signer of French
origin, she was quite limited on where she
could go. The French were racist I learned.
A very subtle, almost British covertness,
with their indirect discrimination. Or
maybe it wasn't racism, just a blinding
arrogance how much better they believe they
are than the rest of the world. As my
Belgian friend once told me, 'Comment un
Français se suicide-t-il?' How does a
French person commit suicide? 'Tirant dix
centimètres au-dessus de leur tête.' Aiming
four inches above their head.

So, she moved in with the middle-aged
crying man still in love with her. Well, he
was no longer in love with her by word, but
still fawning over her by action. I didn't
care; I knew she didn't like him and I
stayed with her most nights. Things were
tense between him and me, but never to the
point of open hostility. I'm sure Claudia
enjoyed it.

The apartment wasn't the nicest place
in the world, but it made staying with her
easier. Given I had to commute more than a
walk down the street to see her now though.

An idea of us hadn't come up for some
time until one evening I was laying there
naked in her bed watching her get up and
put on some pajama bottoms and a shirt. No

bra and nipples showing, she sat at her computer as if I wasn't there. Her Eastern European coldness was getting more normal for me.

She clicked and read, clicked and read. This email and that. And then I watched her face become somber. It was a face as if watching a terminal patient die.

Her boyfriend had just broken up with her.

It was a letter attached to an email. A letter to break up with her that was dated a year before and sent with an email to tell her he had written it a year before. What a winner. He couldn't break up with her in person when they were together, but wrote the letter, said 'see you soon,' then sent the letter a year later when she was far and away.

She opened up then; she told me they had barely even seen each other over the past three years, and that she knew it was over the last time they had seen each other. She talked about how she had fallen in love with him. They had met through mutual friends. She hated him in the beginning and then that hate turned to attraction and later, love.

They were all part of the same artistic circle in their little Romanian city near Hungary. He was a guitarist. A rockstar that was even part of a tour in Germany once. I was so impressed I wanted to vomit. If I hadn't been so happy to be finally connecting with her, I probably would have.

We cuddled for a while after that,
light caresses with soft fingertips was all
that was said.

I felt for her. She hid her pain well,
but I could feel the torment inside of her.
The death of something she truly loved. I
knew she would always love him and I knew
she would never love me that way. She may
love me one day, but never like she did
him.

I died a little inside too. But I held
her. Kissed her forehead and held her. This
was not my night to be selfish.

#

I woke up with Claudia. She had a
cheap mattress with no bed frame or box
springs. It was sleeping on comfortable
ground. It was June, and she lived next to
the top floor of her apartment building. It
had a view, and it had the effect of a
sauna. We slept with just a sheet, and
barely that sometimes.

She was being the sweet girl she had
grown to become with me, kissing me,
nuzzling me, and occasionally popping
pimples that popped up on my forehead from
time to time. She loved it. It was our
little thing. One of those odd things you
think about once you lose somebody.

'Ew,' she said, 'Got one.'

She put her fingers in place; I could
feel the sting already. She would look me
in the eyes, make a grimace as if she was
the one in pain and then push and pull the

skin until I could feel the fucker pop. It seemed to hurt worse when somebody else did it, but she would always give me a kiss afterward and I rarely kissed myself after popping a pimple so it was worth it.

'I saw you changed your relationship status to 'it's complicated.'' I said

'Yea, but I think I will delete it. People keep asking me questions now.' She said.

'Well, isn't that why anybody puts anything on Facebook?'

Silence. She never admits when I'm right.

'Not that I care about Facebook, but why change it now?' It had been a few months since the letter from her ex and she had never changed her status. I also noticed she put up a song called 'Stupid boy.' I knew that one was about me. She always called me 'boy'.

She didn't respond.

I also noticed she wrote her status to say she needed time and space.

'Do you love me?' I asked.

She pretended to not hear me and kept looking for new pimples.

I looked away; I had woken up perturbed.

'You asked me that last night.' she said.

'Did I?'

'Yeah, you don't remember.'

'What did you say?'

'I said no.'

We were silent for a minute, then I

got up. I put on some pants and went to go
grab a bowl of cereal.

I kept silent as I ate my cereal and
she sat across the table from me and
watched.

'We talked about this for over twenty
minutes last night.' she said.

I could tell she had been bothered or
upset about something, I just hadn't known
about what until now.

'You also asked me if I wanted to move
in together once you got out of the
Legion.'

I kept eating. Some of my newly opened
flesh wounds still burned.

'I had a dream about you last night.'
I said.

This time she was quiet.

'You moved on and left me for somebody
else. You didn't even seem to care.'

'That's not what I want right now.'
she said.

'I don't know. Sometimes I just don't
know if this is good for me.'

'I don't know if I'm good or bad for
you,' she said, 'but I want to be good for
you.'

I was too pissed off to have a real
discussion about it. The feeling of
betrayal and the pain of unrequited love
still lingered with me from my dream. I
would wait until I was drunk then let the
floodgates open to let her drown in it. It
was never on purpose to handle the
situation that way, but it became the way I
handled my emotions with her. I was strong

and silent while sober, angry and loud when
drunk, always feeling ashamed and guilty
afterward, always hoping she wouldn't
remind me of what I had said or done. I
never acted that way except with her.

I left in a passive-aggressive
silence, punishing her for not loving me
back, for attacking me in my subconscious.
I knew my dream was trying to warn me to
run from this girl. That she had the power
to destroy me just as quickly as she had
saved me. But it was just a dream. I would
walk it off and come back to have her and
the dream again that night.

She sent me a text ten minutes after I
had left saying she was in a 'don't trust
anybody' state. I wasn't sure if it was
because of her ex, or something else in her
past. I wished she would open up to me,
tell me why, tell me more than that. But I
felt she was afraid to lose me, that she
wanted me to understand her. I felt closer
to her. I didn't respond, but I did still
love her.

My clothes didn't smell too bad. I was
sure the guys would be up for a drink.

7

After 6 months of being together, I gave Claudia an ultimatum of committing to me or walking away from this guessing game of a relationship for good. I would have stuck it out as long as possible, but my friends thought the ultimatum was best for me and my happiness. I listened.

She didn't like the idea at first and was saying goodbye. She didn't understand the need to put labels on it. I didn't understand what was so bad about it. Everybody thought we were together until she corrected them. We did more than just fuck each other now. She was just as much a girlfriend as I thought a girlfriend should be. It felt sad even thinking this way. It felt pathetic saying it out loud.

She reluctantly agreed. She still kept the same ground rules as before, but now I could tell the world she was mine.

Nothing much changed really.

She still told me she didn't care if I slept around. Great. The perfect woman. And the whole idea bothered me. I've never met a woman who had said that. I wasn't sure if it meant she was sleeping around or planned to herself. It was that, or she really didn't care about me at all.

One drunken night I came home and confronted her about it. She said that when she's with somebody she doesn't need to sleep with anybody else. I didn't either, and so I didn't despite my free pass. 'As

long as you wear a condom with them' she
would say, 'And if you fall in love with
somebody else or it's somebody I know, then
I want you to tell me.'

This level of maturity was more than I
could handle. It drove me crazy not knowing
what she really meant by all this. A smart
man would've thanked the gods and enjoyed
his cake, but I wasn't smart. I was her
'Stupid boy'.

#

It was August now, and we were in
love. She finally said the three words I
had been fighting for since the beginning
of the year. It felt good. Damn good. I had
won. Shit.

I always found something to complain
about. Now it was with her living
situation. She was still living with the
same guy she used to sleep with. It drove
me crazy after months of staying at his
place, walking by his open bedroom door,
and looking at the bed she used to mount
him on. Then there were the Romanian
parties where the two of them acted like
old pals. I just wanted to scream out the
secret I knew between those two so
everybody would feel as uncomfortable as
me.

I was tired of the daily routine.
Every day, it was the tedium of military
life: cleaning, formations, and uniforms.
Everything I hated about the military and
nothing of what I like about it.

My physical therapy wasn't every day
now, and I needed something to fill my time
besides Claudia and drinking buddies. I
tried learning a few things like the guitar
and Linux. But like most things in life,
I'd be overly passionate about it in the
beginning, then burn out and set it down
for an indefinite period. I learned a few
songs in case I needed to be that douchebag
at a party. And I kept Linux as my
operating system but gave up on trying to
code.

So mostly I just felt like I was
rotting away in Malmousque and started
thinking about being medically discharged
from my broken dream of being a superhero
that fell from the sky to kill people as a
member of the infamous French Foreign
Legion. I had been thinking about it since
early spring. They discharged people once a
month, not including summer. Nothing
happened in summer in France and when I
talked about the idea with my *chef de
section*, he said three months wasn't enough
time to start the paperwork before summer.
I'd have to wait till fall.

My leg was getting better, but not at
the speed I was hoping. The doctors said I
would always have a limp, always be
limited, and that metal rod in my leg would
have to stay.

They asked me what was next for me.

I said I had no fucking idea.

They told me I would never be a
parachutist again, and with my leg, I would
never be in a combat company again or able

to do anything that involved heavy lifting or strenuous exercise.

Well, I didn't join the Legion to drive buses or sit at a desk, so I saw the door for my exit was opening if it hadn't only been cracked before.

Fortunately, I still had plenty of time to stew things over, even when kicking you out, paperwork holds everything up. The only thing that saves us from the bureaucracy is its inefficiency. I would still get a paycheck until fall, probably winter.

We drank wine and enjoyed the rest of summer.

8

I was officially released from duty in the second week of December. I took two bags of clothes and items to Claudia's and set up shop.

Claudia's dreams hadn't been going as well as she wanted. She didn't like school. She thought she was too good for it. She couldn't find work, at least acting work. She was still taking care of the same girls she came here to France to take care of. It was definitely a defeat for her, but not one she ever admitted to.

She seemed constantly stuck between wanting to improve in life somehow, but then thinking she was already better than everybody else. I wasn't sure how she pulled it off, but it was easy enough to ignore or laugh at internally.

I wasn't sure if she saw me moving in as a defeat. She had asked me to, but she also had that same conflicting aura about her that told me she may be constantly bouncing between the pros and cons in her mind about whether she liked the idea.

I saw an old lady selling stuff as I was walking to her place. She had a small wooden kitchen island on wheels for sale. I gave her a few euros, and she gave me the table. I gave her more than the table was worth and she thanked me for it by giving me a book in English she had found.

It was a pocketbook about etiquette from the late 19th century. I found it

charming and kept it in my inside jacket
pocket from then on. It would give me
something to read when sitting at the bar
alone. I could look around and be amazed
how far we've fallen from grace or at least
proper etiquette.

For Christmas, Claudia and I went to
visit the family she worked for in
Perpignan. It was an older man named Jean,
older than I had expected and his kids were
still kids, not quite in the double digits
of age. He joked about how people thought
he was their grandpa. I laughed too; it was
a good joke. He was a nice man though, and
his new internet wife was coming over from
Indochine. I think she was his third
internet-wife.

Jean's oldest daughter from his first
marriage, when he didn't need to order
women online, married rich. He was a
producer of music, and we spent Christmas
dinner with them. Christmas dinner in
France is on Christmas Eve. We opened gifts
there; I got drunk and played the piano
with the music producer.

Then he took over to play a lovely
song for his wife and we all listened.
Maybe it was the candles or the wine, but I
felt warm and fuzzy as he sang. In that
moment, I envied somebody else's life.

Afterward, we listened to his wife's
music. The warm and fuzzy turned to nausea.
I bet every woman this man has married or
loved has forced him into making an album.
When will he learn to keep business and sex
separate? *Laïcité.*

But the man seemed happy, and I had everybody calling him Porn Jesus by the end of the night because of his robe. It was a long, dirty white, and transparent. His junk was there for all to see and he didn't care. We drank, we smoked, and we ate lots of cheese.

9

A year had gone by and I still didn't know where Claudia and I were together. But I also didn't care as much anymore. It was comfortable and habitual. The idea of losing her didn't hurt as much as it used to.

I had to find something to do though as being jobless was not something I was used to. And I couldn't see myself living off my meager pension while playing the guitar and learning Linux.

I grew up with a Southern Protestant, hard-working attitude. Unfortunately, I was far from that. I felt lost on a deserted island of what to do. I had joined the service like any good Arkansas boy did, right out of high school. Now, I found myself with no pieces of paper that said I was smart, beautiful, or talented.

So, I did what most anglophones do in foreign countries when they can't do anything else.

I decided to teach English.

I found a school in Barcelona so I could get certified. Really, I just needed an excuse to go to Barcelona. Pinchos, sangria, and beautiful woman who weren't all taller than me.

I signed up for the class and left the same week.

I stayed with a local guy who rented out his room to me for the month. It was right in front of Park Güell - a beautiful place.

Barcelona was far from a disappoint itself. The people, the food, and the Sagrada Familia and other architecture felt right to me.

Barcelona was heaven. The cigarettes were cheap. The beer was cheaper. The drugs were stronger and more varied than what you could find in France. Cute girls on a terrasse or on *Las Ramblas* were always there to laugh at your accent and give you weed. I was never a smoker before, but even I did it every day there.

Unfortunately, my level of English was a disappointment. I did not understand how ignorant I was in my language. What the fuck had I learned after twelve years of school?

I became good friends with most of the class. We would work hard during the day and drink well at night.

There was an Irishman that nobody could understand but me. There was a monster of a Scotsman we called Shrek. And a Saskatchewan who became like a little brother to me. He came from Regina. It always sounded like 'vagina' when he said it though. And he said it often.

'So where are you from?' said the cute girl at the bar.

'Regina.' he said.

'Como?' she said.

'Vagina,' I would interject. 'I came from one too.'

Most of his past life experiences and stories revolved around Regina. By the end

of the month, I had told all of Barcelona
that I came from the Vagina, that I went to
the University of Vagina, and that I loved
Vagina.

There were more girls in the class
than women, and they would sometimes let
their hair down with us. I made some
connection with all of them, but never the
full connection. When dealing with the
opposite sex, you never quite knew how to
behave. They say they have a boyfriend,
then get drunk, dance, and take you home so
you can touch them but not fuck them. I
enjoyed the variety though; they were
anglophones from all corners.

There was the princess from California
who enjoyed teasing. The tough sheila from
down under. The Julia Roberts look alike
from Boston. The English one who was fun to
drink with but wore makeup that could scare
away predators. The giddy one from Scotland
who looked like she just came from some
pagan cult rite meeting. She even taught
the class a 'deer' dance. We all had to
teach something our first day. I taught
people how to jump out of a plane. They
were quite entertained with that too.

I loved all these women in their own
way; some I showed it more than others. The
one I got closest to and turned in my free
pass with was from Texas.

We had a party at her apartment as she
lived in this spectacular city. We all
stayed up drinking and dancing. Towards the
end of the night, once most had left or
passed out, we began the drunken intimate

conversation that happens between two people. That conversation that would never usually make it far because of reasoning or social correctness.

We held hands. We kissed. We made fun of the couch pillow that had a picture of her boyfriend sewn onto it. Her mother had made it. Her boyfriend was in bed asleep with just a door separating him from his unfaithful girlfriend.

The next day we shared looks of remorse and nostalgia, and half-breathed attempts at talking about whether it was something to act on or let go.

We said nothing. We let it go.

#

It was towards the end of the month and we were standing on the roof of the school taking our first coffee break when the Aussie started with another one of her monologues. It always seemed to be the same thing, or at least the same tone. How teaching kids in Australia is great, but she just needed to do something different. Or how nobody really knows what they're doing here.

'I just don't understand him.' she said.

'Ah,' I thought. 'It's about her boyfriend.'

'He just doesn't seem to notice me anymore.'

Everybody listened and feigned concern as she spoke. Or just sipped their coffee and looked away.

'Why is it that men do that? I mean, the first few months they can't get enough, and then suddenly it's like I'm not even there.'

The women gave their 'mm-hmm's and just nodded in approval like an African-American choir after the preacher laid down his hard truth about the Lord.

She went on for a while. I tried talking to the Irishman to not get involved.

She was too loud.

'Well,' I said, making sure I had her attention. 'For every beautiful woman, there's a guy tired of fucking her.'

I didn't believe that what I had said was original, but the others laughed as if it was the first time they had heard it.

She gave me a glare that said she hated me. That she'd love to smack the shit out of me if I gave her what for. I got a flashback to the Italian-Spanish-French girl back in Marseille. I'm not a hateful person, but I enjoyed fantasizing about hate-fucking her. I gave a smirk to tell her I wouldn't say no. I complimented her.

'Don't you have a girlfriend?' she asked me.

'Yep,' I said. 'It's been over a year now. And we used to fuck four times a day. Now it's only once or twice.'

She just steamed and walked back inside. The rest finished their cigarettes and coffee a little more awake than they had been before.

10

I passed my test and was officially certified to teach the Queen's English, or at least the international version of it. I wasn't the best in the class, that went to the more bubbly characters, but I was happy with myself as I was the only one without a college education in the group and did well.

So, with a diploma in hand, half a smile from a good time, and a bit of confidence to do something new in my life, I went back home to Marseille.

#

Unfortunately, work was not as available in Marseille as it was in Barcelona, and I didn't find it right away as most of my former classmates did. So I still had some free time to kill with old friends while waiting for responses from my job applications.

'So, how's Malmousque these days?' I asked.

'Shit,' said Easterhouse. 'People keep fucking up and now we can barely go out. We have to wear uniforms all day and sign out every time we leave.'

'Well, what are you going to do?'

It wasn't necessarily a rhetorical question, but it played out as one.

Both Murphy and Easterhouse were soon to be getting out of the Legion. We sat

around and drank beer in a bar down the
street from Malmousque and enjoyed some
biltong that Easterhouse's father had just
sent from South Africa.

'Why don't they sell this here?'
Murphy said.

'French,' we said. It was the answer
to a lot of our woes now.

'We could make it.' I said. 'It's
basically the same thing as jerky.'

'We could probably even sell it.'
Easterhouse said. 'Think about how many
anglophone legionnaires would buy it.'

'Yeah, probably.' I said. I was tired
of Easterhouse always trying to make money
out of people, especially his friends, but
I agreed, we probably could sell it.

'Where would we make it though?'
Murphy asked.

'I would say mine, but the humidity
wouldn't allow it to dry as much as mold.'
I said.

'And how's things with Claudia?'
Easterhouse asked.

I could tell he was hoping for bad
news or looking for me to blame her for us
being unable to do the biltong business
from my apartment.

'Good,' I said. 'We're good.'

Murphy said nothing and showed little
to no concern. We had to be drunk and in
dismay to complain about the women in our
lives. We could often sit and drink and say
nothing for hours. He was a true friend.

Claudia and I were now living together
in our own apartment. It was a nice little

place in *Le Panier* of Marseille. It used to
be a nice neighborhood, one of the nicest
neighborhoods in Marseille. And according
to what history I had heard and read, it
was the oldest neighborhood in the oldest
city in Europe. It was on a hill right by
the water, looking down on the famous *Vieux
Port*.

Unfortunately, being stuck between the
old port and the new port, it was now
hostile territory. The Corsicans, Russians,
and Arabs were now constantly fighting over
who the neighborhood truly belonged to. I
felt at home in the militant tension.

Easterhouse, Murphy, and I sipped our
beers and thought for a while on this
biltong business idea. Occasionally, there
would be a blurting out of random thoughts
about what could work and what wouldn't.

'We could call it Trois Frères
Biltong,' Easterhouse said.

Murphy and I laughed, it was simple
but clever in its simplicity.

We shot more ideas around and just for
fun imagined ourselves as business owners.

Then we all started doodling on our
beer napkins. I always carried a pen with
me; the other guys got one from the
bartender. Maybe it was the sun and
alcohol, but it started to come together
and seem like a good idea.

#

I finally got work teaching. No
schools would hire me. Getting hired was

something that doesn't really happen without a formal education and a few years of work experience. Not to mention, every anglophone in France came here and taught as a living. It made sense since this seemed to be the only country in Europe that still couldn't speak the language despite learning it throughout school. It also made sense that they just didn't really care to learn it.

That wasn't the problem though in the big picture; it was more to do with the labor laws I came to learn. It was risky for an employer to take on somebody new, more than risky, it was expensive.

Luckily, France had a way to lower their unemployment numbers and help the unemployable feel employed. You declare yourself an entrepreneur and you can contract your work like any business would, only you are your own business: manager and sole employee.

I found this guy who had just started a language school that took a chance on me. Classy fellow. Arab descent, but French in every way. Perhaps he liked my look more than anything, but I was glad to have the work. It didn't add up too much, 20 hours a week was my busiest time through him, but apparently that is the maximum for teachers here, fifteen being normal. Unfortunately, as a contractor of sorts, I got paid by the hour and not on salary as an employee which meant I was making just over half the minimum wage (legally).

I wasn't complaining too much though;

I was still living my former life of long
nights with the guys at the bar and was
working on my insurance payout from my
military insurance. That along with my
pension and disabled veteran pay, I was
somewhere near breathing level and lived a
spartan life.

#

Easterhouse, Murphy, and I also
started importing biltong from Spain,
bagging it in a nearby restaurant and
slapping our sticker on it for resale. It
was going well. We weren't making any
money, but it was a laugh and we didn't
expect much.
Murphy and I didn't expect much,
Easterhouse was Mr. Man with the business,
scheduling the meetings, declaring himself
the manager, and already looking for
investors of big money to create a company
with the sole intention of selling it all
once it got up and going. Given, he was
near 40, while Sully and I were mid-20s, I
suppose age played a role as much anything
with our attitudes towards the fledgling
biltong empire we were creating.
Both Murphy and Easterhouse were out
of the Legion by this point as well and
relied solely on the business and their
payouts to live off of.
It wasn't but a few months in when
Murphy and I decided we had other
intentions and visions for the company than
Easterhouse. If it would be something real,

we wanted it to be ours and ours to keep.

Easterhouse left with a buyout of half made up business expenses and a promise to not start up something new within the next six months.

It all happened quick and with mixed feelings, but not with any regret.

Up to this point we had been doing things off the big brother radar, just informal contracts with two bars and then selling it to friends and friends of friends. By the third month, we were up to thirty kilos at our home bar. It was a well-established bar in Vieux Port, and they were selling it without profit as friends of ours to see if the French would buy into it. At an even two euros for fifty grams, they bought it well.

Murphy and I took it easy as we always did, we got together and discussed things over a pint and concluded that since I'm already slaving away as a teacher, he'd take charge of getting the paperwork in order for the business. Once everything was in place, we'd both jump in full time, until then, we'd just keep the importation, stickers, and packing over the weekend.

11

It was in the spring, around the end of March, just after I finished my certification and started teaching that an old caporal chef at Malmousque gave me a ring.

'Slaughter?' he said.

'Oui, caporal chef.'

'It's GP.' he said, *Caporal chef de Malmousque.*'

'Oui, caporal chef,' I said. 'Ça va?'

'Si, si,' The French speak French, but sometimes they take after their southern cousins. 'Onyx just had puppies. I thought you might want one.'

Onyx was this caporal chef's dog. It was a mixed black lab, almost as wide as she was tall. During a three-month stint GP had in Guyane for his jungle training refresher course, I looked after her.

She was an older dog, and it was surprising she could produce a litter considering she could barely walk. But she was a dirty old bird swimming every day and shaking that water off in front of all those other dogs regularly. I wasn't that surprised.

I grew up with dogs and I had always wanted a dog of my own but never allowed myself to have one. I always said it was because being in the military I was never sure to be in the same place for very long and always gone more than home, but I was sure it had more to do with committing to something that required responsibility.

Given the circumstances with a steady
lady, a job that didn't move, an apartment,
and the plans to establish a business, I
figured I wouldn't be going anywhere.

I came over the next day and picked
the dog I wanted. A chocolate lab, just
like the dog that carried me around by my
diapers, I would even name her Cocoa after
my first furry caregiver.

#

Unfortunately, that dog got bought, so
I chose a black one with a white front. She
was majestic. I wanted a female for the
tamer, more protective qualities.

Then an officer came and called
priority.

I went back to the base a third time.
I sat on the ground and watched these now
running and playful runts step on shoes and
piss on each other. It was magical.

I looked at the brown one, the one I
wanted first. He was too fat anyway.

The puppies kept running around in
circles, playing chase while saying hello
to every person around.

Then I saw the second one, I had even
put a collar on her to mark her as taken.
She was pretty, and I already missed her. I
tried talking to GP, but he couldn't say no
to an officer. I took off the collar.

I must have sat there for another
forty-five minutes. People and fellow
legionnaires came and went and the puppies

came making their circles.

One puppy then broke off and came running towards me. He didn't stop. He just kept running and then jumped at my chest. Then ran around me and continued jumping on my legs and trying to jump on my chest. I think he was trying to get to my face, but even sitting down and jumping from my legs, it was too high for him to reach.

This little guy was a fighter. Smaller than the rest and standing out from the rest. It was a boy, not what I wanted, but he looked exactly like his sister who I had chosen with the black coat and white paws.

I collared him and called him Maverick.

I came back six weeks later to take him home. Claudia didn't like the fact we hadn't talked about it, but I didn't really care.

12

During that same summer, the wine was flowing, and the sun was shining has it had been the year before. It felt different though. I felt tired. It didn't feel so much as fun as it did an escape from life. I had the new job, the new puppy, the lady I wanted, and the friends who were always looking for a drinking buddy or a good time. I got into a little trouble, but never too much, and things were good, but I was in a state of doubt, misery, and reflection.

The new job was not nearly as entertaining and easy as I thought it would be, mostly because it took as much work finding work as it did doing the work.

The puppy was the joy, but was still a little creature that required more responsibility than I was used to and cleaning up shit with a hangover wasn't glamorous even when it wasn't your own shit.

Claudia and I were never on the same page. We were still having sex every day, still doing some things, but most of the time we weren't together, and when we were, it was at the house, both on the loveseat with screens lighting our faces rather than each other.

My friends were consistent, nonjudgmental, and always up for a laugh. I felt lucky despite a good part of my friends leaving the area since they left the army, there were still a few of the guys in, and a few that stayed around after getting out. We kept our traditions even at the expense of ourselves.

Claudia was never much of a fan of my friends, but she rarely said so. She was never one to judge, at least openly, and never one to control someone else. I could never tell though if she just didn't notice, or just didn't care.

There was no doubt a few times I came home drunk and she would slap me for saying something stupid, but she never punished me or brought it up the next day.

The only time she ever really criticized or commented on one of my friends was with my former business associate and first friend at Malmousque, Easterhouse.

Despite kicking him out of the business, we all remained friendly afterwards. I had my personal issues with him. He seemed fake and seemed to take advantage of his friends. But he had a way about him that won people over. It was an art. He could do the unthinkable and quickly give the most sincere apology afterwards. Time and again, we would all experience some of his antics. Stolen shoes from a guy in the same barracks as a gift. Borrowing two hundred euros and then paying you back in unwanted computer accessories that are worth half the amount. Despite this, I remained friendly with him in a very commonsense way, avoid money and don't trust him with anything that truly mattered.

It was in that summer though, not long after he left the business and he came by the apartment when we arrived at a final chapter. People always came by the apartment without calling first. Claudia hated it. Especially when it was him. Those two never forgave each other from their spat over a year ago when arguing over what was good for me.

He came in with another dramatic story.

I said I didn't care.

He upped the drama and story.

I said I didn't give a shit.

He made it my concern, but I wasn't buying it.

Claudia was in the room on the couch but keeping to herself. Eventually she turned around and pointed out that I didn't give a shit. He responded by saying nobody asked her and told her to fuck off.

I jump in and did the 'Ho, ho, ho' Santa Claus 'take it easy' routine.

She set her computer to her side and really started going off on him. He followed suit and stepped towards her with the same venom. At this point my military police training kicked in and I was grabbing this corn-fed boy that outweighed me by two times by the back of his elbow and guiding him towards the door.

He could have easily pushed me off or fought me off, but the door was close by and still open and I got him through without a fight. Or he let me push him through without a fight.

He left in a huff.

Claudia still hadn't sat back down when he came back and hollered at me through the window. His usual apology routine. I said, 'Yeah, sure, okay.' I had enough.

It would be the last time I really every spoke to Easterhouse. I was a bad guy for that for some time. A lesson I learned early in adulthood is that you are always the bad guy in somebody's story.

#

This incident and falling out eventually led to a falling out with a few people, after a few months it would all fade away, but one friend, an Englishman and neighbor two floors above me would cancel our trip together to India. Something we had planned on a drunken night doing coke and listening to Queen live at Wembley '86.

He took Easterhouse's side on the mere fact that friends should come before women. Admitting Easterhouse was a piece of shit, but there are principals. It was a shame. I had been looking forward to the trip. It would have been my first real vacation as an adult.

Despite Kay's flaking out, I bought the ticket. Solo. Claudia and I were just waiting for the other to end things, so I didn't ask her, and she didn't try to come or try to stop me.

I thought despite our differences, she
would still be willing to take care of
Maverick. I was wrong. So I called on
friends. I had a handful of them doing
rounds to feed and walk him and check up on
things at the apartment. They agreed
without hesitation and Murphy said he'd be
the *responsable* that made sure Maverick was
always looked after.

I felt bad leaving Maverick behind. He
would have Claudia at home for a consistent
presence. She wouldn't be the most
comforting and entertaining company, but he
would have a new playmate visiting every
day for those needs. I felt bad for leaving
Maverick, but I think his 6-month-old
puppy-mind somehow knew more than anybody
what I needed.

I would go to India alone. Travel.
Meditate where Buddha reached
enlightenment. And trek the Himalayas in
Nepal. I would find the enlightenment I had
been searching for since adolescence and
get away from all this booze, drama, and
bullshit of everyday life.

Having it all felt like nothing.

13

I flew out of Marseille in to windy turbulence, only to land in rainy turbulence in Paris. Then had a four-hour layover which was okay. The first thing was finding out how to get to my correct terminal since the normal shuttle wasn't running. I must have walked around two hours hitting roadblocks. They exhausted me. My leg was hurting, and I hadn't slept the night before.

I found it though and had a nice nap in the waiting area. Then I waited on the plane and watched other people board.

There was a family with the mother trying to guide the kids and the father trying to carry all four handbags for each member of the family while giving half dirty, half apologetic looks at everybody he passed and tried not to smack in the face with his daughter's bookbag. The mother got the kids strapped in and reached for the children's bags to grab them some crayons and a Gameboy, while daddy put the suitcases away, and afterwards their kids' school bags into the overhead compartment. He sat down on the other side of the aisle of his wife and kids with a heavy sigh. The people that were stuck behind him gave a lighter sigh and continued marching down the narrow walkway to their own chairs, some thinking they will do their best to not be the person to hold up the rest like that, some thinking they were going to

fucking take their time for some spiteful
revenge on the rest still waiting to be
seated.
     Then there were the professional
flyers with their suits and computer purses
and perfectly sized roller overnight bags.
There were the young couples with their hip
clothes and smiles and holding the hands of
each other down the aisle. And as always, a
few obese ladies rubbed every arm that
didn't move in time with their oversized
love handles.
     We all strapped in on this flying
piece of metal watching the others, playing
the lottery of transitory companion.
Please, we say, let me get somebody
attractive or funny or quiet. Looking up at
them as they pass, are they looking at the
seat number over my head?
     For the first time in a long time,
someone greeted me with a 'good evening' in
English. I got a middle-aged guy who would
sleep for most of the flight and read his
book. On my other side, a girlfriend of
some guy who was sitting behind her. His
hand would be in my face this whole flight
caressing her face. Don't worry, buddy, I
have no interest in your lady, and I'm sure
she loves you.
     I felt relieved to be away from my
love. I felt happy that Claudia never
looked that ridiculous with me. I felt sad
that I felt relief and knew she did too.
Were we lovers or strangers? Was it
possible to be both? I felt pity for
myself. I still wanted her to love me. I

was her slave, and she knew it. I felt like the stupid boy she always said I was.

The plane took off, and I could see the lights of Paris fade away behind us just before we bumped through the clouds and out of sight of Earth. I was leaving my world behind. Not for good in the idiomatic sense, but for good in the most basic sense. My good. A voluntary and self-surgical lobotomy with fear, isolation, and reflection as the tools.

I was a fool, a damn fool, but there was no turning back.

I was about to wake up in a new world.

14

I did not sleep on the plane. Which including the next-to-nothing sleep in Marseille, I was tired. Arriving in India raised my spirits, however. Upon leaving the plane, I went for a smoke. I intended to quit when getting here, but I was glad I still had a few left from France. Mostly because while I was smoking I met a French woman who got me into town, showed me around, gave me a few pointers, and got me to a hotel. She also introduced me to a company cheaper than most to buy a bus ticket to Agra. So I hung out with her until the early afternoon. We walked around the bazaar, had lunch, and then grabbed a tea.

'So,' I said. 'If there's one thing I should know about traveling in India, what would it be?'

'Don't be a tourist.' She said.

I laughed.

'You will get harassed a lot here.' She said. 'Whenever they start, just tell them you come here every year for three months.'

It would prove to be the best advice one could get while in India.

She eventually left the same day to go north to her yoga class. I went to my new home to shower and take a nap. I intended to go back out for the night, but I ended up forcing myself to sleep through until four AM the next morning. I was okay with

this to be well rested fully rested and
have a full day to explore Delhi.

Delhi proved to be just like the
movies: busy, loud, colorful, dirty, but
charming in its own unique way. I feared I
would get hit by a bus or car or rickshaw
or ox before I left, but luckily I had the
energy to dance my way through the chaos.
The nonstop of these people was exciting,
overwhelming, and exhausting even as a
spectator sport. I had no specific place in
mind to visit in Delhi, but I was not too
concerned about it either. India was a
place for exploration.

Self-exploration and time alone.
That trip really started in Marseille,
where I found this scared little boy
feeling inside of me scratching at the
walls of my outer shell that were becoming
thinner and thinner. It came and went in
waves, but I realized I would get something
out of this trip, to face whatever these
creatures were inside of me: face them,
talk to them, and hopefully befriend them.

The city still slept between five and
six in the morning. There were people
working in the streets, but most places
were closed... including my hotel. I
thought to go to see some temples, but then
thought best to stick around until eight
for the hotel to open so I could pay for
another night. I could have just kicked the
guys awake, the hotel staff was sleeping on
the floor in the 'lobby' as I left. But I
decided to wait and whenever they got up, I
would ask for a map and some breakfast

before I started my day.

I walked around for the next couple of hours, drinking my tea and getting acquainted with the nearby area. No drunks were walking home or girls getting in their last customers. Just tea and spiritual men handing out blessings like Halloween candy. I had my tea and realized I had never been a tea drinker before, but this tea was something incredible. Coming from a big pot on the side of the street that probably hadn't seen a sponge too often, I can only guess what the secret ingredients were.

Not much else going on, I sat down with one of Gandhi's people. He had a few bowls and incense sticks burning before him. He kept smiling. He was a beautiful old man. Smaller than myself with red war paint on his face and a white robe. He didn't speak English, but we still had a conversation. I asked him about my gods, lust and toxins. I assumed he told me about his. He gave me a blessing and touched my forehead. I gave a few rupees to the guy; I wasn't sure if money was part of his god equation as it is for most peoples, but a man still has to eat. He didn't look down at the money, just kept smiling and stared at my eyes until I started to walk away.

I found out later he painted a red dot on my forehead. My spiritual journey had begun.

#

Being a regular of public

transportation now as a big city resident, I headed off to find the metro. I was the only white guy on there. Not many tourists here. Not any personal space either and staring seemed to be written off their social etiquette contract.

I found myself at the Baha'i temple. Shaped like a lotus, it seemed like a religion of all religions. That was the scariest thing I could think of, or the most inspiring. Inside was just a huge empty room with benches and mats. No shoes allowed. Must wear long sleeves. And silence. These seemed to be the only rules of this temple. What the world could learn. I had to go buy a long-sleeved shirt, most holy sites it would seem avoided overexposed skin.

There were people of all sizes and colors inside, praying and meditating. I sat in the middle and just absorbed the environment. I wasn't sure how this spiritual enlightenment journey was supposed to happen. I sat there for a while. I thought I felt something. God perhaps. Calmness. Anxiety. I wasn't sure, but I stayed a little while longer until I saw a tourist taking pictures. Then I remembered who I was and left.

#

After the temple, I visited a few more sites; the Lodi Garden, Parliament, and an Indian Arc de Triomphe. I even ran across some temples with swastikas. I knew the

swastika was an ancient symbol from this
area, but being a Westerner, I still
thought of Hitler and his band at first
sight of one.

I was also a Westerner and wanted to
see all they had in the market areas. I
bought a rug. One of those nice handwoven
rugs that really catch the eye in a room.
The guy was overselling it. Giving me the
details I didn't ask for and even told me
they run over it with a truck a few times
to demonstrate its quality. Apparently,
there are classes of rugs and being run
over a thousand times by a truck puts you
up near the top.

I bought a sari for Claudia. I wasn't
sure where we were at the moment. The whole
year so far had been pretty off and on, and
she almost seemed happy to see me go. The
first time she seemed happy in months.
Well, it was probably over, but I still
thought she would look good in a sari, if
not for me, then for the next guy.

I also grabbed some tea, spices, and
four marble candle holders. It was all
ridiculously cheap, and I sent it all home
by mail. Gifts were done. One less thing
for me to worry about during my trip. I
also bought some sandals, which were needed
here. It is not hot but warm - and much too
warm for boots. Plus, I was already tired
of taking off my boots every time I walked
inside a place. That and holey socks at
holy sites was a bad joke.

Being back in Bahar Ganj - the bazaar
area, I could see the huge difference in

tourists. I found it a shame that they are more attracted to cheap shopping rather than temples and modern Indian culture such as experiencing the metro.

Delhi is a huge city. It would take too long to see it all and my tolerance for cities and crowded areas is low. After the initial excitement of a new area, it becomes animalistic and I can feel the heat and nervousness run through my chest, to my feet, to my fingertips. I had my fill as a silly tourist and I looked forward to moving on.

The kindness of some people was absurd. The man for my bus ride to Agra was beyond anything I had ever experienced with humanity before. Others I still questioned despite their polite, friendly way, I knew they wanted something. That could explain why I spent five hundred euros on gifts and gave five hundred rupees to a widow.

I got back to the hotel in the early afternoon and had lunch.

15

Once again, I started my day with no sleep.

What kept me from my slumber though was an encounter with a beautiful and young, but older than me, Spanish woman. I had met her briefly at the hotel while having my lunch. She was at a table beside mine and we got to talking. Later that night, I came back up to have a drink for my last night in Delhi. She was with an Austrian girl who also stayed in the hotel. We had our dinners and then I proposed going for a walk to find a bar. They agreed, and we found ourselves in a place not too far from the hotel.

The streets were quiet and nothing like what you would expect from a city. There weren't streets and signs, just buildings with nothing in between. We saw the word 'bar' on a building and given the environment we figured it would be the only place to find something like that nearby. We found out it was just another hotel. But they had a bar with actual tables and booths. They also had some music. I think it was one of those top 40 hits CDs because it sounded awful and after two hours the first song played again. We didn't stay long because guys kept coming over to hit up the girls, or me, they talked to me a lot, maybe they saw me as a rich man with these two girls and wanted me to share.

I felt like I was connecting

with both of them and at one point both
were playing footsie with me. I liked them
both so I played it cool. The Austrian girl
was blonde and seemed more of the book
type. We had some great conversation about
books and science. The senorita was just as
stimulating in a different way. Dark-
skinned, dark hair, and dark eyes, she was
the spiritual one. She was in India to head
south and volunteer teach for six months.
We all held the conversation between us
fairly well. They seemed friendly and not
too competitive with each other. I felt
special that either was even interested.

After the third group of guys
made their attempts, and the CD had made
its full cycle, we grabbed five forties and
headed back to the hotel. We went to the
rooftop terrace where the kitchen and
tables were to have our drinks.

The kitchen was closed, but the guy
was still up there cleaning and he saw us
sitting down and pulling out our cold ones
from the plastic bags. He watched us for a
minute and came over.

'I'm sorry, sir,' he said, 'but you
can't drink here.'

I told him to grab a cup.

He did, and he sat for a few minutes
with us and had a few drinks. He was quiet
and mostly just listened and laughed. He
left in good spirits and told us not to
worry about any mess, that he would take
care of it in the morning.

It was a small round table made of
curved metal rods and had chairs to match.

It was nice out, not hot and not cold. I must have drunk three forties and the girls barely drank one each.

Until this point, I didn't think too much about what was happening. Even with Claudia and I parting ways in a 'We need space' sort of way, I didn't plan on looking for romance on this trip. I was just enjoying the company, and it was good company. It's always good company with a pretty girl that can hold a conversation. I got lucky and had two sitting in front of me.

I played things out in my mind and figured having both of them here would prevent me from having either. It would eventually get to where everybody tried to hold out waiting for one to leave until nobody left and then we all just passed out with nothing happening. I figured it was for the best that way since I really didn't want to betray Claudia despite her relationship rules and the space we were currently taking. I was feeling a good buzz at this point too and was sure I wouldn't be able to resist if one of them really came onto me.

Having broken the seal, I needed the little boy's room. Both girls' rooms were up on this top floor and Solé, *la senorita*, said I could use hers to save me walking downstairs to my room.

I pissed. Washed my face. And was preparing my words for an awkward goodnight.

When I came out of the bathroom, Solé

was standing in the doorway. She looked
beautiful and my body felt warm in a way
opposite than earlier that day. Rather than
feeling nervous, I felt at home.

She was chewing a piece of gum. I
walked up to her, not past her. I asked her
if I could have a piece. She pulled out a
piece from her pocket and stuck it in my
mouth, then slowly pulled her finger out
which I caressed with my tongue until it
had made its full exit.

This broke any control she had, and
she pulled me in.

We pulled back smiling and went back
out to continue talking to our Austrian
friend. I think Sandra knew something had
happened because she felt more neutral in
her way of talking and soon left to go to
bed.

Solé and I didn't stay out much
longer, and both went back to the same bed.

She started by going down on me. I
wanted to give her an award. She knew she
was good, but still seemed insecure about
it.

'Te gusta?'

'Yeah,' I said. 'It's good.'

She looked at me and gave me eyes that
said 'really? That's it?' She went back
down and rose me to heaven.

She came up after, took off the rest
of her clothes. She had a body. She laid
down beside me and I caressed her and ran
my fingers up and down her. I particularly
enjoyed the crease between her lower ass
and thigh; it was enough to make you

believe in God. I teased her, fingered her,
and then her self-control went out the
window again. She was waking my guy back up
and strapping on his rain gear before she
strapped on herself.

We went at it for forty-five minutes.

What a beautiful mess we were in a
dank and musty and poorly lit room.

I noticed a broken condom when I went
to pull it off and it was one of those 'ah
shit' moments that quickly turned into an
'ah fuck it' moment.

We stayed up the rest of the night
talking and fucking, naked and beautiful,
warm and young, passionate and carefree.

I had to leave then; she was upset and
thought I was lying. I wasn't. I had to
pack and catch my early morning bus. She
gave me her email, and I took off having
one last glance at that Spanish goddess
wrapped up in those dirty, white Delhi
sheets.

#

I got my bus by six AM. The trip was
rough at first. I mean both the roads and
the fact of trying to sleep with no luck. I
believe it took two to two-and-a-half hours
just to get out of Delhi. Stopping here and
there until the bus was full, and I was
even more uncomfortable. Eight people on a
four-person seat - I was glad to have a
window. When I finally gave up on sleeping,
I just stared out of it.

It amazed me how poor and dirty India

looked, and yet, such a natural-feeling habitat. I had seen all in one day: goats, sheep, cows, oxen, monkeys, elephants, and camels. The bus ride was long and annoying, and it didn't help that I was tired and uncomfortable.

I arrived at Agra by lunch and grabbed a tuk-tuk to a hotel. Unloaded and changed, I went back out for a bite, a terrible exchange rate for some spending money, and a train ticket I was not too happy with.

I hired my tuk-tuk driver on as my go-to-guy for my stay in this big, small town. After first taking me to his friend's hotel to get a room, we went to the Red Fort, although I found out later, the actual Red Fort was in Delhi. Agra Fort seemed just as red though.

He stopped just in front of the fort and I told him to come back in two hours to pick me up. He started to watch me walk away; I wasn't sure if he was just going to wait or go find more clients and then come back.

I finished a bottle of water I had been drinking. It was one of those plastic liter-and-half bottles with a blue sticker around the top of it. I crunched it up and started looking around for a trash can. My driver came up from behind me, took it from my hand, and threw it on the ground. I looked at him, probably in a funny way.

'This is India!' was his answer. Then he bobbed his head side to side as I noticed the Indians do when they give affirmation of something.

'This is India, all right.' I thought. I first came across this fascination in Delhi. Sitting on the side of the street, there is trash all over the ground, but then you have some old lady in rags come by and sweep it up. No government employee, but she takes tips if she sweeps something from under you. These sweepers eventually all meet in some central location, which becomes a big pile of trash. Not an official dump, just somewhere in the middle of town. Then you have the scavengers that stay in the pile of trash and take apart the clocks, the tires, and whatever else they find salvageable. Once there is nothing left to salvage, they burn it. It all seemed highly effective to me, and all without government aid.

The Indian people didn't seem materialistic at all, perhaps because of religion or just being poor. They had stuff, plenty of it, but they didn't seem too attached to it. Use it, break it, throw it on the ground.

#

After a day of visiting Agra, tombs, forts, and craftsmen, I found myself sitting across the river of the Taj Mahal, watching the sun set on this world wonder. Unfortunately, because of the pollution, the sunset was not as majestic as it could have been. I washed black out of my hair that night.

The perfect plan was to have today go

as it had, wake up early the next day for the Taj Mahal, and then be on a train by lunch. Today had gone as planned, but my train ticket was not until midnight the next day, which meant I would have a whole day to kill in a city I had not taken so much to liking. The people seemed snottier and less friendly, be it at the hotel, street stands, or museum. Agra fort was nice and I cannot deny that beauty, along with the other Islamic architecture. I was especially looking forward to seeing the Taj Mahal up close the next day. I didn't plan on getting up early for the sunrise as I had an entire day to kill. So, I planned to sleep in and check out this *merveille du monde* all afternoon, then pick up my train ticket, have a walk and try not to spend too much money. Finally, I'd catch my train I hoped to sleep most of to wake up further east. Further away from tourists and the frustrating Indians that encircled them.

16

I wanted to hear Claudia's voice, but I had nothing to say. I was still having those moments of feeling scared and lonely during my trip. But the feelings also felt good, like curing an illness - painful but necessary. I wanted to cry.

I had been fortunate though. My first day, I met Roux - the French yoga lady. The next day, I meet Solé and later Sandra. And as I was finishing my day today, I met another French woman - Valentine, who would take the same train as me out east. Four women, three days, all of which were beautiful, intelligent, and charming. All of which seemed to share interests with me that Claudia did not. All of which I believed had an attraction towards me, at least it was more fun to think so. And I wanted to call Claudia. Do I love this woman or not? Two more months to find out and find out everything else I'm supposed to find out.

I figured if I learned nothing out here about myself; it was fun to watch these Indian people. The past two days I had watched Indian men holding hands, grabbing asses, sitting in each other's lap, and hugging each other in a way that seemed much more than platonic. They never touched women and women never flirted or seemed alive here. I guess this would be ideal in the west where women were constantly complaining about being seen as

sex objects and being continually hit on by
men around them.

I then had a few imaginary arguments
in my head about this. With the current
political drama around Muslims in France
and women wearing hijabs at the beach,
maybe it wasn't such a good time to bring
this home.

That and people would complain, the
French in particular, about anything and
everything. An impossible people to please.

#

I woke up the next day feeling rested
and much calmer. I had a cup of my newly
beloved tea, packed my bag, and then killed
a few hours around town waiting for my
driver to get to the hotel. I came out
wearing my Indian shirt and got a
'Fantastic!' review. I said 'Thanks.' I
doubt that's what he was looking for.

The Taj was as wonderful as a world
wonder should be. Though I found more awe
in it the evening before from across the
river than up close. Even the greatest
wonders are more fascinating from a
distance. The right distance. Not too far,
not too close. But I guess you have to put
yourself too far and too close before you
can know the right distance. Am I talking
about people or architecture now? I wonder
how the Taj represented the favorite wife
for whom he built it. And then how did the
other wives feel? How could a woman follow
that up? 'I hear you say you love me, Shah,

but where's my Taj?' I wonder if he
regretted building it after that. Probably
just said fuck it, built his cask next to
hers and laid down next to his dead
favorite wife. 'None of these birds were
like you, Mahal.' I also wondered if he
would have seen the wonder in his dead
favorite wife if she hadn't died so young.
Perhaps he didn't get close enough to her.

I spent more time walking around the
garden than I did around the Taj itself. I
was also quite the sight for some tourists.
They asked me to take pictures with them. I
should have charged them. Some of them were
the over-friendly, grab-assing men. Another
was a man with his son. Where are the
Indian women? They're there, but they're
not.

I followed up my trip to the Taj with
a dinner which was half sauces, some rice,
flavored bread, a few veggies, and a glass
of yogurt. All of it was spicy beyond
pleasurable and I imagined the yogurt was
to keep it all from coming back up.

I couldn't head back to the hotel
since I had checked out in the morning, but
I still had another five hours to wait for
my overnight train. It had been another
long day. I was about ready to assassinate
the next person who stared at me or tried
to sell me something.

The way the commerce worked here was
very communal. Charming but mostly
annoying.

You stepped out of the train station
to be greeted by drivers. Who took you to a

hotel who had people that tried to guide you to stores or restaurants. At the store, you had a greeter that took you to a seller who took you to somebody else, who just showed you to another seller, until you were finally done. Then a transition guy took you to the cashier where you had another street guy trying to lead you to another store, restaurant, or hotel. They shared all of this end money through commissions. I respected they shared everything. I couldn't say I was a fan though of being constantly followed, lead, or conned.

And after you have talked to twelve people to buy one thing, you tried to come up with creative answers to the same questions.

'Where are you from?'
'What are you looking for?'
'What's your name?'
'How do you like India?'
'Do you have a girlfriend?'

Nice questions all leading to one thing. I thought about making a sign that answered all these questions with a subheading that said I had no money.

#

The train would take seven hours to get to my next destination, all of which I shouldn't sleep. Twice I had been warned not to eat or drink anything on the trains here for fear of getting roofied and being robbed.

The thought of sleeping still felt
nice though and if it hadn't been for the
noise, I would have dozed off right in the
station. This fucking country, it had the
ability to give you spirit and just as
quickly take it. I'm now left here in my
fatigue, frustration, and vulnerability
thinking about Claudia. Thinking I should
look for an internet cafe to see if perhaps
she had sent me an email.
    Solitude.

#

    The trains were reliable and on time,
but they purposely oversold tickets. They
had certain cars where they had no limit on
tickets. They sold these cheap tickets and
allowed you to get on or hang on at your
own risk. Most bought their tickets and
then went to one of the bed cars that had a
fixed number of tickets and stole
somebody's bed. I couldn't blame them when
the cheap cars literally had people sitting
on each other, hanging out the window, or
riding on top of the car itself. I asked
the guy in my bed to get out, and he did so
without too much fuss.
    Despite the warnings, I would sleep. I
had a lock with me and attached my bag to a
post on my bed. I was on a top bunk, so
somebody would have to be obvious to snatch
it. Plus, I kept it under my legs.
    I couldn't sleep though. Something had
upset my stomach since my first day in
Agra. Diarrhea mostly, with gas. It wasn't

the most horrible room-clearing gas, but it
was uncomfortable in feeling and the
diarrhea was consistent, cleansing. I
suppose my digestive system came to India
as well to sweep out his demons.

After two hours, the cleansing process
went into overdrive and it tried coming up
the other way. I jumped out of bed and onto
the guy I kicked out of my bed, now
sleeping on the floor below me. He said
nothing. He just looked up at me and then
laid his head back down.

I did my best to step and weave my way
through the rest of the sleeping crowd to
get to the toilet.

Locked.

No time, there were no closed doors on
the train and I just stuck my head out into
the cool passing night air and let it go.
The wind threw the vomit up onto the side
of my face. I reached up to wipe it off and
almost fell out of the train with my one
shaky arm holding me up. I fell to the side
of the train door and then just held myself
there for the next half hour that felt like
several hours.

The guy in the bathroom finally got
out. Which was good, because now the
diarrhea was back and I didn't feel like
sticking my ass out the door, but I would
have done it if he hadn't left.

The bathroom was a hole in the floor.
No seat or water, just a closet with a hole
in the floor. Looking down, you could see
the tracks passing quickly below you. The
train seemed to go faster when you had such

a narrow and direct overhead view.

I squatted and held myself up against the wall behind me that was wet.

It all came out in a horrible and disgusting way but felt like an orgasm in the release. Covered in sweat, I wondered how close diarrhea and ejaculation really were, and I didn't mean in physical proximity to each other.

I went back and forth from the train door to the bathroom for the remaining four-and-a-half hours of the trip. I was going from the sweatbox that was the bathroom to the open door of cool night air and it felt like jumping into a pool from a hot tub. The pleasure attached to the pain.

The guy on the floor slept on my bed with my bag as his pillow.

17

I got to Khajuraho in the morning
still sick, but with nothing left to force
out. It was a small town and much quieter
than the India I had experienced so far. I
found a hotel and convinced the guy to let
me check in early and just stay for the
day. I had bought another overnight train
ticket when we arrived at the station so I
just wanted a place to take a shower, brush
my teeth, and leave my backpack for a few
hours.

I had also met another Spanish woman
while at the station and had a friendly
conversation; I thought my luck with
Spanish women was no accident. I seemed
just as drawn to them as they did to me.
The language, the look, the personality.
Then the Spanish girl's boyfriend showed up
just as I was about to ask her to tour the
sex temples with me.

I went to a small stand to see what
type of medicine they kept there. This
wasn't a pharmacy or drug store, but just a
guy in a box selling everything from
batteries to pills to toilet paper. I
bought a little of each and exchanged more
money. He had an impressive exchange rate,
so I converted most of my money there with
him. The pills I bought had nothing to do
with my stomach but were just painkillers.
I had always been a fan of painkillers and
after my flight here I figured it would be
nice to just kill myself for a few hours

rather than live through another rough and long aerial expedition.

I talked to him for a bit about sports and my stomach. He didn't have much for me but recommended I go to the temple in town.

I was skeptical, but he said it worked for him and I agreed to do it. I couldn't just walk in and asked to be cured though. I had to offer fruit in exchange. He suggested a melon that grew there. It started to feel like more trouble than it was worth, but I listened as he explained the process.

I went to the temple with my fruit. It was a small chapel-sized temple with just a few small pews on either side, some candles, flowers, and an old man sitting at the end. I came in and he looked at me. I assumed he didn't speak English, and he didn't. I rubbed my stomach and gave an unpleasant face. He pointed to the fruit; I tried to offer it to him and he shook his head. Then I remembered what the guy at the pharmacy had told me, so I broke the melon in half and handed over half to the Hindu medicine man. We each took a bite, and then he sat the fruit on the altar with the other offerings.

He picked up a flower and some other small grains and leaves I didn't recognize. He wrapped the surrounding flower and tied it all off with a blade of grass and handed it to me.

I thanked him and left staring at this dark pink flower wrapped up in my hand. I went back down the street to the hotel to

take it with some water. When I walked in
the guy saw the flower and asked me if I
had an upset stomach.

'Yeah,' I said. 'Does this stuff
work?'

'Did you bring an offering?'

I told him I did.

He said it was the best thing he's
ever had for his stomach.

He gave me some water and laughed as I
ate it.

Valentine, the French girl I had met
in Agra, walked down from her room at this
point. I hadn't seen her on the train or
after, and it was nice seeing a familiar
face. I knew nothing about her and wouldn't
call her a friend, but just the fact that
it was a face I had seen before was
comforting in familiarity.

So I asked her if she'd like to visit
the sex temples with me.

She agreed, and we headed off.

It was nice having a companion; she
had also come alone. She was a journalist
in Paris and wrote a very revealing book
about Sarkozy which had apparently gotten
her into a lot of trouble. Not so much
legal or financial, but her paper had put
her on a hiatus and after which she had
found out that someone had tapped her
phone, so she had to get out and away for a
while. It surprised me since Sarkozy wasn't
president anymore, but apparently, he still
had future intentions to run.

She was a good walker and seemed about
my pace when visiting. It can be difficult

sometimes to find a good partner to visit
museums and sites with because of different
interests and different levels of time
people like to stare at something. Ours
seemed about the same and the sites were
fairly bare with people.

There were a few tourists, but often
we would be the only ones there. There was
no sexual chemistry happening between us,
but it did feel very much like having a
girlfriend spending the day together like
that.

The temples themselves were everything
I had hoped. Scenes of porn chiseled all
around the outside, offerings for
fertility, impotence, and pleasant sex. How
do we not have this in the west? In a world
of constant stimulation, why don't we take
the time to worship what is so beautiful
and is responsible for so much creation? I
wasn't sure that Valentine saw it the same
way. She found it intriguing, much like a
person studies something that has nothing
to do with themselves. I would see that a
lot in people in my travels. People open to
seeing new things but not connecting to
them. Just another day at the zoo. Just
another photo to show to your friends with
an interesting fact attached.

I didn't hold it against her, and we
had one thing in common on our walk that
day. We came across a small collection of
houses. There were no tourists around and
the women were smiling, the first time I
had seen that since my stay in India. The
children were playing and coloring on the

ground. Valentine tried talking to some locals, but none of them spoke English or French.

I knelt down and started coloring the ground with the chalk just as the children. The mothers smiled, Valentine smiled, the children laughed, and I laughed. I felt happy for a moment.

The sun was setting and so we hurried to see the last temple on our plan before heading back to the main village. The setting sun painted everything around us orange. The temple was orange; the desert was orange. I was orange and my shoes outside at the bottom of the temple steps were orange. I was still feeling the high from my coloring session and floated on a cloud for the rest of the orange evening, from temple to hotel and eventually the train station.

Before leaving, I thanked the medicine man.

18

The days were blending, and it was getting harder to remember which day of the week it was. I wasn't sure if it was a Wednesday.

I slept on the train this time and slept well. My headache from the first days was next to nothing, and I woke up with an appetite. I grabbed some cakes from a vendor and waited to see if I could spot Valentine stepping off the train. We took the same train again but again didn't make the effort to be in the same car. She seemed uptight about seating arrangements and there were no open seats next to her assigned seating. I didn't bother. I wished her a nice trip and told her I'd see her in Varanasi and went to go find my bed.

I was back in high spirits and reflected on my trip. India was such an interesting country and fun if you had the energy for it. I guess you could say the same about any country though. Despite the trials with an upset stomach, I felt lucky things had been going my way. I hadn't made any exact plans before arriving. I knew I would land in Delhi and that I had my only scheduled stop two weeks later. Everything else was up in the air. I made half-assed plans to see the Taj, the sex temples, and Varanasi in between, but no reservations or real planning went into it. I was on time for my timeless timetable.

19

Varanasi. When I think of India, I think of Varanasi. The city that Shiva gave birth to. A holy city, and therefore a city without alcohol. Shit.

After the usual routine of hotel check in, I looked out my window and saw people singing and carrying a dead body over their heads through the street. I went downstairs and followed them. I followed them all the way to the burning ghat and watched as they prepared her body and the pile of wood she was to be burned on. The prayers and the small tears. I watched as the son opened her mouth and stuck his torch in it. I watched.

After a moment, a little boy came running past me and bumped into me. I asked him to explain everything to me. He took me by the hand and said follow me.

He told me that everybody came here to burn their loved ones, that there are only seven things that don't get burned. Animals are gifts from God. Priests pray every day and are therefore holy. Pregnant women carry flowers. Children are still innocent. There are also lepers and a few other exceptions. The reason that these select few are not burned is because they need not be purified.

We walked up some stone stairs. Some old women were holding out their hands asking for money. I waved them off. The little boy stopped and looked at me.

'You should give them money.' He said.
'Why?'
'They are widows,' he said. 'They have
no money and no family left. They have no
money to buy the wood for their fire and
they are here to die.'
I gave the women some money, and the
boy turned back around and kept leading me.
He showed me the way to the holy fire.
'This fire has been burning forever.'
'Forever is a long time.' I said.
'I know,' he said. 'It has burned
nonstop for thousands of years and will
continue to burn forever. All people
brought here are burned with this holy
fire.'
I stared at the fire pit for a while.
They built it into a wall with a concrete
roof and had its only opening facing the
river.
We walked closer to the river, and
from our height I could look down the bank
at the multiple pyres burning. There must
have been five or six that I could see.
'Hundreds of people are burned here
every day.' The boy said.
I said nothing for a while, then he
continued.
'After they burn them, they throw them
in the river. Except for the priest, kids,
cows, mommies and other animals.'
'What happens to them?'
'They just go straight into the
river.'
He was a good tour guide, and I knew
there would be a price, so before he asked,

I gave him a chocolate bar and a hundred rupees.

I also found myself at the end of a festival. They built the city around the Ganges, and if dead bodies weren't enough, the people also built small shrines which they then paraded through the town and threw into the river. Boats, music, dancing, fireworks, a bit of artistic fighting, floating candles, and rice being thrown at your face all in this party city. Good times. Without a drink.

To end my soirée, I met up with a group of people that were traveling around as well and asked me to join them for dinner. A Spanish couple, Valentine, a French guy named Arthur, and a Dutch girl named Lotte. It was strange being so sober, like a diluted, watered-down version of myself, but I still found I could speak all three languages and make people laugh. I felt strangely normal.

#

I tried to find some spirituality given my current location. I bought a bird and released it. It's supposed to release karma, and I could see the spirituality of that, but I imagined it was just a hoax like most things there with the Indians and tourists. Release the bird, then they caught it and gave it to the next guy. I couldn't complain too much though since it is all relatively cheap to do and you can't put a price on good karma and spiritual

release.
    After releasing my bird, I went down
for a walk on the Ganges; I had already
taken a sunrise boat ride that gave me a
full riverside tour of Varanasi, but
walking past the calm Hindu cows, the holy
men, and the average Joe washing his
clothes in the river felt like a more real
experience. I saw one man bathing in the
river and so I went for a swim too. I was
with Arthur and Lotte, and they didn't take
me seriously until I was down to my
underwear and handed my sunglasses to a kid
playing nearby. It was dirty. Almost like
they threw hundreds of dead-burnt people in
here every day. I found out later that the
real reason it was so dirty is because of
the industrial plants just up the river. It
is considered one of the most polluted
rivers in the world. A Frenchman died the
previous year after letting some water get
in his mouth. I didn't die, but I found it
funny thinking if I had. It also seemed
funny that the most holy river in the world
was also the most polluted.
    Towards the end of our walk down the
Ganges, we turned into town and into a
bookstore. I found an English translation
of the Bhagavad Ghita. I read the
introduction at the store before buying it
and felt an immediate connection with the
translator, Juan Mascaro. He spoke about
releasing birds and swimming in the Ganges
and even that synchronicity was not lost on
me. More than that, it was his way of
writing that spoke to me. I bought the book

and looked forward to the read. Afterwards,
I talked to the teenagers in the bookstore.
Everybody sat on the ground here, which was
a pain for my leg, and the injury blocked
it from moving the way it normally should.
So, I stayed standing and talked to them
that way. They spoke English and French.
They explained to me that everybody in
India either spoke Hindi or English, plus
their local language. He advised me not to
waste my time learning local languages
since there were so many and only apply to
such a small amount of people. I still had
him teach me a few basics for Varanasi and
for a laugh, but he reassured me that most
Indians spoke English, and I had little to
worry about during my travels.

20

Varanasi was a pleasure. It was not nearly as stressful as the first days and provided a bit of the spirituality I came to India looking for. I made a few friends and had a business offer to be a French contact for importing clothes and other Indian made products. I also sat with some Israelis as they lived up their vacation after serving their mandatory military service. They came to India for the cheap drugs. I was still nowhere near where I wanted to be, but I was ready to head that way.

I had breakfast with my travel friends before seeing them off. I would miss the company, but glad to be on my own again. I didn't believe I disliked people all that much, but I've noticed I like them less and less individually as my life went on.

#

Bodh Gaya had Tibetan monks and many other Buddhists from around the world. Varanasi was the capital of spirituality for Hinduism, Jainism, and even significant for Buddhism, but it is Bodh Gaya where Buddha himself reached enlightenment and was where I planned to follow in his footsteps. It was the Vipassana 10-day meditation retreat that I scheduled as my only planned stop. It was this course I built this entire trip around.

On the train, I had read the Bhagavad
Ghita, and on arrival, I started my tourism
of the mountain where Buddha meditated for
six years, where for twenty-seven days he
didn't eat or drink. I'm sure most
scientists would find that impossible. I
thought going that long without alcohol
could starve any soul that wasn't already
dead, but I was looking for life in another
extreme with this trip. The destructive
phoenix I was trying to create before did
not leave me with the wings I had hoped,
and I was looking for answers in this
Eastern philosophy I had always admired. I
told myself that I was worth trying to
save, at least worth one attempt, and
nobody can do that but me. No amount of
alcohol or drugs or feminine affection or
psychoanalysis could save a man but
himself. It was a battle for my soul. One I
didn't believe would be easily won, but the
only fight worth getting bloody for if
there ever was one.

I climbed the mountain, which on its
own was as pleasant as climbing any other
small mountain or hill. I didn't see the
Dalai Lama, but I saw his room right down
the cliff edge from Buddha's meditation
cave. I also saw a lot of monkeys.

I fed the monkeys and then thought
about a little boy I had seen when I was on
the bus from Delhi to Agra. He was one of
many that stood outside bus stops begging
for money through the windows of the bus.
He earned his coin not in serving tea or
snacks, but with his monkey. He had a

monkey that could pull a few tricks with a
stick. I was impressed, but I didn't give
him anything. I had been in a bad place
with my stomach and fatigue and comfort at
that point. I stared at the boy for a long
time and he stared back rather than moving
on to the next customer. His skin was dark
like most Indians there, but his eyes
glowed green. It was mesmerizing and
entranced me. I wanted to take him home. I
wanted to give him a life better than
begging for change on the side of a bus.
I'd even take his monkey. I had always
wanted a pet monkey when I was a kid. The
boy seemed to ask me for help with his
eyes, and with mine I promised him I would
come back for him one day to take him home
with me. I knew that was another broken
promise made about as quickly as the bus
left the station. It made me sad, but also
hopeful that one day I could rescue some
kid like that. No year waiting for a
Chinese baby. Give me one that already
knows how to use the toilet and has already
had a rough start. And no waiting list,
just a homeless orphan I'd kidnap. I'd
figure out the paperwork later.
        I rented a motorcycle for my traveling
in Bodh Gaya and started making the rounds
of other touristic sights to include the
pile of rubble where a maiden offered
Buddha sweet milk rice. I didn't know what
the fuck it was all about, but I saw it.
Walking the steps of Buddha all right, but
I didn't have a sweet milk rice maiden.
        There was a school nearby, and I

visited that. It was the second school I
visited, and this one had a building. The
other was just kids sitting on the ground
with a teacher and board in front. They had
a building because they asked for donations
and had a website to ask for more Western
money. I took a tour like a rich tourist
and told her I'd wire some money from home.
I didn't have any intention to do so. I saw
sadness and poverty, but I still don't
enjoy being begged for donations. If I
donate, it's anonymous and without asking.
I'm an asshole. I know. Jesus save me.
Buddha save me. Muhammad? Vishna? Somebody
somewhere?

Driving back to town, Bodh Gaya was a
much smaller and quieter town. I looked at
all the Indians again. The top heavy buses
with people hanging out windows and stacked
on top. The young men with their young
ladies riding side straddle. How classy I
thought. It reminded me of some medieval
movie where the princesses and ladies of
the time would ride like that on the back
of the horse.

I went back to my new home as that
orange sun started to settle. I had my tea
on a community balcony at the hotel, along
with a few cigarettes and a book.

The next day I'd be off to see the
famous Bodhi tree and temple and whatever
else I could find to do in the actual town
now that my outer excursions were done.

\#

After checking out an 80-foot statue
of Buddha, I found an internet café in town
and figured I'd check up on the missus. I
had kept my promise to myself and to her
about the space, but there was a part of me
hoping she had written.

Claudia wrote. She seemed okay. She
told me she went out drinking and dancing
one night with a mixture of my friends and
hers. Good for her I told myself. And then
I wondered how things would be when I got
back. Would there be a change, and if so, a
positive or negative one? I can only
imagine a positive one, but even positive
change can be painful or hard to accept.

After reading her email, I went to
Facebook to look at her. Past the age of
wallet photos, I had been on a year-long
break from owning a cell phone and any
other social media. My way of telling the
world to fuck off. My bosses didn't like it
too much though.

So Facebook was to look at the photos
of my lady that any random guy could look
at without an account. She was still
claiming my dog as her own. She did that a
lot in an annoying way. If the dog shit in
the house, barked, did anything not to her
liking, it was my damn dog to look after.
Go to the beach or the park and people come
up to say how cute he is, and it is all
hers. Not mine, not ours, but hers. I once
reminded her she never wanted the dog, and
I got him without her and against her
wishes. She said nothing, and I never
mentioned it again. I had also just left

her with the dog for two months while I
chased phantoms of peace and solitude.

     After her doggy posts and comments,
she had more pictures of her ex. Not
remaining pictures, but new photos of him
on his rock-and-roll tour. A Romanian rock
star. I guess a rock star is a rock star
even if he is in a country most people
can't find and he isn't quite a star yet.
But he's only forty. He's still got plenty
of time to figure out the part about how to
be famous. She was never shy to remind me I
was nowhere near his level of excellence,
but it's okay, she loved us in different
ways.

     I have always questioned for different
reasons whether she truly loved me,
assuming I knew what true love was. One of
the main reasons would be because of her
ex. She had always stayed in touch with him
and even put up pictures of him on her
Facebook. Facebook itself means nothing.
Keeping in touch is okay with somebody you
were once close to. But is it too much to
ask that she posts a picture of me instead?
Of her current boyfriend who is far away in
a distant land rather than her ex-boyfriend
who should be far away from her thoughts. I
couldn't help but think when seeing her
post these pictures it meant something more
than an 'old friend'. She posted them
because she missed him, not me. She thought
of him. Looked at his photos. Thought of
him more. Thought of him fondly, proudly,
... lovingly. So much fondness, pride, and
love that she must display this to all her

friends and family through what is the most popular broadcasting social network there is.

I tried to give her all my love. I was not sure if it was not all received or not all appreciated. Either way, I had to be honest with myself and face a truth I had known from the beginning with her. A truth I had always known, but refused to accept.

Claudia was not the one for me to fight for. She will not love me. Perhaps she is shallow in the sense that I am unsuccessful. Perhaps we are just too different in spirit. Perhaps I was not good enough for her. Maybe I didn't treat her well enough. I had my moments where I was not the best boyfriend, but looking back, they all stemmed from the anger I felt by not being loved and appreciated the way I wanted to be. The way I did for her. I know to mention these things with her; she will only point out the childishness in getting upset over photos on Facebook. Demeaning the true intent of the argument.

I could respond to her email now with a note saying that things are definitely over. It would give me the time to get over her while I'm away, to meditate and walk it off. Six weeks of solitude would put me in a good place coming back, but making that decision on an emotion would be just as immature as making every other decision I had made in life. Plus, she had my dog. Her dog.

She may or may not have loved me, but I did not want to end things badly. She was

a good person and was never purposefully
wrong to me. Unfortunately, her heart was
not in India with me. It was with another
man and has been the entire time. No amount
of fleshly sins can compare to that kind of
hurt. A hurt I have felt for two years. I
had hoped and waited long enough. A change
was necessary, but I planned to make this
decision with a calm heart to not be
betrayed by raw emotion.

These signs were small, but to
overlook signs is to ignore the soul of the
world. Was it selfish to want all of
someone's love?

I continued to drift through positive
changes that were painful and hard to
accept. Here I was in India looking for
some answer to the emptiness in my life.
Just a few years before, I had made the
move to Europe with the same goal. Was I
closer now than then? I didn't even know if
I believed half the shit I told myself
about the world, about creating, about
fighting, about loving, about living, or
about my being. If there was some answers,
I thought I would be closer to finding it
now.

I wrote a bad poem for Claudia and
didn't send it.

21

I woke up the next morning feeling a lot more at peace with my feelings for Claudia.

I read the poem I had written for her just to see what all the anger and tristesse was about. It seemed ridiculous. Pathetic. Morning me despised evening me. Strong me hated weak me. Iron me hated vulnerable me. I took myself as a man of mercy and gave myself a condescending yet concerning pat on the back. I took the poem, shortened it up and rewrote certain parts to make it seem more like a poem rather than a child crying for his mommy.

Whereas before my imagination left me wondering what she was doing and thinking, I now didn't care. Something broke. It broke often. I often just didn't care. I thought of a word I had read in a book once. Actually, I had read it more than once. It was everywhere in the book. Abusively, but it made sense.

'Maktub.'

#

Claudia replied to my poem.
Twice.
The first was to say that the poem was 'nice.' It was the best I had come to expect from her, so I was happy with the result. She followed up by saying that she still needed to clear her mind and think

about things. The love between us could
conquer worlds. I didn't get too upset
about it. It was a bit heart-breaking, but
not at all surprising, and I was still in
my 'Maktub' feeling.

The second email was a poem. Written
by some guy named Matt. It seemed
irrelevant to me. I didn't like it. It
seemed too easy, too fairy tale for my
taste, but it was a nice thought.

I didn't say it; I didn't act, but I
needed my space too. After these few
emails, the space was driving us apart, and
I just wanted to say 'fuck it' and let it
happen. I would soon be locked away for ten
days meditating. Then I would come out as a
super buddha who flew above all these human
sufferings. I'm sure Buddha said 'fuck it'
too. The untold story.

Six weeks left. I was anxious about
the meditation; I wasn't sure if I would
kill myself in there or come out nice and
clean like a newborn baby. I almost wanted
to get it over with so I could go for a
walk in the mountains. Nepal was becoming
more and more the focus of my trip rather
than India.

#

I was sitting on the second-floor
balcony having my tea and cigarette,
staring at the setting sun. A guy came up
from behind me and sat at the table with
me. He had the long dreadlocks and baggy
pants. I saw their type everywhere in

France too. I was never sure if they were
artists, homeless, or both. I suppose
uniqueness was their aim, but it never
seemed all that unique to me. It wasn't as
bad as the hipster saga that was so popular
though. Hipsters. People that find
themselves unique while blending into the
crowd. Into a crowd. A group. Every monkey
has their troop.

       The guy smiled.
       I gave a nod and half-wave.
       'Beautiful out, isn't it?' he said.
       Damn, I knew I shouldn't have made eye
contact.
       'Yeah.' I said.
       'I noticed you up here last night. You
in town for a while?' He spoke with a
Spanish accent, but spoke English well.
       'Where are you from?' I asked.
       'Spain, well, Mexico and Spain.'
       'How's that?'
       It always fascinated me when people
said they were from two places. Either they
considered two places home, which is
admirable in its own sense, or they were
just some dickhead that enjoyed showing how
full of culture they were because they once
spent a stint in a foreign country or their
great grandmother's dog-walker did.
       'Spanish parents. Lived in Mexico
where I mostly grew up, then back to Spain
where I live now.'
       He gave a no nonsense answer. Not a
bad guy.
       'You?' he asked.
       'Soy Gringo.' I said.

'Neighbors then.'
'Indeed. You don't hate me, do you?'
'Ha. No.' he said. He seemed genuine.
'I traveled up there, good people really.
Just a bit…'
      'Yeah, I know.'
   We got to talking for a bit. I told
him I was living in France and loved
Barcelona. He concurred his admiration for
Barcelona and his 'meah' feeling for
France. He had a cigarette, and then
another and talked about how he was always
going off and on. I didn't mind sharing the
cigarettes. He was a good conversation, and
like most things, the cigarettes were
cheap. I enjoyed the cigarettes here too.
Cloves or something unique about them.
      'So you are doing the course up here
too?' He asked.
      I had avoided the meditation course.
Sometimes I felt proud of myself for
seeking some sort of spiritual
enlightenment or peace with myself, other
times it felt like some hippy, bullshit
holistic idea I should be embarrassed to
even mention. With this guy I shouldn't
have been too worried about his judgements,
but I was still hesitant to mention it. He
won me over though and it looked like he
was going too.
      'Yeah, you?'
      'Si,' he said.
   We had been speaking back and forth
between English and Spanish. His English
was much better than my Spanish, but he
entertained my attempts to capture the

language.

'How much do you know about it?' I asked. 'I read everything I could online. It seems straightforward, but can't help but feel I will still be surprised when I get there.'

'Have you ever quit smoking before?'

'Yeah, couple of times.'

'Good. Then you know how hard it is. No smoking there.'

'So you've done it?'

'I did it in Spain. This one here will be my third time.'

I had a lot of questions for him now.

'So what should I know?' I asked.

'You don't need to know anything. You just gotta show up.'

This sounded like the bullshit they warned you about with cults. I looked at him and tried to see through his answer. No arrogance or beguiling, but he seemed happy, anxious yet calm.

'Is there anything you could tell me?' I asked.

He looked at me.

'I'd like to tell you all about it. Really.' He said. 'But I truly believe it's best for you to find out for yourself, for the full experience.'

'No expectations, eh?'

'Right.'

We sat for some time more; the sun had well set, and we each lit up another cigarette.

We talked more about my plans for Nepal after. He said I planned it perfectly, because after completing the course you would be focused and want more time alone. I hadn't really planned at all; I didn't even have a plane or bus ticket to Nepal yet. I just wanted to go and had the time. But I felt like a master planner.

He started to leak some information. Letting me know it would be hard in the ways I imagined. No talking. Light eating. No smoking. No drinking. And forced time for yourself, no distractions, to think and not think. He said I shouldn't worry about my leg. There aren't any rules exactly for how you sit and I could use a chair if I wanted. He just recommended not using the back, sitting up helps with the experience.

All this opening up, I told him about my unsettling feeling. This feeling I had been carrying around that eventually led me to this course.

'This course is like cleaning the brain.' he said.

'Brainwashing sounds good.'

'Ha, no. Clean. Not full of shit. The opposite of 'brainwashing.''

This guy was speaking my language now.

'That unsettling feeling,' he said, 'is like hunger.'

I listened.

'When you are hungry, you are looking for something to eat.' he said. 'Sometimes you are an hour away, sometimes five. Either way, once you walk inside the restaurant you are relieved because you know you are about to eat soon.'

It was strangely poetic and settling

what he said. Sitting on the balcony in
Bodh Gaya with the course two days away he
said, 'You are in the restaurant. We are in
the restaurant.'

22

Another sleepless night tossing about over Claudia. I had fucked up fantasies of her sleeping with other men in our bed, in an almost mocking way, while I was here. Yet when the sun rose again, and I faced a new day, I felt almost nothing of the sort. Indifferent to what she may or may not be doing. What good is there to think about it? There is nothing I can do about it. Reason over worry, over emotion, over heart. She was most likely not having orgies in a celebration of my absence. I was probably only feeling anything because of withdraw. Even from an ice queen, a man can have withdrawal symptoms. I couldn't deny the symbolism of my love for her. Madly, deeply, obsessively. Then no attachment. I was still holding out that the following six weeks would release me from this too.

I had no big plans for the day. I spent it eating a tropical pizza and reading. I checked the internet to see that my package had arrived in Marseille; I imagined Claudia got it without too much trouble. My course to enlightenment started tomorrow.

Just sitting in Bodh Gaya gave me the peace of a real quiet life. Where doing nothing really is doing nothing. It didn't mean video games or movies in bed. It meant listening to birds sing and the wind blow. Just sitting still.

I thought about home. Just being able
to be back in my bed, under the covers,
with my shit food and lit-screen
distractions. A comfortable environment I
knew. I even had a dream of going back home
before Nepal and then debating whether to
come back and finish my trip. I didn't come
back in my dream.
Silence. Seclusion. A gift and a
fucking test of a man's endurance.

#

The visuals of Claudia and this
imaginary lover continued the next night.
No orgies this time. Just one man that I
would come home to find out. I would then
take the bed, the couch, everything 'he'
had touched and throw it out.
'Whether she loves me,' I said to
myself. 'I doubt she'd bring this guy to a
place where everybody knew we were
together.'
'No, she is fine.' I told myself. As
if the quality of her state had anything to
do with whether she was destroying my
quality of state.
This paranoia, this evil in my mind,
might make me go crazy after six weeks
rather than enlightened. Connecting the
days, I could see why the past few nights I
had been like this.
Besides losing the girl and most of my
furniture with her, I saw myself losing my
friends over it. Insecurities, weaknesses
like this, running wild over myself from

just a few days alone.

I had a lot of work to do starting tomorrow.

#

I slept well. So, I sent Claudia one last email before I was to truly disappear for ten days. I made a reply to her email about the package. She still hadn't received it. I made up a small story about a young girl reading 'Le Petite Prince' in braille and sent it to her. I told her about my days in Varanasi and then I told her about my perturbing thoughts that involved her. I finished by telling her about the Spanish guy I met and spoke with. I told her I was in the restaurant.

I emailed her with more than enough angst as I knew I would not be able to see a reply for so many days. I would only think about the response the entire time I waited for a chance to check it.

I had a nice big breakfast after that. Packed and left the hotel and checked in to the Dhamma Bodhi at 11:30.

The registration was simple enough, a name in a book. My room, my home for the next week and a half, had four stone walls, two low beds, a toilet, a faucet, and a bucket. It wasn't the first time I had washed myself with cold water from a bucket, and I knew it wouldn't be the last on my trip. I enjoyed the simplicity of it and wondered if I would have a roommate. I didn't imagine they would since there was a

no-talking policy during the course.
      It was damn quiet here. It was the
middle of the day and I could hear crickets
outside my window. My anxiety turned to
excitement. I felt comfortable. I felt
ready.

23

The course seemed like nothing but pain until the last day. I came to learn many things during my stay. As far as my obsessive worrying over Claudia, I spent many nights pondering, contemplating, and stressing. Some nights were just rambling, emotional thoughts similar to before starting the course. Sometimes my thoughts were more rational and analytical. Debating how she felt about me and what I should do under every outcome. It wasn't until the ninth night, after another long day, while I was walking around in circles in a small garden, that I really felt and accepted what I considered being an absolute truth. That I should not expect Claudia to love me as I love her. That in fact, it is a selfish love to love someone and expect them to love you in return. Doing this only showed that I loved myself more. As strange as a concept as that was for me to comprehend. I looked at most relationships around me and saw it all much clearer. From the outside and inside, I knew it to be true. Pure love is love given with nothing expected in return. I imagined the men and women of faith would say true love, real love, is like God's love.

Give.

Give.

Give.

And that is what I planned to do from here on out.

For the emotional torment, I learned
my way of dealing with it had been wrong.
Surprise. The answer is not to express
these emotions or to push them deeper
inside. Observation is the key. Equanimous
observation. I was to just be aware they
are there and then watch them fade away all
by their lonesome. I laughed as though this
was some secret weapon to turn me into a
Shaolin monk who would now have flying
superpowers and a stone face. I'd have a
drink and celebrate every victory over
these damn intrusions of emotion.

Which pointed to another pitfall.
Being the emotional child that I was, I
only knew how to express myself when drunk.
Repress. Drink. Explosion. Shame. Repress.
Drink. Explosion. Shame. Repeat until
death. I thought about how much meditation
it would require to eradicate all these
seeds I have sown. I was fucked.

'My less-than-noble mistress.' I said
'Alcohol. You yourself are not the sin, my
dear.'

I felt a tear of sadness running on
the inside.

'You are not the sin, but you
encourage the sin.' I was breaking up with
the me I had always known. 'Craving. Of
cigarettes. Shit food. Ego-driven sex.
Selfish love. You multiply that need, that
craving, my dear. If I am to be a better
man. A man who can die in peace. A man who
can live without the need to be liked by
laughing friends, flirting girls, and
unwavering love from one. I should probably

let you go.'

I said it all as an affirmation, in my newfound strength of solitude and clarity. This clarity was easy in my solitude and in a place of no distractions, but I knew the story would change once I got back home. Back to the girls at the bar. The friends at the table. Claudia in front of me.

My first meal back into the real world would probably be the biggest piece of meat I could fit between two slices of bread. The vegetarian meal and a half per day left a man feeling cleansed, but empty. It's a shit world where something has to die in order for me to live, but I can only conquer one idea at a time.

The noble silence ended this morning after we learned the 'Metta' technique to end the course. I didn't feel as though I had answers to questions, but I felt I better understood the questions. I had enough table space to work through them.

I felt better, and I felt many things behind me. I still checked my email in priority. Claudia had written a few times. She received both packages. Unfortunately, the candle holders broke. She also had some difficulty with the package because I had addressed it to myself. The rug came in well though, and she was quite pleased with it. I thought about the trucks running over it.

As far as our love story, she tried to tell me not to worry and that we would figure things out when I got home. The most meaningful sentence I read was where she

told me the story I wrote her made her cry.
    Almost.

24

Four in the morning, I left my voluntary prison of silence and solitude, of war and peace. I left it behind me to face the same world in a new way. Another Hindu festival was beginning, and I started my search to make it north to Nepal.

The train wasn't possible. The bus was down to one, overcrowded, and required too many overnight stops. I decided to take the modern travel method of a plane. There was a small domestic airport nearby that could get me to Calcutta, and from there I could leave the next afternoon to Kathmandu. I had this new fear of flying that only showed itself this trip, but flying would be the most logical and dependable way to arrive and give me the time I needed to do my trek in the Himalayas.

I bought my ticket from a travel agent. He said he was a travel agent, but when I arrived at the airport, they couldn't find my seat. After a few exchanges of kind and unkind dialogue and contacting half of India, they found my seat. This little airport in Gaya was unorganized. There was only one desk to check in and like a construction site, there were four guys watching one guy work. This one guy was trying to juggle six to seven people at a time. What a sight.

After that adventure, I went through the security checkpoint. I had forgotten that my knife was in my bag and I

immediately got the attention of all the
boys. It was a small airport. Literally one
gate, one plane in and one plane out. I
believe my knife was more action than they
had seen in a month. They really didn't
know what they were doing.

To make their poor souls even more
miserable, they started to question my
camelback.

'What is this?' three people asked me.
I guess they wanted to make sure I heard
the question. More people came over.

'What is this?' they were getting
louder and angrier but wouldn't give me a
chance to speak.

'Water.' I said. 'Water.'

I looked at them like the idiots I
thought they were.

'Water,' I said one more time for good
measure and to match their enthusiasm of
questions.

Blank stares.

Hindi talk.

Suspicious stares.

'Water.' I said.

Then they pulled out this fancy
biochemical detector. They must have been
too excited to use the equipment. I thought
I would have to throw away my camelback
now. I was about ready to anyway, but I
doubt that would have prevented them from
tossing me in prison if they really
believed I was a terrorist. The Indian
justice system was not the most reputable
in efficiency or quality. They will
imprison you on suspicion and hold you to

wait for a court date. That court date
could take one to five years to take place.
During that time you would have already
served your time and more for charges you
may or may not even be guilty of, with
people who actually are there for a good
reason in a shithole with no bed or toilet.

They scanned everything thoroughly,
all of them staring at this one little
piece of equipment waiting to pull out
their guns and handcuffs and become
national heroes.

They opened the cap and stuffed the
entire scanner right inside. They looked at
it for five minutes, waiting for something
to go off, then looked up at me waiting for
me to tell them how to operate it or to
admit I had liquid explosives in my
camelback. I knew how to operate it. Why
would I ruin the fun though? People were
the best entertainment, this being one of
the better shows, and it was all free.

They looked back at their scanner,
then two of them started to look in the
black box it came out of, probably for
instructions.

I tried to grab their attention to
remind them it was water.

'Do you want me to drink it?' I asked.

'Drink!' they said. They felt very
authoritative in this. I wanted to give
them a 'good job' for such power.

I put my hand out for them to hand it
to me. They shoved it into my chest. I
laughed and took a drink.

'Mmm… water,' I said with a mocking

smile. 'And look! I'm not dead!'
       The one female officer there smiled.
       I grabbed the rest of my stuff, gave a
half salute, and went to find a quiet place
to practice my meditation and observe,
without attachment, my anger rise and fade
away.
       Anicca.

#

       The flight was short and sweet. By the
time I got my bag though, it was dark. As
expected, no tuk-tuks at this airport. Only
prepaid taxis. I took the cheapest one to
the cheapest nearby hotel. The airport was
quite a distance from the town center, plus
traffic in the most densely populated city
in the world was insane. And did I mention
the Hindu festival going on? It would have
cost 1000-1500rs and extra time to get to a
cheaper guest house than the ones around
the airport. So for a one-night stay and a
lunch time flight for the next day, I paid
the 500rs to take a taxi to a nearby guest
house. The cheapest being 1600rs. After
looking at the room and being disappointed,
I got in a three-way argument with the
hotel manager and taxi driver. I got the
room for 1000 and my taxi driver promised
to take me back to the airport for only
300rs. Not bad, I guess, but Bodh Gaya was
half the price and twice the quality.
Difference in cities, I suppose.
       Thanks to a pleasant walk through the
ghetto I was staying in, I calmed down

after my money struggle. The music was loud and everywhere, but the streets were nearly bare. I wondered if everybody was resting for the big festival the following morning. I looked for an internet cafe on my outing to book a guesthouse in Kathmandu. No dice.

I kept walking around and realized I was the only white person around. Good experience, but unfortunately, last-minute traveling made it difficult to take full advantage of an area.

Arthur and Lotte were also supposed to be heading to Nepal. They would already be there by now. Another reason I wanted the Internet. It would be nice to send them an email to see where they might be.

They were a funny couple. Not a couple per se, they met on their travels. Yet, like so many other couples who meet traveling, they were fun to watch. A guy alone meets girl alone. They become travel companions. Boy wants girl for lovey, sexy reasons. Girl laughs and keeps boy at arm's length. She likes the company, the free meals and freeboard, but drags along for weeks. It's so obvious to anybody seeing it from the outside, but they must think they are playing quite the quiet game to themselves.

I also wanted to check in on my own delusional love, Claudia, and see if she replied to my afternoon email. I told her about my 'truth' realization on Love. I was not anxious though, I felt no hurry or worry to read and reply as before. It was such a relief to be so calm, even given my

dispute over the hotel and the awkwardness
of being the only tourist in this rundown
neighborhood.

I meditated. However, because of a
full stomach from two nice-sized egg rolls,
the overly loud music, fireworks, and just
general Indian traffic noises I only pushed
out thirty minutes. The music would have
been pleasant I think if played softly. I
was just hoping at this point that I would
get some sleep.

The meditation brought to light
another positive benefit. After waking up
at 4am and having a full day, I felt okay.
I was also proud at how my legs and back
felt much stronger than they were ten days
ago, even five days ago.

On a more disappointing side, I picked
up a pack of smokes. The first of many
pillars has fallen.

Well, time to relax, watch some TV,
smoke a cigarette, and dream something that
would no doubt resemble Bollywood with the
Indian pop music in the background.

I hoped to find a nice guesthouse in
Kathmandu. A warm shower at least. I didn't
mind cold bucket baths, but I felt I
deserved some warm water and a clean floor.
No offense Air View Guesthouse, but the
view of the air in the room is not worth
1000rs.

I laid my head down, and the music
changed. My eyes shut with the walls
rattling to Indian rap.

25

My three days in Kathmandu weren't that exciting. I was sick out the ass again. Vomit to boot. Cold rooms and freezing showers.

I did my shopping, bought everything I needed for my trek and found out not being prepared had its downfalls. I didn't have a permit to trek, nor a permit to enter the protected areas I would be trekking through. The equipment was cheap and easy enough to find. Too easy to find really, it was the only thing being sold it seemed, besides massages, food, and booze. I liked Kathmandu, but I didn't take too much advantage of it.

I met an American and a Canadian while waiting in line to get my trekking permit. They were prepared and had their travel insurance cards and bags packed. I talked about heading up with them, and they said they would wait for me if I got my affairs in order quickly enough.

I didn't. I told them I would see them the next day or two on the trail.

When I finally had everything ready, I grabbed a seven-hour bus ride to Besisahar. The trekking would begin tomorrow. I prayed for my stomach and hoped for my leg.

#

It was a rough day of marching. Nauseous and weak. Leg. And too much

weight. I stopped earlier than I had
intended but found the area enchanting. It
wasn't a village, but two metal shacks
owned by a family. The family stayed in one
shack and rented out rooms in the second
shack for travelers.

It was beautiful, quiet, and peaceful.
I stopped in the early afternoon, so the
sun was still shining its warm rays against
the cool wind. I couldn't eat anything so I
took a book down by the nearby river and
read for a few hours. I thought I'd take my
bath in the river, but after washing my
face, I couldn't imagine putting my whole
self in there. Despite the tropical
landscape and warm sun, the water would
have been ice if it was still. Looking up
the river, I could see my objective. The
mountains. The real mountains. Ice-capped,
white and gray, and reaching into the
clouds.

I wasn't sure if I would make it in my
current state. There was a comforting
thought about just making it as far as I
could and then laying down forever. It
didn't scare me and a part of me looked
forward to the idea.

Usually when I think about death,
there were a few things that kept me from
taking any real action towards it. The
first was usually my dog. We were still in
the infantile stage of our future together,
but there was potential there I couldn't
ignore. Who would take care of him if I
wasn't around? He would no doubt get
adopted or put in a shelter, but I didn't

trust people or the world enough to take care of him the way I wanted to take care of him.

After my dog, I worried about my mother. She always worried, and I was sure my death would crush her to oblivion. The thought of her crying had guided me to stay on this side of the line more than once. Whether I deserved to live I would always debate, but I had no question about whether my mother deserved to cry anymore than she had to. But given my way of living, we barely spoke twice a year, and she could probably live on for a very long time before she ever knew.

One last thing that usually crossed my mind when debating my life is what to leave behind. Are fading memories of myself enough for me? Or should I write a message? If I wrote a message, it would become a book, and that book would never get finished since I never finish anything. A catch-22 to keep existing.

Enjoying the sounds, the air, and the view, this freshness of pure nature, I felt at peace with leaving my loved ones and with no message. I almost felt that this was the real reason I had come here. Like the old widows in Varanasi, I came to this world to find peace with myself and then face my end. There was no logical debate to be made, I offered nothing to the world, and took much more than I gave. They say taking your own life is selfish because you are taking away from your loved ones. I saw my existence as selfish, because I took

away from my loved ones more alive than I
ever would gone.

I even started to think my whole life
was coming to this point. I joined the
military to get away, and when that wasn't
far enough, I joined the Legion without a
word to anybody to inch closer to the final
goodbye in a step-by-step method.

Now it would soon be time. To take the
final step of fading into everything and
nothing. I felt at peace and I slept well
that night.

26

I felt much better the next day. I had
Tibetan bread and jam for breakfast with
more chai. No vomiting or runs, and I was
almost pissing like normal.

I made it to a small village for lunch
where I had some spicy fried pasta with
tuna. It was nice and needed, and I held it
down. My body was sore and my leg had some
rough patches, but it didn't seem too
dilapidating. I ran into the American and
the French-Canadian girl (of Vietnamese
origin) I had met at the trekking permit
line. She spoke to the goats for our
entertainment. They both seemed like good
people and like-minded. It was welcome to
have the company.

I finished the day early again, only
walking for about five hours in total. I
could see how out of shape I was. I even
unloaded a pair of pants and shirt at my
previous stop to take off some of my
weight. I doubt it really changed much of
the weight, but I figured two pairs of
pants and a few shirts was enough. It was
the socks and underwear I needed more than
anything and I doubted I'd bathe every day.

The views continued to be amazing as I
advanced further and further into the wild.
I was told that the circuit I was on would
lead me through thirteen different micro-
climate zones, starting with tropical where
I was now up to the mountain tundra at the
top of the mountain pass I was planning to

cross.

I pretended to be a photographer to
myself, taking pictures of landscapes,
village locals, and colorful spiders I had
never seen before. It was a cheap pocket
digital camera that did no justice to the
image, the idea, and the beauty of all that
my eyes were trying to capture. It was
living poetry, a poetry that words would
always come short describing, and I wanted
to drink it all.

#

We were following a river and
continued to do so. The walk with my two
companions was exactly what I wanted it to
be. During the walk, we each had our own
pace, usually within sight of one another
and taking small breaks together along the
way.

Matt, the American, was well read in
philosophy and knew the names of ideas I
did not know had names. We would take these
philosophical breaks from time to time
while we waited for our third companion to
catch up. She was slower in pace. A small
girl, but she never not smiled, her spirit
seemed unbreakable. I looked at myself, and
though I compared my mental and physical
strength to be a fraction of what it used
to be, my spirit seemed healthier than
ever. I wasn't entirely sure what a spirit
was or if it even existed, but something
felt right in me despite the years of
inactivity and substance abuse after

shattering my femur in the Legion. Whatever this spirit was, it was no doubt the only thing keeping me going.

Maybe Matt could enlighten me on this subject. Until then, I would continue to search for my answers in the waterfalls and flowers that populated our mission.

#

We walked, and we walked. Too many waterfalls to count and the climate zone was changing. We were near 2600 meters now and the pine trees and smell of the much cooler air gave me nostalgia of my youth. The annual Thanksgiving trip with my dad and brother to deer camp. It was always one of my favorite times of the year when I was young. Besides waking up before dark to sit in a tree freezing my ass off for hours waiting for a deer to come to us and only seeing squirrels, I loved the day where nobody would hunt and I would run through the woods alone, creating stories in my head of fantastic villains and devastating wars that I had to save the world from. I still got the urge to grab a stick and sword fight imaginary enemies whenever I found myself in this reminiscent state.

Unfortunately, the weather didn't get warmer as we climbed higher and higher. The same effect seemed to work on the water. The only advantage I could see from taking showers with a hose from the river was how warm you felt in the cold after the shower was over.

I was using work gloves rather than
any gloves that provided warmth or water
protection, and I was entering a state
where I could not feel my hands for the
foreseeable future. My sleeping bag was an
old army summer-weight bag that did not
keep me warm at night in the Himalayan
mountains. Coldness had become my closest
friend.

I could only laugh at myself and how
unprepared I was. I shivered until I was
too tired to care and finally fell asleep
wondering how many more nights I would have
to feel like this, and if I would even make
it back in time to catch my flight.

I laughed at myself more.

27

We started our fifth day of trekking, leaving Timang. The day started well as we went non-stop for the first three hours. Finding a nice place to grab some water, I figured a water break was in order. I finished my water while I waited for the others to catch up.

Like clockwork, Matt was about five minutes behind me, and Cathy about five minutes behind him. It had been a fairly easy morning being mostly flat, uncharacteristically flat for Nepal. Out of the trees, we sat down on a rock near the river and basked in the warming, rising sun.

'Feels good to get a nice walk like that.' I said.

'Yeah,' Matt said, 'It feels like we are finally making some good ground, we should make it one town further than planned, I think.'

'Is our turtle up for it?' I said looking at Cathy.

She smiled. 'Yep.' she said. She was always smiling; I didn't know how she did it.

I got up to fill my water bottle and put in the water-purifying iodine capsule. I think I'm supposed to wait thirty minutes for drinking it. Matt got up and filled his too. He had a bottle that filtered and purified it immediately.

Cathy didn't need any more water. I

think she could walk for days without trouble. She probably just kept at our pace to keep us company. She was French-Canadian, which meant she spoke both English and French fluently, French with more ease than English, but we mostly spoke English, unless Matt wasn't around, then we would talk a bit in French. She also spoke Vietnamese, her parents moved to Canada as adults, and so she grew up in a house that spoke all three languages.

What connected with me about her was her demeanor. It was also her look, but mostly her Zen poise and presence. The whole small, cute Asian and Zen thing could be attractive enough on its own, but she reminded me of a character from a book I had read when I was younger. It was a fantasy type book, not books I read often, but I must have read about 20 books by this one author named R.A. Salvatore. Most of the books I read by him were about a character named Drizzt. They were good stories. Then I read one of his books that went away from the normal direction of these fantasy books. He made a cleric, a medicine man of sorts, the protagonist. Apparently few people do that since clerics are usually the less exciting characters, but he did, he wrote five of them I think for the series, and I read all five. The heroine and girlfriend of the series was a small Asian monk, very Zen and very strong. I fell in love with her in the book as the protagonist already had. I started to imagine Cathy staying behind us so should break boulders with her bare hands. It was good to have a badass monk in the group.

Matt was a manager during the day, an aikido trainer by evening, and a philosopher by study. He made a good protagonist too. I wondered what that made me on this adventure.

I had a Snickers bar while listening to the two of them talk. The sun was out, and it looked like we would walk in it for some time, so we took off our coats and started to get ready to head back out. I gave them the 'ready?' look and Cathy confirmed it by getting up and putting her bag on. Matt kept to his bottle of water and told us to head on up. He would refill and then be on his way.

Cathy and I started ambling away and exchanged a few words about the area and the trip. We hadn't had any deep conversations yet, and I thought she was the more reserved type, friendly but reserved. She probably thought I was reserved too.

We were in a flat area and so after about 200 meters I looked back to see if Matt had left yet. He had and wasn't too far behind us.

It didn't take too long before the flat dirt road turned into a rocky up, up, and up climb. This is usually where I got out ahead. Not because I am physically stronger, I think it was just the old army mentality of 'attack, attack, attack' when facing a hill.

It was windy and steep and I knew I

would lose them quickly if I went on too
long without them. So after about 30
minutes of walking up, I stopped to make
sure they weren't too far behind. After
five minutes, I didn't see anybody, so I
sat on a rock to give a little relief from
my bag without taking it off. After about
ten minutes, I saw Cathy, her slow and
steady pace was inspiring, no heavy
breathing or signs of struggle. Just one
foot in front of the other, a look up at
me, and the same smile she has carried the
entire trip.

I was worried though when I didn't see
Matt with her. It's true after the first
couple of hours he usually lost momentum.
So Cathy and I waited another 15 minutes
with no sign of Matt. I started to head
back down. I eventually found him and we
headed back up to where Cathy was waiting.
Matt looked exhausted, and we decided to
stop one city shorter than planned.
Originally, our plan had been Pisang.

We waited ten more minutes for Matt to
rest, but it wasn't enough. He promised to
catch up soon. I waited a few more minutes
anyway and let Cathy get a head start. I
gave him my second candy bar and told him
to eat it for the energy boost. After he
finally agreed, I left and saw him start
not long after me.

It was another steep climb, steeper
than before, and it looked like there were
a few different ways to get up. I took the
more direct, steep way to avoid the
Nepalese train.

These Nepalese guys were no bigger
than me, smaller even, and they were
carrying logs on their backs up these
hills. As if climbing with that weight
wasn't enough, maneuvering through the
forest trail we were now on couldn't have
made it easier. I wasn't even sure I could
carry that weight. It was incredible. I
took a picture. I remembered the guys in
the Legion from Nepal, and now I knew why
marching was never a problem for them. I
thought I was tough carrying the same bag
as the big 120k boys that populated the
Legion, but the Nepalese guys, like me,
being half their weight, even made them
look bad. Mountains and heavyweight meant
nothing to these Gurkha warriors.
        It was a good climb, but I didn't stop
until it leveled off, which only took about
15 minutes taking the most direct path. I
hadn't seen Cathy when going up, but I
assumed she would be okay, and sure enough,
she arrived just after I did.
        This time we waited nearly thirty
minutes before I headed down to look for
Matt again. I walked all the way to where
we left him and I didn't see him. I took a
different trail back up and still no dice.
We asked every passersby if they had seen
him and it seemed he had never passed by
this way.
        It was getting dark and cold, and it
had been an hour since we started waiting
for him. We assumed he found another way
and made the decision to wait for him at
the next town.

Sure enough, he had made it to town. He found a main road that the trucks used and followed it the rest of the way. He was waiting for us at the town's edge. He had made it so early that he checked every guest house in the town for us before settling on one and then heading back to the town entrance to wait for us.

We called it a day and headed to the guest house he got for us and had dinner and a few beers. The beer went straight to my head. It felt nice. Intoxicating.

'Fuck.' I said. 'It feels good to sit down and have a drink today.'

'Yeah,' Matt said. 'Sorry about that.'

'Maybe we should stay closer from now on.' Cathy said.

We agreed. There was tension in the conversation as we all seemed frustrated and demoralized. We ate. Matt left to grab a shower and head to his room. I got another beer and Cathy stayed with me.

'You think he'll be okay tomorrow?' she asked.

'I don't know.' I said. 'Yeah.'

'I understand what you mean about it being in his head.' She said. 'But we can't really know for sure, can we? I mean, altitude sickness is a real thing.'

'Yeah,' I said. 'I suppose it is. I had never heard of it until tonight, but it makes sense.'

'This is easier for you, huh?'

'No,' I said. 'But maybe it is easier for me in a mental capacity than it is for him. I've just always had trust issues with my head.'

She laughed.

'I mean we are barely over 3000 meters now, how likely is it to get any problems, right? Plus, he took the medicine preventively for it yesterday and the day before yesterday.'

'Yeah,' she said. 'Started mine this morning.'

'What does it do exactly?'

'It's just for symptoms. So you don't get headaches and stuff from the altitude and lower oxygen levels.'

'Hmm. So if you take the medicine, you may never know if you have symptoms or not.'

She smiled. 'I guess not.'

She told me more about this acute mountain sickness. Seemed shitty and had me worried that once again my lack of planning or preparing in any way would get me killed up here. I kept that part to myself. I still partly believed that it was mostly in Matt's head and that it was an excuse to not go too far too fast. After he mentioned cutting tomorrow short as well if there was too much climbing, I wanted to give him a bit of tough love. 'Matt, it's a fucking mountain. It will only get steeper… quicker.' I planned to make it to our scheduled stop tomorrow with or without them. I could wait for them there, as it is a mandatory stop for all trekkers before going higher for the altitude change and acclimatization.

I was honestly worried that if we went

any slower, we wouldn't make it all. I
hoped wherever he was hurting, physically,
mentally, or spiritually, he would feel
better tomorrow.

I was done thinking about it though. I
was feeling tipsy from the altitude and
beer and there was a common room with a
stove which kept the place nice and cozy.
It was nice feeling my face and fingers
again.

28

Thanksgiving.

It wasn't much of a holiday for me anymore, and if Matt hadn't said anything, it would have gone by another year unnoticed. It was one of my two favorite holidays growing up. The other one being the fourth. Very American of me. Considering how un-American I was in so many other stereotypes, I was bound to have my roots planted somewhere.

Matt was doing much better today, and it helped that most of the walk was flat. We got to Manang with no trouble and looked forward to our first day off from the trek. A day for the body to catch up with the challenge it hadn't been prepared for.

When I got to the center of town, I filled up my water bottle as usual and waited on a bench in the center of town. It was a town. Most places up to now had been small villages with small guesthouses and a small shop to buy the basics. Manang was a town on a hill. A nice square hill. It had a theater. It even had a landing strip. Small planes that only came every two or three days, but this place was class. It was the designated stopping point before going higher. Being over 3000m, it is where most people stopped to acclimatize before making the rest of the climb or it was for the few who doubted their commitment to the journey; they had a chance to fly back down.

'Will!'

I turned around and saw a familiar face. An Israeli girl I had met in Kathmandu. We had had a drink on top of a hotel too, but it didn't go like the night in Delhi with the Spanish girl. Her and two Germans had started their trek a day before us. They arrived in Manang the day before and were on their day of rest. She was wearing sandals and a smile. Fucking Israelis.

'Aviva.' I said. 'Good to see you.'

'Yeah,' she said. That smile was incredible, so large, so disarming. 'Where are the others?'

'Matt and Cathy are just behind me.'

'Go to Tilicho lodge. That's where Friedrich, Herman, and I are. We'll have dinner tonight, they'll be glad to see you too.'

'Cool. Sounds good.' It would be good to see them. So much more enthusiastic and cheerful than my past two days. The mandatory day of rest must do wonders.

Matt and Cathy showed up not long after. Matt looked exhausted again. He crashed on the bench and I took the time to tell him about meeting Aviva for dinner.

We checked in to the guesthouse and grabbed a table for dinner after our showers. Aviva and a few others were already up there. We got a table next to theirs. Unsurprisingly, Aviva had made friends with everybody in the guesthouse and trail it seemed. She was a star. Not in a snobby, fucked up way, but a real star.

Pure light that you couldn't help but see
against all the darkness. She had a way to
make the entire room glow and made
everybody feel special all at the same
time.

We laughed and traded stories of the
trek. Aviva must have been quite the laugh
all the way up the hill too. She gave us
all we needed to know about Manang; they
had internet, shops, an ATM, and a medical
tent with a mandatory briefing on Acute
Mountain Sickness. And then we laughed
more. I felt like a kid about to piss my
pants I was having such a good time.

I saw a deep-fried Snickers bar on the
menu. I was skeptical, so I split one with
Cathy. I heard about them being popular in
Scotland. I would have my first far from
there. After a Yak burger, why not, my
stomach threw his arms up in the air about
my food intake a long time ago.

I was looking forward to my rest day.
It seemed being in the heated rooms I
became more aware of my body and how much
pain it was in. Especially my leg. Yeah, a
rest day was mandatory for this broken
person.

Cathy, Matt, and I stuck around the
restaurant talking. I had a few beers. We
talked about the AMS and how oxygen becomes
less and less after 3000 meters. We were at
3500m now. Matt was still claiming to have
symptoms: headaches and fatigue. I laughed
and said I had a headache and was tired
too. That's normal. It's dehydration and
climbing a fucking mountain. I was tired of

talking about this sickness as if it was
the great challenge to overcome. I bought
some Diamox today just in case though. The
others recommended I take it to avoid
problems. I didn't want to. I wanted to
test this idea and see if it was real. I
came from a zero sea level area, lived in a
zero sea level area, and was by all
accounts a prime candidate. I told them not
to worry; I'd rely on military training and
water. I was one of those dickheads again.

Aviva and Friedrich mentioned taking a
detour to Tilicho lake. They said it was
the highest lake in the world. Aviva and
Friedrich would separate from Herman, their
other German companion. He had a porter and
schedule and seemed to be mostly doing the
trail for the sake of a bucket list check-
mark. The porter idea seemed appealing to
Matt and Cathy too. I wasn't sure how I
felt about the whole porter thing. Hiring a
Nepalese local to carry your big-ass bag
for you seemed kind of fucked up. But
fifteen bucks a day was a lot for them and
helped their family and their shitty
economy. Matt assured me it was an all
around good thing. He was probably right,
but I didn't like the idea.

We talked about Tilicho lake. It sold
me. I saw it as a test. The base camp to
the lake was only at 4000 meters, but the
lake itself was a half-day climb of over
1000 meters, then back down again to the
lake at an even 5000 meters. The Thorong La
pass that was the pinnacle of our adventure
wasn't far from this at 5416m. Both

required steep climbs and immediate
descents on the same day. The lake would be
a test. If I climbed it and handled it
well, I could go into the pass with
confidence. If I failed, it would make the
pass more intimidating, but I would have a
little more altitude training. It would be
a blessing and a curse. I liked that. I was
never a gambling man, but I always gambled
with my well being.

The beer was feeling good and my
negative feelings of the past two days, of
Matt's struggles, were fading away. We sat
at the table with our maps and high hopes,
planning the detour and where to get back
on trail without losing too much time. We
figured we could push it and do it in three
days or take our time and do it in four. I
was against more time-taking, but three
days would be a good push. I figured if
Matt took a porter though, it may be
possible.

All hurt feelings aside, I finished my
beer and wished my two friends a good
night.

Climbing down the stairs, I felt a
bolt of lightning through my leg. I was in
trouble. I climbed down the rest of the
stairs, only descending one leg and
clutching the side rail to drag the other
one behind me. I made it to my lightweight
summer sleeping bag and shivered to sleep.

#

I woke up for the first time without

the sound of an alarm clock. It was still
only 7am. Not much had happened since I
fell asleep. I mean a lot had happened in
the world. People died. Babies were born.
Talks of revolution were shouted and
whispered in pubs. People fell in love.
People had sex. People drank. People
watched TV. People watched bad TV. People
fell out of love. People searched for the
meaning of life on Google. But for me,
nothing happened in the waking world.

My dream, however, woke me feeling
furious. Another dream where Claudia hurt
me. I always had dreams of her hurting me.
This time through my family. Funny, I
hadn't contacted her since my arrival in
Nepal and so she was contacting me through
my subconscious. She was a Romanian witch.
In all fairness, she had already told me
she was.

In the dream, I can only assume we
were living together at my dad's home. My
little brother was there, and my cousin,
Jordan. Claudia fucked both of them and
married my brother. Now all three of us
were in love with her and distrusted each
other - including her. And Claudia seemed
to live it up as Mrs. Independent, doing as
she pleased despite the consequences. Her
attitude reminded me of a spoiled teenage
girl or a scorned ex-lover who never got
over her last breakup. I found out later in
the dream that the latter was correct.

Broken and angry, I still saw how
ridiculous the whole situation was and
ended it. I start by vocally dismantling

the situation. This stopped the immediate
hatred among my brother and cousin. Claudia
responded with much louder and colorful
responses. Using her beauty to her
advantage. When this didn't work as she had
hoped, she put on this big show. Literally
a show. Stage and all. People from the
neighborhood showed up. She apologized to
John for not being a good woman and wife
and promised to be good to him from there
on out. This worked, and even I felt bad,
and later angry again. My brother, he
deserved better than me. But he also
deserved better than her.

Luckily, the anger snapped me out of
my trance and I acted again. This time not
vocally or in a show as she had done, but
through writing. I immediately started
writing everything. How everything
happened. Claudia caught wind of this and
knew I would paint her as the bad guy.
Everybody's a bad guy in somebody's story,
sweetie. She also didn't like that I had
given her no attention since her show. She
was better at this game in real life. Even
my imagination couldn't keep up with her.

She was distraught and sought me out.
The entire dream took place in and around
my old house, so it didn't take long for
her to find me. She tried destroying my
computer to end my attempt at telling the
story. When she failed, she appealed to the
side of me that loved her. First, by crying
and saying ever since I walked into her
life, I had ruined it. Second, by pleading
to allow her to try a life again with my

brother.

It seemed sincere. And out of hurt, sympathy, and ultimately love, I left. I went to an apartment in the city telling no one. Blytheville was not a big city. It was not even a city; it was a town. But it felt far away.

Sitting alone in my new apartment, I knew I had done the right thing. I would miss them, but there was no place for me in their lives anymore.

Then I fell back asleep. It was only about fifteen or twenty minutes, but it sent me to another home movie. I did that a lot. Sometimes on purpose. Just by hitting the snooze five or six times, I could watch a few different movies every morning. Sometimes it was a series. It was the only thing I liked about waking up.

I had an erotic dream this time. I didn't remember much, but I woke up happy and confused. That one was much simpler to analyze. I hadn't released the pressure at all since my trek started. The pressure had been building, but it was just too damn cold to do anything about it.

#

These dreams reminded of other vivid dreams I had experienced so far on the trek.

I was walking past my bathroom back home in Marseille in the apartment Claudia and I shared. I glanced in to see Claudia doing something in the mirror. I then saw

another man in the mirror beside her.
Shocked by this, I took a half step back to
get a better look. I realized that man in
the mirror was making the same movements as
myself. The only conclusion was that it was
me in the mirror. I was the other guy.
Despite knowing this, I did not recognize
myself. I saw I had shaved which threw me
off, but even after this I spent five
minutes looking at myself trying to figure
out what was different. Trying to see who I
was. After some time, I just shrugged and
accepted this stranger in the mirror.

The night before that, I woke up
terrified. I had lost sleep because of it.
Resting the whole night eyes wide shut.

I was sitting in a high grassy field
in the middle of the night. I was not sure
why, but I felt the need to keep a constant
surveillance on the two-story farmhouse
about 200m in front of me. There was also
somebody 100m to my left doing the same
thing. He was not somebody I knew in real
life, but in this dream he seemed to be a
teammate of mine. Despite the military feel
to it all, I had no weapon of any kind and
I had no clear objective in mind.

To my right was a clothesline. On my
first scan of the area, there was nothing
hanging on it. However, on a later scan of
the area, I saw something. I keep my eye on
it to make out what it was in the dark.
After a few minutes with no clear idea, the
wind blew, causing this thing to bounce and
turn on the line. As the gust passed by and
caused this thing to bounce slowly, it

turned towards me. With a glow, possibly
from the moonlight, I saw the face of a
Japanese cat doll staring at me. I
continued to stare back, scared of this
strange occurrence, but curious at the same
time.

Eventually, my attention was pulled
away by the shadow of a man behind the
glowing, smiling cat. How did he get there?
Who was he? Where did he come from? How
could I let him get so close without being
aware? I sat perfectly still and monitored
him. Maybe he hadn't seen me yet. He
started to move closer to me, but
unhurried. I could still not see any
defining details, just a dark silhouette of
a man. I started to question myself. What
was I supposed to do about this? Why
couldn't I see his face, but the damn doll
was so clear? What was I doing here?

By this point, the man shone a light
in my direction. He kept the light focused
on my area, but I was confident I was still
well hidden. He started to move toward me
again, keeping the light in my area. Fear
took over, and I became paralyzed. Then an
inner voice took over and told me to sit
up. I obeyed. The light moved to my face,
barely revealing myself above the high
grass line. Paralyzed in fear. A deer
caught in the headlights. I had failed. A
feeling of defeat washed over me. Death was
a welcome certainty. The man moved quicker.
Was there no last escape? Could this be a
dream? I told myself to move. Move! I told
myself to shake out of this and run. I

shook, I woke up. It had all been a dream, but the feeling lingered with me as had the image.

#

I took the rest of the day to stroll up a hill without a bag. Going up was okay on my leg. I also learned in my Acute Mountain Sickness briefing that going up and down hills helped. I still couldn't understand how people didn't realize that where we were in Nepal and everything was up and down. I took a hike to a nearby lama to receive a blessing. I liked these old Tibetan guys. They had something figured out. I knew in idea what it was, but when you saw them, you just felt it. They had good spirits. You knew a good spirit when you met one.

He didn't ask for money but 100 Nepalese rupees was less than a euro and I would have given him more if I had seen him begging on the side of the street in Marseille. He gave me a pat on the head with a wooden block while saying a bunch of things I didn't understand. Then he put a string necklace around me. It was supposed to be good luck for getting over the pass. He probably knew I would need it.

I stayed up on the top of that hill until sunset. I could see the small town of Manang about 500 meters down. But I mostly stared at the glacier on the other side of the valley. I had never seen anything like it. It was overwhelming. It was beautiful.

The day had been beautiful.

I climbed back down to meet my companions for dinner. I hadn't seen them for the most part of the day.

Matt broke the news he wouldn't be leaving with us tomorrow. I saw this coming. Cathy also felt sick now. Well, shit. It was a down conversation after such an up day. The weather was supposed to be cloudy and snowy tomorrow and my leg was still causing trouble. Now, I was making excuses. It was contagious. Tomorrow may turn into another rest day. Fuck it. I would like to continue, but if waiting one more day meant I would have company, it was a fair idea.

I also learned that if something happened to me at this point in the climb, they would have to send a helicopter. But they wouldn't send a helicopter unless you had traveler's insurance and a $3500 minimum credit card. I had neither. Matt said if something happened though, he would call it in under his name and then figure out the details once I made it down the mountain. He also lent me a couple thousand rupees since the ATM didn't exist. I hadn't thought of the money thing either, so I was out of cash and not even on the other side of the mountain. Preparation was key. I seemed to lose keys a lot.

29

Matt stayed.

I felt him leaning in that direction from the dinner the night before. I wasn't feeling that much better, but I just didn't want to stay in the same place for that long when we were only halfway up climbing up the hill. This lake I had only heard of also enchanted me. It seemed more worthy to see, to achieve than just walking over a mountain pass.

I packed my bags planning to head out on my own. I was disheartened by leaving my pleasant company, but something drew me much more than companionship.

As I was waiting downstairs to say goodbye to Matt, Cathy came down packed and said she was coming with me. I could see almost a pang of lost love in Matt's eyes. Not a romantic love, but a loss of something that didn't see the end he had envisioned and hoped for. He made a few 'Are you sure?' attempts to ask her to stay, and I could see the discomfort in her to tell him 'Yes.' They had been together since they met on a website to meet fellow trekkers in Kathmandu. They had each come on their own, but came together almost immediately and just as quickly made their plans together. It was nice to see people come together like that and I was glad to have been a part of it, even in a spontaneous, add-on sense. I felt guilty too, since it was Matt that invited me

along and had me join his team, and now I
was splitting it apart. Matt would leave
the next day to continue on the path to the
pass, which would put him ahead of us. We
spoke hopefully and optimistically about
crossing the pass together and how he might
wait for us at one of the base camps for
such a reason. Though it was no promise,
and none of us assumed it was such. We said
'See you soon,' but we meant, 'Goodbye.'

Cathy and I left. It would be a full
day getting there. Longer than any day we
had had so far. Up to this point of the
trek, we had only walked about five hours a
day with breaks in between, sometimes
frequent and sometimes long. It made a day,
a short day, but a day. I felt confident
with my drive and her steadiness. I
imagined getting there, running up the
mountain, and then getting back on track
without a loss of breath or time.

I felt that way until the first two
hours were over. Up and down and up and
down. Was it left or right here? Was this
even a trail? My motivation became a desire
just to get to the base camp before it
snowed too heavily.

#

There were two villages we passed
along the way that provided a place to stay
for people making the trek, but the steady
tortoise won the race.

'Good to go?' I would ask.

A smile and 'Yep.'

The trail was windy, cold, and the last leg of it involved walking across a landslide area. Considering that there was not even enough trail to put one foot, I wondered how the villagers brought large cattle or supplies through here. I kept imagining one little rock turning into an all out landslide as we walked across it. The entire mountainside was nothing but small rocks. Forty-five minutes of leaning against these small rocks so as not to be blown off the inch-wide trail by the extreme wind and gusts, I looked down and envisioned the fall quite a lot. It would be one hell of a slide. One hell of a ride.

We made it. We arrived at Tilicho base camp, got our shack, and then headed to the common area where we found Friedrich and Aviva. The common area was like many other places we stayed at. It was a large room with a kitchen in the back. It was the only room with a stove to heat the area and it is where everybody who stayed there would stay until it was time to go back out to their rented shack and sleep in their sleeping bags.

There were people scattered around the open space, some at tables reading, some at tables eating, and some at tables drinking tea and staring at the larger concentration of people near the front of the room. This is where we found Friedrich and Aviva. There were probably a dozen people in this little circle.

Friedrich was under the weather. They had just finished their climb to Tilicho

Lake that day and already come back down.
Friedrich was now feeling the wrath of
Acute Mountain Sickness. I believed his
story. He didn't seem the type to use it as
an excuse. He had himself curled up on the
floor with a jacket over his head. It
seemed mostly like a headache, but he
couldn't eat and was having some nausea. I
believed more than anything his ears were
the worst of it. He was happy to see us,
but hid under his jacket most of the
evening before finally heading to bed.

Aviva was still her cheerful and
friendly self, but not as emphatic as she
had been before. She was concerned about
Friedrich. She was eager to continue the
trip, but just as ready to stay and wait
for Friedrich to rest as long as he needed.
Cathy and I also met two of their new
companions, two Israeli boys who would go
along with them. They wore sandals too.

'Where's Matt?' Aviva asked.

'He still wasn't feeling well. SO, he
stayed another night in Manang, and will
head up to the pass directly rather than
the detour here. We're hoping to catch up
with him.'

Aviva told us about the lake.

'It's the most beautiful thing I've
ever seen.' She said. I looked at the
pictures she took. It looked inspiring, but
far from the most beautiful thing I had
ever seen.

'It's amazing.' Cathy said looking at
the pictures.

'So was it a tough climb?' I asked.

She looked at Friedrich. 'It wasn't too bad, but it is straight up. We didn't go up too fast, but it was still such a change that even I felt dizzy once we got up there. Friedrich seemed okay at first, but even after the climb down he's only gotten worse.'

'That's scary.' I said. 'I wasn't too convinced of this mountain sickness thing, but Friedrich… I didn't see him falling victim to it.'

'Yeah, he wasn't taking the Diamox before, but now he's going to.' She said.

'How long did it take you?' I asked.

'It only took three hours to climb up, then once you get to the top, it's only another thirty minutes to the lake. We stayed up there for an hour and then climbed down. Going down only took an hour.'

'That's not too bad, I guess.'

'It's not too bad.' She said. 'But most people say it's harder than the pass itself. So if you do it, then you should be okay for the rest of the trip.'

'That's kind of comforting.' Cathy said.

Most of the night though, I spoke to a young-old couple from Canada and the Czech Republic. The man was in his forties; she was in her twenties. They had met when he was backpacking in her home country of Czech. They had been together since, just walking. They lived out of their bags and had been to many parts of the wild world to trek, to camp, and I imagined, to make

hairy armpit love. They were now planning
to climb to the lake, but rather than head
back down to the main trail, they would
just continue through another trail that
stayed around the same elevation. They were
trekking across the entire Nepalese
Himalayas. They were already well into
their trip.

I wasn't too interested in their love
story or personal lives as interesting as
they were, but I listened hoping to get
around to her violin. She was a very thin
girl and carried a bag twice the size of
mine that included a violin. She had played
it her whole life. It was her art. It was
something so valuable to her that she
strapped it to a bag and carried it with
her across the Himalayan mountains.

She played a piece for me. I was
seduced immediately.

She played another. I wanted to open
up and tell her everything. I wanted her to
know that I had always wanted to play.

She continued to play a few more
pieces, and I just listened. This is life.
This is magic. This is the unexpected when
it is most needed.

I thanked her for the music and
complimented her strong character for her
liberating and honest lifestyle. Then I
left her so others could talk to her; she
was now the center of attention. The girl
who carried a violin to the top of a
mountain.

I went to sit down and eat. Cathy
joined me. We had a quiet conversation

about the following day's plans. We both
felt okay and if we really could climb up
the hill and back down by morning, we would
try to get immediately back on the trail
rather than stay another night here. As
usual, she was up for it if I was. I
figured we could turn three days into two
and be back on the main trail and only a
day behind Matt.

After dinner, we headed to our
unheated, uninsulated shack. Which wasn't
that bad since it protected you from the
wind and anybody planning to hike the
Himalayas would no doubt have a nice warm
sleeping bag and not a summer weight
sleeping bag.

I grabbed my shower gear and braved
the cold wind to have yet another cold
shower. No water. Thank God. Baby wipe bath
it was. Just like my war days.

#

Chinese neighbors and an unexpected
return of the regurgitation fairy defined
my sleep. The neighbors were loud and
inconsiderate, but not up that late so it
was just a frustration about their
existence and inconsideration that
disturbed me more than the actual
frustrating and inconsiderate disturbance.

I also woke Cathy up in my running out
the door to give a refund to the local
chef. I couldn't have been any easy person
to bunk with during this trip. I felt bad
about that, but I just pretended it didn't

happen and she didn't ask more than once if
I was okay. We understood each other pretty
well.

We didn't let the excitement from the
evening slow us down the next morning for
our climb to Tilicho Lake. It took less
than three hours going up. What made the
trip much easier than I had thought must
have been the climb without the weight of
all our belongings with us. It almost felt
like running up the hill. We still took our
time. Cathy maintained her steady pace and
I would run up ahead and then wait. She
felt bad about making me wait, but I was
glad to do it, since I didn't want to climb
too fast and pass out from lack of oxygen.

I didn't notice until the top that my
head was spinning. Then the spinning went
to annoying pain, and I sat down and drank
half my water telling myself it was just
dehydration. Cathy felt fine, and I didn't
mention my headache.

Once the walk leveled off, we faced a
wind that came from hell. It was the wind
that could freeze hell that I had heard
used in so many expressions before. It felt
like blades cutting through you. I told
myself thirty minutes of this, and we were
there. I put my head down, made sure Cathy
was with me, and charged ahead like an
adventurer discovering the back door to
Hell.

My watch said it had only been 7
minutes since we started this last leg of
the trek.

Then 12 minutes.

We crossed one guy coming back alone from the lake; he was almost running. Or gliding. I think each time he took a step, the wind lifted him off the ground and carried him another five feet forward. I was already looking forward to the return.

Fuck, it was cold. I decided it must be a scientific fact that no amount of clothing could protect you from this cold.

18 minutes.

This lake better be fucking worth it.

19 minutes.

Cathy is a little behind me, but still moving forward and in sight.

25 minutes.

Is it over this hill?

25 minutes and 30 seconds.

It has to be this hill.

26 minutes.

Stop looking at your watch. Thirty minutes could mean thirty-five or forty minutes.

27 minutes.

As you climbed the last hill, the lake just opened up to you. It was just over a thousand meter climb. You stand on a hill on a mountain at 5200 meters and look down at the highest (largest due to a technicality) lake in the world at a cool 5000 meters.

What breath I had left, what momentum rested in my feet, died. I was left speechless, utterly stunned by the overwhelming beauty. All the waterfalls, flowers, birds, and cute children could not compare to this sight. I didn't understand how a still body of water could be one of the most beautiful things I had ever seen, but I did not question it.

Cathy arrived, and I watched her feel what I had just felt. I hugged her. We both looked out over the lake for a while, the wind and cold seemed nearly irrelevant.

Then it became very relevant again, and we hid behind a small shack that I imagine provided coffee and snacks during the tourist season. We took turns jumping out into the wind and trying to get a good picture. No picture made sense. No picture could capture what we felt. Perhaps there was some high from the walk or altitude or struggle that created this delusional effect that there was something more to this lake than there really was. I didn't care. I knew I could never capture this moment with a photo, and even though you can photo-shop beauty and contrast and color into a photo, I wouldn't try to fake the nature of what I was witnessing.

We stayed for a while, but we didn't stay long. It was so damn cold.

#

It didn't take us too long to get back down the hill. We did about a five-hour hike. Not a bad day, but it was early afternoon.

'How do you feel?' I said.
'How do you feel?' She said.
'I'd like to keep going.'
'Okay. Me, too.' She smiled.

'We don't have to go far, but two hours will get us past the landslide area while it isn't too windy or snowy and will help cut off a day to the pass.'

She looked at me to say, 'I already said okay.'

I then continued to explain to her my genius plan of adding a couple extra hours to each day to cut off one entire day.

Patient girl.

As we walked, I thought about how my stamina improved with these longer, colder, and steeper days. I thought about home. I missed Claudia and my Maverick. I missed being inside. Warmth and pajamas and all three of us cuddling. Even if she was on her computer and I was on mine and the dog was in between us sleeping, or begging us, or throwing the ball on our laptop to remind us he existed. I thought about our Romanian upstairs neighbor, Petru, or Pierre as he preferred to be called. Different in so many ways of what I would normally call a friend, and one of the few people I would consider a true friend. I thought about pizza always being fifteen minutes away. And showers. Long and warm showers.

I looked around and then thought about the rest of my trip. After the pass, I was looking forward to the easy climb down. The last climb up to Poon Hill for a look at the mountains I would have just finished walking through. A chance to say goodbye to my journey and the mountains. I would appreciate the occasional break or meal

with new friends. I would miss the
solitude. Especially the solitude. The
solitude before the thrust back into the
life that felt so far away and missed.
        I was looking forward to all of it.
One experience made the other experience
richer. Without one, the other was dull,
almost a ghost of its true self. Yet side
by side, having both created so much value
in the essence of both. It was a strange
combination of having everything and
nothing. To choose one meant to lose the
other, selection meant rejection. It was
like the strings of my new friend's violin.
Playing only one string sounded stupid.
Varying it up gave you a melody. It can be
even more magical if you knew how to go
from sharp to flat in one song.
        Living this double life wasn't about
half-assing two things. Or maybe it was. I
knew I wasn't missing out on things at
home, but I knew I was appreciating them
more here, away from them, then I would if
I was home. It wasn't trying to have my
cake and eat it too. That shit didn't make
any sense. Sure. One existence could
eventually devour the other. That was the
risk, that was the game, the compromise.
Independence v. Dependability. Adventure v.
Comfort. Solitude v. Companionship. I would
spend the rest of my life half a stable
man, half a rolling stone. Compromise
didn't mean settling for one friend of five
she approved of. It didn't mean having one
or two beers and avoiding the reason
alcohol existed. That isn't compromise,

that is defeat. I had it figured out. The
sun was setting, my legs were moving, and I
had it figured out. Or I had just lost my
mind. Either way, it felt good.

30

Thorung La Pass was only two days away, and we were stopping at Letdar for the night. Our aim for the next day was the High Base Camp. It would put us at 4850 meters. I was pushing it. I was pushing her, but I was ready to get the pass over with. I was more worried about running out of money than I was about getting over the pass. There was apparently a town on the other side, Jomsom, that was much larger and had an ATM. I was on a tight budget until then. There was that and the fact I wanted to relax and go home.

'Two more days…' I thought.

Cathy was staying up well now, never having to wait for over three or four minutes for her to catch up. I was sure the pass would be easy for us. The going down will be Cathy's turn to wait for me. My leg was getting worse and my knee was still causing problems from Manang. I almost couldn't bend it, especially when stepping down. The climbs had always been up and down to this point, and I feared what an all day descent would feel like. If the other side of this mountain was as populated and crowded as people had said, I would just catch a bus down. Fuck walking down in misery and pain.

I should focus on the pass first though, or I may go down in a helicopter.

#

Today was the eleventh day of the
Annapurna Circuit. Considering the detour
to Tilicho lake, we were ahead of schedule.
From the High Base Camp, we would make our
final ascent, the peak of our journey. With
only a 600 meter change in elevation, the
climb itself should be easy enough. I've
woken up between 3:30 - 5:30 every morning,
and if I was not walking by 7:30, I was
pacing the room. Walking had become my job.
I finished my boots. The soles were coming
off both. For my left foot, I had a hole in
the front that let an unpleasant breeze run
through my toes and up my leg, while on my
right, I had the back half flying off, not
as airy as my left boot, but the flip-flop
effect was no sunny beach. I tried taping
them with some duct tape that I had
brought, but it never lasted more than an
hour or two. I was hoping the soles would
hold out until the end. I'd like to show
Claudia.
          Cathy and I walked into the High Base
Camp and found Matt, Friedrich, and Aviva
waiting for us. They purposely walked a
half day in the hopes we would catch up, so
we could cross the pass together. A
touching gesture that would soon lead to
another farewell once on the other side.
Matt, Aviva, and Cathy would take a Jeep-
taxi down the other side. Friedrich and I
planned to walk down, and we would
doubtless end up going about the same
direction and pace.
          I didn't know why, maybe it was the

lack of oxygen, maybe there was a string of
childhood lighting up in my head, but for
the joyous occasion, I prayed. A man of no
faith or God who was trying to find peace
in life or death. One who grew up on
Protestant Christianity in the bible belt
of America, turned away from it to find
faith in other religions, and found a deep
attraction to Eastern philosophy. Of all
philosophies. Of reality and reflection.
But in this moment, if there was a spirit
in a dualistic sense, I figured on the top
of a mountain - hungry, tired, and cold -
that would be the place to get in touch
with it and see what was out there. What
was in me.

#

To whom it may concern,
    I am a pilgrim on the road to finding
myself. I have been told that is the answer
to my problems in life. Finding myself.
Tell me if I have been led astray. Pity me
if I have led myself away. Help me turn
problems into solutions. Correct me when I
turn knowledge against myself. Show me the
wisdom that will help me help others.
    And since I got your attention and I
don't do this often.
    Take care of those that have been
treated unfairly by life, who feel like
they don't deserve what has happened to
them, and who sulk alone in couch corners.
Those poor bastards may never one day fight
the good fight. And aid those that can only

see the shit in themselves and in every
action they take, sometimes taking every
world problem on themselves. Both are
exhausting, endless wars within ourselves
that may take our lives before the doctor
announces our time for us.

Let the overworked and underpaid enjoy
more than a weekend off. Especially in
those places where half the weekend the
town is closed. And for those that still
find too much time to shop with stores open
or closed, help them find a new pastime,
like drinking or baseball.

Train not just me with the good fight
within, but also the kings and queens of
this world who have conquered so much
already and have yet conquered themselves.
And for those who have achieved the
greatest victory, help them off the street
and out of the bars of life because they
feel like shit for not conquering the world
around them.

Laugh at us when we try so hard to
create things, whether by a tool, a
computer, or an art-form. Laugh at us, but
give us the courage to fucking do it
anyway, even if we know somebody could do
it better than us, and a million already
have. And then laugh at the legends in a
lunchbox that have turned their inspiration
and skill into a reason for making
themselves feel better than others.

Feel sorry for those that eat too
much, drink too much, and just find
themselves with only their bowl of ice
cream or their bottle of wine as their

lover. *But also feel sorry for those that
live such a censored and controlled
lifestyle, who see themselves as heroes and
expect admiration.*

*Have mercy on those who can only see
themselves. That the world and people
around them are nothing but a blur and a
boring movie playing in the background.
Don't let them suffer too much in their
eventual silent and empty atmosphere. And
have even more mercy on those that just
give it all away. That see nothing in the
mirror and give themselves away for free.
Mercy that we may one day realize that if
we have a glove, but are hungry and not
cold, that we trade it for an apple.*

*Comfort us into understanding death.
To accept death. Not to look for it, but to
admit it is there. To realize that we all
die. Die alone. And whether we have only
one death or many deaths, help us remember
that it all ends. Rich or poor, pretty or
ugly, smart or stupid. Help us realize that
just this very fact should be enough to
make us all be a little fucking nicer with
each other until that unknowing and
unpredictable end arrives.*

*And love. God, what have you done with
this love? An equation that nearly rivals
your own. Warm those cold souls that see
love as the only solution. That tie their
happiness to it and use it to think
themselves masters of others for it. That
feel envy, and poison themselves and
torture themselves because they still can't
see that everything, including love,*

changes. And light a fire next to those that are so afraid of love that they reject every opportunity for the hope of finding the right love or a greater love or who are too afraid to experience it due to the pain that is sure to come with it.

Show us that the universe is more than just a scientific explanation and that human beings are more than just creatures with needs to be satisfied. And it would be cool if you could have a talk with those fanatics that kill people with you in mind and make our lives miserable because they put too much blind faith in you.

To you that is listening, dare us to take up the sword to fight when it is time, and to light the fire when it is time. Lead us to recognize, understand, and accept ourselves. To find the middle path that Buddha did. To swim with the stream of the Tao like Lao Tzu did. To realize that we hold both our fire and our sword with our two hands, two opposites that are equal, symmetrical, seemingly the same, but separate. Let these two hands help us build the way toward wherever the fuck it is we are supposed to be going to.

Thanks for hearing me out.
Amen.

31

The praying was a laugh. I don't know if it worked or not. I had a rough night of sleep. Cold. Some difficulty breathing and more knotted stomach pains. I didn't release the pressure this time through the form of regurgitated supper, but I had plenty of gas and diarrhea. It has graciously stayed with me all day.

It was a big day of personal achievement for me. The day started at five a.m. Not too early since I was already up half the night. I had my usual breakfast of oatmeal with apples at 5h30 and waited around until 615 for the others to get ready. It was cold. Too damn cold. Colder than should be allowed for a human to voluntarily commit himself to, but I did. Then I was testing my patience and maximum levels of frustration as I waited for the others to get ready.

The sky was lit up with a baby blue Tarheels color, but we were on the wrong side of this mountain tip as we started our ascent. We were stuck in the mountain's shadow for the first hour up. The mountain didn't protect us from the wind though and the wind was freezing. It froze my water. It froze the entire camelback. It froze my toes. I wanted to keep moving so I wouldn't break them by misplacing my steps, but I waited. I was still waiting for them. I guess I shouldn't complain; they waited for me for a half day to catch up. The difference was that they had apple pie and hot cocoa. But I waited. Every fifteen minutes, I waited fifteen minutes. And that was just for the second person. I couldn't understand it. I saw myself a fat-ass and broken with a metal rod in my leg, a screw in my knee and another screw in my hip. I drank, and I smoked, and I didn't take altitude medication. Yet, I was flying up this hill compared to them. What had the army done to me?

Another hour. Same shit. The warmest mittens in the world couldn't keep my fingers alive. I know cause I bought them. I could see them there, but I couldn't feel them.

And my face. I couldn't feel it well enough to even speak properly, much less feel all the snot that was freezing on my upper lip.

On a positive, my pack was light, or at least I couldn't feel it too heavy on my shoulders and lower back like I usually could. Also, I was wearing all my clothes.

After about an hour of stop and go freeze yourself, the sun was high enough that I found a spot along a natural rock wall that hid me from the wind, but allowed me to stay in the sun. I waited twenty minutes before seeing Aviva. I was unnerved. The wait frustrated me as I could not understand how they could be so far behind in such a short amount of time. After a quick conversation with Aviva asking about the others, I decided I had waited long enough - the others had each

other - Aviva and I would continue up. She
agreed. She stayed up fairly well and
responded well when I was motivating her.

I stayed with her until we saw the
prayer flags flapping in the arctic wind.
It was a finish line. There were still
mountains around us higher than us, but we
felt on top of the world.

We danced. We took photos. I smoked a
cigarette with a local. We talked to other
trekkers including a Dutch couple we had
seen throughout our trek. It was a moment.
A beautiful moment. I wanted to make love
in that cold world because it was such a
moment.

Cathy arrived about forty minutes
after us. Matt and Friedrich showed up
twenty minutes after her. Friedrich being
the support for Matt. He was struggling
again. I felt sorry for him until I
realized he wouldn't want sympathy. He
wanted support and appreciation. So I gave
him both and felt good about it when he
accepted it.

We all made it. Aviva gave a running
and jumping greeting to each as they came
up the last stretch. Their exhausted and
smiling faces made running on frozen toes
in below freezing weather a joyous moment.

I was proud of all of them. Probably
the lack of oxygen talking again. It wasn't
Everest. It wasn't worth writing a story
about. It was tourism. Selected tourism,
but still tourism.

When Friedrich arrived, we had to do
our clapping push-ups. We planned this.

Doing it without a shirt was not. It was cold... But we got some laughs. Some stares, and even some cheers.

After a few more photos with the group, we started our 1500m descent.

Mostly uneventful.

My knee was still causing trouble, but it was a beautiful view. The weather began to steadily get warmer. After the victory of crossing the pass, we had an earned and relaxed climb down.

Matkinah was beautiful and settled in a valley. We visited a monastery. Friedrich had been there before and told us about it. Him and his parents had climbed this half already, but never did the pass, now as an adult and no longer a teenager with mama and pop, he wanted to do the full thing from the other direction. And he did.

We found a guesthouse for all of us, and I had a victory beer.

I also had two dinners. A grilled garlic chicken. It was good to eat decent food again. And two hours later, a veggie burger. I spoiled myself with the mood being content and the air feeling spiritual. We took warm showers and felt accomplished. Then we made plans that separated us and would ideally bring us back together.

I put another pint in front of me.

32

The following day was a big day.

It started with goodbyes. Matt. Cathy. An Italian I never really knew. The Dutch couple we had met a few times. Aviva decided to join myself and Friedrich on the climb down to fully complete the circuit.

We would all go our separate ways down the hill. North Americans in jeeps. The Dutch on bikes. Clichés, but good people. Glad I had met them, but always funny to see the reality of the cliché when placed in front of you. Friedrich was a German. Aviva was Israeli. I was a confused American. We probably fitted our clichés too.

We had breakfast together. Took our pictures. Hugged. Smiled. And left.

It was good to be back on the road again. We got to Kagbeni in three hours. We visited a monastery with dogs and children in Tibetan maroon and yellow outfits. They had their shaved heads and enlightened smiles. The dogs barked at us.

We saw stolen American logos and names. Hill-ton, their guesthouse really was on a ton of hill. Applebee's was exactly the same spelling and logo. We had lunch there, tea and sandwiches.

Then we fought a sandstorm for two hours walking to Jomsom.

Friedrich was a newly certified pilot for Lufthansa airlines. Apparently, you can go straight into pilot training from high

school in Germany and the company pays for
all of it. I was jealous. I liked Germans.
I thought about a German sweetheart that
wanted to break all the rules with me.
Maybe I'd move to Germany. Things seemed
all right there.

Friedrich talked about his school as
we walked. Then he talked about the
nightmare it must be to land a plane in
this area. Jomsom had an airport, and he
was doing the simulation in his head. A
valley squeezed tightly between two
mountain ranges, with this wind, only a
small plane could fit, and small planes
were the hardest to control in rough
environments.

I got scared thinking about it. I had
a rough flight from Marseille to Paris and
then going to India. I still hadn't
shrugged it off or enjoyed it as I once
always did. I felt my stomach in my throat
just from simulating the flight in my mind.
Maybe I needed to seek psychological help.
I wasn't sure what had happened to me, but
I no longer took pleasure in flying. I felt
like a pussy, but I couldn't help it. I
couldn't reason or trick myself out of it.

We got to Jomsom after a few hours of
walking like Laurence of Arabia through the
sandstorm. What should have taken eight
hours to walk, we made it in five. Much
faster than before the pass, Friedrich and
Aviva were more my pace.

It was only about four when we arrived
at our destination, but we had pushed it.
It tired me.

I found my ATM. Then I relaxed. Then, I found an internet café. This place was civilized.

I checked my email. Judy, Jackie's grandma, my best friend growing up, had passed away. People kept dying when I was too far away to visit them. I loved that woman like my own grandmother. I stayed on that moment for a while and looked at everybody in the room, accepting the reality of their death for them. It was sad. Another funeral I've missed. We always forgot or put it in the back of our minds we would die. Oh, Judy. I'll never forget you saying, 'Lying through your teeth,' as you would catch Jackie and me getting into more trouble.

I didn't know how to respond to Jackie's email, so I didn't.

Sometimes I thought about how long it has been since I left Arkansas and how it has changed.

Claudia also sent a few emails.

The first four were very sweet and loving. Even saying, 'I love you (today, but we'll see when you get back.)' Well, at least I knew it was not somebody pretending to be her. The last one was not as affectionate though. It was sent two days ago and five days after the first four. I had been out of touch for a while. I didn't miss it.

She said she hoped I was having a good time. It was maybe passive aggressive. But I did unfairly put a lot on her. She had work and school. Both part time, but she

was a serious woman, and every minute
counted. Then there was Maverick. He held
true to his name.

She said I should get home soon and
come back to the real world.

I didn't respond to that either.

33

We took our time getting up. Waiting until the sun was up before for moving around. We were on the downhill side. I got up first and had my breakfast in a near empty kitchen. It was a solid breakfast.

Not feeling so tired, I faced Claudia and sent her a response. I decided against trying to actually justify or reason with her last email, but just wanted to comfort her. I usually write good letters, but this one said, 'I miss you. Be home soon.' I hoped that would hold her over until I got home, or at least to Pokhara.

Friedrich, Aviva, and I planned another long day, but took it more relaxing. We stopped halfway at the apple capital of Nepal, Marpha. It only took us an hour and a half to get there, but we stayed for a while. We had apple crumble, apple cider, and apple brandy. It was strong and sweet, and it was good. It was a beautiful morning of just sitting, talking, and laughing. I also finished a book. I would have to find another book store to exchange for new books. I must have read about 11 books, always carrying two or three on me and then changing with other people or with stores along the way.

We ended up staying for lunch before we made progress further down the trail. I was drunk and didn't want to move, but staying wasn't the best idea even if it was the apple capital of Nepal. The walk was all right in the beginning being slightly drunk, but after two hours, the accelerated hangover kicked in and I was feeling knotted and had that annoying pain in my head that came with drinking alcohol.

The hangover with the wind and general fatigue from two weeks of trekking made the afternoon long. We ventured off the main road for half of it, which was nice. There were apple farms, pine trees, lovely smells, and more flashbacks of home. You could see the change in microclimates as each day passed, and we descended hundreds of meters at a time.

This side of the pass was more populated. China was building a road for them to make trade easier with India. Nepal didn't mind, but us nature-tourists, we disapproved and always tried making our own trails away from where vehicles could now pass. I was glad Nepal was getting an upgrade into the modern world, but walking along roads, even dirt roads just made the trip feel like walking to get somewhere rather than walking to be lost somewhere.

That's when the motivation started to fade and fatigue and soreness started to settle in. I wanted to get this bag off my shoulders and my feet off the ground.

Even with our relaxing morning, we still did over eighteen kilometers.

My knees were shot.

I got a new book and started reading it while waiting for dinner.

#

We left Larjung this morning, adding an Italian sailor to the group. We had met him at Marpha while having our apple brandies and crumbles. Then crossed him again last night at our guesthouse. He had his own boat in the western Mediterranean. He could never take more than a week off, so this was his third trip flying over here to complete the circuit, just doing legs at a time. I don't think I had ever been that motivated about something.

He was an interesting guy though. I didn't take to him too much at Marpha, the apple capital of Nepal because he interrupted me while reading and drinking to say hello, but giving the guy a chance last night at dinner and walking with him, he had some wisdom and spirit about him. He was about forty, but had the vigor of a much younger man. Despite that, he kept calm like a much older man.

We talked about women. We were on the same page there and even though he was the type to oil his long dark hair back every day, I could see we were of similar breed. He must have thought the same. He offered me a job on his boat with a promise that in a year I would have my own boat. I considered it.

Myself, the sailor, sailing from port to port, carrying my charm and STDs from one bar to the next. Speaking my languages and seducing women of all shapes, sizes, and colors. I tucked his email in a safe place.

We were still walking on and off the
main road. The map said it was a trail, but
it was obviously behind Chinese production
and we constantly worked our way towards
any side path we could find.

My boots were getting worse and worse.
Three quarters of both were hanging off,
but in opposite directions. I was tripping
on them and flip flopping everywhere. The
sound was driving me insane and the
conscious effort to not trip over them was
wearing me more than the boots themselves.

We were on the other side of the river
from the main road when I saw a bus. I
didn't even think about it. I yelled back
to my friends. 'See you in Tatopani.' I
then took advantage of the bus stopping to
let a woman off to run across the first
wire bridge I could find. I waved the thing
down for a ride.

The more I thought about it, the more
I was glad I did it. I felt like shit
leaving like that, but they knew about my
knees, and that day and the next was a
fifteen hundred meter descent. My knees
were reason enough, but I also hadn't
washed my clothes in a few days and they
needed it badly after the sweat and
sandstorms.

The bus ride was an adventure. I sat
on the floor, bags in my lap, rocking back
'n' forth like a ship on the high seas. The
road was rough and the driving slow.
Nepalese were vomiting and the guy sitting
on the chair beside me covered his mouth
the whole time. Luckily, the trip for me

was only about three hours. It would have been six to eight walking. With a stop for sleep along the way. My friends would catch up tomorrow.

We only stopped once along the way on the bus. During that stop, I got to talking to some younger guys. They were excited to speak to an American it seemed. I was a long way from home. They asked me if I smoked; I lifted my cigarette in response, then they pointed to a ditch about twenty feet away. It was full of weed. Naturally growing marijuana. I had seen some on the climb up, but didn't bother. I was never much of a pothead. I'd do it sometimes. Mostly when drunk and with others, but it was never a habit. They pulled some off, rolled two joints, and the three of us smoked until the bus was ready.

I arrived in what seemed like a haven, a tropical island paradise. I had just jumped a few more climate zones with that descent. I grabbed a nice place. I would have a private room for the first time on this trek. A big bed. Still no sheets, though I guess that didn't matter, but it still felt like a king's chambers to this peasant. There was a garden outside my glass door and the kitchen downstairs had good food.

To continue my luxury, the guest house offered a laundry service, I knew it would still be hand washed and hung dry, but at least it wasn't me doing the scrubbing and hanging this time. I dropped off all my clothes but a pair of shorts which I hadn't

worn yet and an undershirt and jacket which
I considered cleaner than anything else
that I had.

I strolled through town and smiled. I
stopped into an internet café and checked
my email. Already Cathy wrote saying she
was in Pokhara. There was another email
from a guy named Ron about the biltong
business. I wasn't too concerned with that
at the moment. And one from Claudia
responding to my Jomsom email. She seemed
happy with my words. Not only did she put
me in the clear, she said she would wait
for me with welcoming and loving arms. I
didn't think she had that in her. My
disappearance was just as good for her as
it was for me it seemed.

Continuing my exploration of this big-
small town, I found a boy who repaired
shoes. A shoe repair, the chance. The gods
were smiling on me today. I dropped them
off and went back to my garden resort to
have cake, masala tea, and some well-
deserved alone time with a book.

The night was still young after my
cake and tea, and I felt rejuvenated by my
blessings. There was talk of a hot spring,
so I went searching. It was a fifteen-
minute walk, but I found it. I felt light
in my flip-flops, purposely intended flip-
flops, and short shorts. The spring was
nice. There were two Nepalese guys there
trying to sell beer, popcorn, and
chocolates to the tourists there. I grabbed
two beers. There was a couple there too,
and they had popcorn. After my first beer,

we started talking. Then she ordered a beer, and we talked. He got a chocolate bar, and he got huffy. I didn't give a shit; the gods were smiling on me this day.

I knew she was still going to bed with him that night, and I said goodbye to her back tattoo as she stepped out. Damn nice body, shame she doesn't share it with more than one man. I finished my beer and walked back in the dark to my little haven, grabbing some bread and lemon water for dinner before heading to bed.

The weather was much warmer already. Just days before I was wearing everything I had, now I was wearing next to nothing. I lay in bed and felt great.

I thought about my trip. It was nearing its end. Reality would soon be back. Claudia was waiting with open arms now it seemed, but that wasn't worried me.

I focused on what I was getting out of all this. Why had I come and had it served its purpose? I learned a lot but nothing that I had expected. I knew that to figure out who you were as a person; you had to make yourself uncomfortable. You had to take yourself out of the familiar. Away from the people you know, the environment you know, the life you know. Who you were in this moment revealed a lot. And the more extreme the change, the better: a different country, a different culture, a different language, all alone. I've noticed I adapted more quickly now. I became more comfortable in these scary and new worlds more quickly. Today, when I left my new friends to go

ahead, I realized it was really an inner
voice wanting to be alone and to get
another glimpse into my soul. I was happy
with whom I was. It was a rare gift to get
to feel that way.

More than anything, I learned that
freedom was having the most important thing
without owning it.

34

I stayed another day in Tatopani,
mostly in the hot springs. I brought my
beer this time. I watched people eat their
popcorn. And they watched me drink my beer.
We were both at the movies, enjoying the
show in our own way.

My friends arrived that evening and
luck would have it they stopped in the same
guesthouse I did. They immediately told me
I had made a good call with the bus. It was
a very long, boring downhill walk that even
had their knees singing. I wouldn't have
made it, I thought.

After they did their post-trek
routine, we went back down to the hot
springs. Aviva was wearing a bathing suit.
She had a good-looking body and the same
magnetic smile. I had always wanted her
since our rooftop conversation before the
trek even began, but it wasn't until our
closeness in that steamy water, I could
feel the heat from her body more than I
could from the water encompassing my flesh.

I got the feeling she wasn't a big
drinker, but she had a few with me and she
got tipsy from the two she had. She was
still the happy, energetic spirit that
carried us through the trip, but now she
was quieter. More still and sent her energy
out in a subtle yet feminine way. She was
sexy. She was a woman.

I watched her get out of the hot
springs and she turned around and watched

me get out. Our eyes didn't lie, but we were both to go to our own beds that night. Despite my desires and sense of freedom in this foreign world, I still thought of Claudia. I thought of her, and I thought of myself. How selfish I had been in my life with the women I had taken for myself. Most of them looking for a good man. Seeing something in me they wanted to keep for themselves, but I never let them. I would give them my heart, let them touch a part of myself, but only for a short time before I moved on. I told myself I wouldn't do that with Aviva. She either saw that or was too timid to make the first move herself.

I was peeling beer labels off of beer bottles, but I told myself that this is one flower I would leave. One flower I would admire from afar.

#

The next day, I woke up. We walked more, and we talked more. We ate. I missed home.

The rest of the trip was downhill, both literally and metaphorically. It was all downhill except for a quick trip up Poon Hill to look at the three 8000 meter mountains we had just walked through. It was a good closure to an amazing trip.

35

The trek was over: 308 kilometers, 100 hours, 19 days, diarrhea every day, and vomiting in the middle of the night at least once a week. But it was all done now. It felt good. I would enjoy my last few days in Pokhara. We arrived yesterday, tired and frustrated, but ultimately with smiles, stories, and laughs. Coming down the mountain, we walked out of the tree line - the weight of the journey came off my shoulders. Not literally, I still had my backpack and satchel on, but the weight of the real world immediately replaced it: car horns, street vendors, harassing taxi drivers, and chaos.

The next day, I finished my Christmas shopping. I got a shave in a barber shop which cost me one euro, and they did it with a straight blade. One euro and not a scratch on my juggler. I had thought about keeping my Jesus beard for the great return to France, but it was ugly, and I thought about Claudia and how I would want her when I got home. I wanted nothing impeding that. I'm sure women love Jesus, but I doubt they want to jump his bones. People don't trust you when you say you love them in an eternal, indifferent way. The way Jesus would have. They found that phony. Maybe it was. You could tell somebody you wanted to eat them, devour them, and they melt like butter to be consumed. Spread them over toast if you wished. If you loved somebody in a possessive, consuming way, you would possess and consume them. If you loved them in a pure way, if you allowed them to be, yet be loved; they would just be, usually without you. Besides, Claudia was an atheist.

I got myself some patches to sew onto my backpack and jacket. Another conquest under my belt. Then, I bought my bus ticket to get back to the capital. Once the chores were done, I went to a small garden right by the lake called Jiva where I had a massage and a tea. It was a beautiful, quiet garden. I had my tea, a massage from a beautiful Nepalese girl for 30 euros and only 30 meters away from my books.

Relaxation was the only thing in sight for the next day and a half.

#

The last day, I had lunch with everybody from the trek. Cathy, Matt, Friedrich, and Aviva. Matt bought me a book to say thanks for leading the way along the trek. It was 'The Prophet' written by a Lebanese-American guy. It was spiritual, poetic, and short. Most of them bought postcards to send home, but then had trouble writing on the back. I wrote most of theirs for them and they seemed impressed. Exposing myself has never been a problem, and even though I was writing for them, I knew I could write from myself and the same feelings and thoughts would apply. They thought it was a magic trick. It

wasn't magic or a trick, just a secret some
of us had.

I packed my bags. With the gifts, I
had to leave most of my trekking gear
behind to include my beloved Legion
backpack, that fucking summer weight bag
that was not intended for mountain weather
sleeping, and my walking poles that held my
weak leg up for so many kilometers,
forward, up, and down.

My last night, I went to a bar across
the street from the guesthouse I was in. I
met a woman and a filmmaker. Talking to the
woman brought the filmmaker over. I told my
stories. She wanted to sleep with me. He
wanted to make a movie of me. I was
flattered, but left without doing either or
giving them any contact to see it through
later. This trip was a transition from one
life to another. And this transition was
over and I didn't want it to last longer
than the three pints it took me to tell it.

Leaving my friends was sad. The trip
was over, but I was excited to be going
back home. A changed man, I thought. No
longer drowning in my despair, but a
trekker of great mountains. A pilgrim of
Buddha, visiting his tree and retreating
for ten days in silent meditation in a
place just outside of town from his place
of enlightenment. I was a sole adventurer,
embracing the solitude and sharing with
strangers and fellow travelers.

I wanted to share this experience with
somebody. Everybody. But I wanted to tell
it all poetically. I didn't feel I could do

that. Then I felt it more valuable
containing it all for myself. Selfish
perhaps, but if I shared it all, would it
still have the same worth? I wasn't sure I
wanted to risk that.

36

My first week back, I mostly hid at home. Claudia and I lay naked most of the time and were happy. Distance did that to people. Everything that were problems before seemed nonexistent. Was it because I had changed or was this just an illusion because of the emotion of the return?

My fragile stomach seemed to balance out, and I was slowly re-acclimating to the real world. It took me a few days to get my lost baggage from Air France, but they did eventually arrive and Claudia adored her gifts, especially the backpack. I knew she would like that one. It was an ugly green with purple linings. It had drawstrings and way too much stuff on it, most of which didn't make it seem like a backpack, but she liked weird stuff like that.

She had it with her as we were sitting on an empty beach watching Maverick play. It was the first day the sun had come out since my return. It was December, but it was Marseille. It was a nice day.

I noticed that when I walked around town, I still had the urge to look at everything as a picture and to say 'Namaste' when I entered a shop or passed somebody in the street. The smells were strong and nauseating. So much perfume, I nearly died the first time I took the metro in the morning rush. I was easing my way in though, even had two beers and a kebab the previous night. Civilization.

I knew I'd have to live again soon. I
would have to start a routine. I would have
to decide about my teaching and my business
before January.

I had two worlds I was living in
simultaneously and I had to do my best to
find a balance between these two worlds.

37

After a couple weeks back home, I decided to let my friends know. We went to O'Malley's, our pub. It was good being back with the boys. Getting drunk. Looking at all the pretty girls, the trashy women, the pretty boys, and the desperate men. The smell of piss and alcohol was still the same, a nice cocktail of smells that burned the nostrils about the way beer shits did.

I went out with them about three times over the next week. Claudia went back to the way she was before I had left. And just like that, life was back to normal as if nothing had changed. My experience, my travels, my learning was still there, but it seemed more like a story now. No different from any other story I could have just read. Learned the lesson, let it hold me for a while, and then felt it fade away, but never really noticing it was gone until it was too far away to call back.

It was as sad as a dead Christmas tree, but I knew the sadness would fade away too.

#

Marseille was the culture capital of Europe this year, and Claudia and I decided to be there for the opening event. Living in Le Panier of Marseille put us at a five-minute walk from the Vieux Port. Fireworks, tourists, locals, drunks, and thieves all

showed up. This all made it nearly
impossible to get into the center Vieux
Port area, but we tried.

We eventually settled for a more
spacious area in the back for some
breathing room and to meet up with a
friend of Claudia's who we were supposed to
meet in town.

She kept checking her phone and
looking around.

'So where is he?' I said.

She didn't respond. She looked down at
her phone again and then looked around.

'Okay.' I said.

We waited around for a while. I was
looking around at all the people and things
going on in the streets. I was just
admiring the atmosphere, but she just kept
looking for this other guy. It made me
wonder how close a friend this guy was to
get my cold Claudia so agitated. It pissed
me off. I hated jealousy, and one thing I
taught myself well being with Claudia was
just letting that shit slide off.

She was never jealous. Too the point
you'd think she didn't care about you. I
got good at that too.

Her special friend never seemed to
show.

'Let's work our way to the middle and
see what's going on.' I said.

We walked in.

She kept looking around, phone in
hand. It was only about a minute before she
ran off into the middle of the crowd
without telling me. Maybe she didn't run.

But she disappeared quickly.

That's motivation, I thought. I should have just told her he was in the middle all along and then followed her. I lost her though. I lost her, and I was still doing the no cell phone thing. I saw cell phones and Facebook as a sickness. So about a year before leaving for India, I had gotten rid of both. I liked it. Most people didn't, especially the people I worked for. It taught me patience, but it didn't teach other people patience. At that moment though, I wished I had a cell phone. So I just walked back and forth between where I lost her and where we were hoping she'd be doing the same thing. She was on a mission though, and I wasn't the goal. She also knew I didn't have a cell phone.

After half an hour of walking around in circles looking for her through crowds and half an hour of just sitting still and trying to enjoy the show, I decided I had given it a good enough effort and went back home.

I called her when I got there to let her know I gave up looking for her. It upset her. I didn't care. Despite letting jealousy slide off, I was upset with her for just leaving me like that for the possibility of meeting some other guy. Anger aside, I thought I did the right thing by heading home to call her. Regrouping wasn't working by finding each other in the crowd's chaos. We needed communication. We had always lacked communication.

She called back about twenty minutes
later, saying she never found her friend
and was heading home. I wanted to laugh.
Laugh at her. Laugh at every girl that's
ran away from a man just for the
possibility of being with another. Mostly I
just wanted to confront Claudia about it.
But I had been drinking and a man can't win
a fight when he's drunk. Even if he wins
the argument in every way, he'll still lose
because, 'You're drunk.'

    'I had two beers.' I'd say.

    'I can see it in your eyes.' she'd
say.

    'You're an idiot.'

    'You see how mean you are to me? I
deserve better than this.'

    'Yeah,' I'd say, 'Maybe.'

    'We'll talk tomorrow.'

    'I don't want to talk tomorrow. I want
to recover tomorrow. I want to talk now.'

    This is the point where she'd already
be turned away to go to bed. Depending on
how loud the argument got, the door would
be slammed at a corresponding loudness. The
above scenario would have only caused a
hard shut. Not even worth a slam. One good
thing about the apartment Claudia and I
were in at the time was that it had no
doors. It had the main floor with the
kitchen and living area, then a larger
basement area. We slept in a large open
area in the basement. You could see it from
the main floor as there was nothing there
but a railing to keep from falling. It also
had a curtain we put up. The downstairs

also had a wine cave we used for storage and then there was our bathroom. People didn't like that we didn't have a door for the bathroom, but at least it was downstairs. The only door to slam in our apartment was the one leaving the apartment. I always liked that.

I had another beer while waiting for her to come home. I ran the conversation through my head multiple times and no matter how convinced I was that I was right; I knew it would end badly for me. I wasn't sure if she would pick a fight, but if she did, I wasn't sure if I could keep my mouth shut. I went upstairs to hang out with my neighbor. She would work up quite a tropical storm of frustration, anger, and fight on the walk up to our apartment. I figured giving her a few minutes to cool off alone would be best.

There were four apartments above me. Right above me was a Romanian named Petru, sometimes Pierre. He was a kind heart in a heavy man's body. Above him was Kay, a French guy that grew up in England. He spoke like an Englishman and told everybody he was English. He was the guy who left me to take my India trip on my own rather than coming with me. Above him was a French and Moroccan couple. The French guy was an alright guy, but we never went past pleasantries. His Moroccan wife was a high maiden of Venus. I wasn't sure how he landed her, but she was a real sweetheart. One of those rare women who didn't realize how beautiful they really were. Above them

was a two-story apartment with roof access
where a Dutch guy who I was friends with in
the Legion lived. I helped him get the
place. It was a nice place, and we would
often drink wine on the rooftop.

I went to see the Englishman.

Kay was up there drinking alone as he
sometimes did. Drinking wasn't really a
vice for him as much as the white powder
was. Drinking was usually just something he
did as he was high. I was the opposite. I
drank, and then drugs came later. I didn't
particularly care for coke. But it felt
good, and it sobered you up damn well when
you started to feel the Earth sliding out
from under your feet. One led to the other.

He wasn't high that night that I could
tell; he was just watching TV. He either
watched Sky News or some music channel,
usually in the background as he was
cleaning. He was always cleaning it seemed.
We hung out. Talked about women. Women was
always something we talked about. It was
rarely about one in particular, just a
general discussion about the experiences we
had survived with them and trying to figure
them out. He wasn't a fan of Claudia. He
never would suggest to end things though.
He would just joke about how much longer we
would have.

Claudia came home about ten minutes
after I went up. You could hear the
building door open and any apartment door
shut no matter which apartment you were in.
I finished my beer and used my second as an
hourglass before heading back down.

It was probably about twenty minutes
from the time she came home before I headed
down. I figured she'd be in pajamas at that
point. Maybe in bed, maybe on the couch,
but definitely on her computer. On her
Facebook. She always played the indifferent
mature woman, but she was still a victim
for attention like every other human.

I opened the door and found the lights
out and nobody there. I walked over to the
edge of the living room to look down into
the bedroom. She wasn't there either.

I guess she went back out. Maybe that
guy called her back.

I sat there and drink alone as I
listened to Bob Dylan. I asked Maverick, my
dog, where she went, but he didn't give her
up. Damn dog. I didn't even finish one beer
before I got a call from a friend asking me
to join him at a concert. Sure, why not I
thought? I knew why not, but I ignored it.

We met up at my place. We had a beer
and caught up for a minute, and he gave me
some MDMA. I had become quite the fan of
the stuff and usually kept that or ecstasy
around, but even when I didn't, my friends
knew the only way they could drag me to one
of those techno, rave music scenes was to
get me to see pretty lights with a bunch of
soft women roaming around.

It was about a twenty-minute walk to
the concert area, and I could already feel
the chill that passed, followed by the
immediate surge of joy. That initial cool
feeling freaked me out a little the first
few times I partook in the happy chemicals.

I always knew it was coming, so I'd go somewhere that was out in the cool open area and not around too many people. The people would freak me out, and about the same time the cool feeling started, I'd also start sweating like a virgin in heat sitting next to a sensual woman. It would take me about the time of a cigarette to watch that part fade away and then embrace the overwhelming ecstasy that consumed me just after. Ecstasy itself was just as well, but I preferred Molly.

We were in the line to enter the concert and I had another little bag of MDMA in my pocket when I looked up ahead and saw the bouncers feeling everybody up and emptying pockets. I reached in and put the little bag in that small key pocket above the normal pocket. They had never caught me putting it there.

I was right again. And we got in.

The long wait in line probably wasn't that long of a wait for normal people, but being high made it seem like forever, and I worked up a huge shit. One thing I hated about cocaine, Molly, and any upper, were the shits. It'd hit you and wouldn't go away. Just build up and become more and more digested until it became diarrhea and your guts exploded.

I ran to the bathroom, held my beer, and tried to look cool while I waited for a stall.

I spilled my guts. It just wouldn't stop coming out. They should sell this for diets. Hell, they should just put MDMA in

the drinking water, what a world it would
be then. I could see myself running for
President and cutting all programs and
using a 10th of the money to put the stuff
in the water system. What a happy world it
would be. Imagine.

They didn't have any toilet paper, and
I had quite the collateral damage around my
asshole and surrounding area. I undressed
my bottoms completely and wiped my ass with
my boxers and threw them in the trash
beside the toilet. Fucking A, what a shit.

We had a good night.

It was a damn good night.

I drank too much beer and too little
water. I was still in the learning phase of
knowing when to cut off the beer and switch
to water with this stuff. You had to drink
something. You never felt drunk when high,
but when you come down, you only want a
buzz to help with the landing. Drink too
little and it'll be depression. Drink too
much and it was a blackout. I was near
blackout drunk, and if I hadn't had my
babysitter with me, I would have went home
in the wrong direction or not at all.

I got home though.

I crawled in bed. I thought I was
quiet. I probably wasn't.

Claudia was there.

38

Claudia was pissed the next day, but not too hostile about it. She didn't tell me where she went or with whom though.

'Just out. With friends.'

She had a way with words. She stopped speaking to me in English too. It had only been French the past couple of weeks as if she didn't care anymore if I understood her or not. I did most of the time though.

I told her about my night, but she didn't seem interested.

'That's stupid.' she said.

It was, but I'm stupid, and she should know that by now. How could she still be disappointed?

We didn't talk for a few days after that and I was feeling wrong and down about it all. The MDMA probably didn't help. Coming back up and into a normal state of emotional stability, I decided to right my wrongs or at least give her a reason to like me again.

I planned a romantic evening with candles, wine, massage oil, and sweet music. I didn't know many Romanian love songs, and didn't like the ones I found, but it wasn't about me. So, I downloaded what I could along with some other love songs in both French and English. I also grabbed a video of a fireplace I put on the USB and had that going on the TV in the living room. I was going to grab her at the door and make love to her on the couch. We

hadn't had sex since we brought in the New
Year, and that seemed wrong. I also had a
couch that was only a week old and we
always made love on the couch. This couch
was waiting to be broken in.

With music going and electric flames
burning, my queen came home to her man
standing in nothing but a bathrobe. I
thought bathrobes were sleazy, but they
were comfortable and I loved having the
hidden exposure.

She stopped and looked around as she
walked in. I smiled, and she didn't. I
grabbed her by the hand and started my
apology.

'Claudia,' I said. 'You know I love
you, right?'

She said nothing. She still wasn't
smiling.

'I'm sorry I'm such a dick sometimes.
I never was good at being good.' I stopped.
I sounded like a bad song or some douchebag
you made fun of on the internet.

She squeezed my hand but then let it
go.

'I'm sorry.' she said.

My heart dropped. I stopped smiling,
and it was my turn to be silent.

'I'm moving out.' she said.

'What? Why?' I understood what she
said and the reason for it, but I didn't
want to.

'I've been planning to for some time
now. I just wanted to wait until I found a
place before I tell you.'

'Is this because of last week?'

'No.' she said. 'I decided this before.'

I still felt like shit, but at least it somewhat explained her behavior on New Year's and made me feel a little less guilty about my behavior. Didn't change the fact and pain of still knowing it was me she was leaving. It was me that wasn't good enough to be with.

I sat there in my bathrobe on the unfucked couch as I watched her walk downstairs.

Shock.

Denial.

Confusion.

I sat there until I finally fell asleep. She never came back up, and I never went down.

#

She stayed in the apartment for a month before she moved out.

It was civil. We went about our days normally and lived harmoniously. There was some awkwardness but no fights or crying. And mostly, I felt okay about it. It had been a long time coming. I figured two weeks out with the guys getting drunk once she finally left and I'd be over it.

I slept on the couch most of the time. A few nights I went out drinking, but I always came home. In my drunkenness, she meant too much to me. I needed to be around her as much as possible before she would be gone forever. When I would come home on

those nights, I would go downstairs to her
bed, our bed, in reality, my bed, and just
lay on her with my head on her stomach. She
would wrap her arms around my head and
caress me.

'I'm sorry we didn't work out.' I
would say.

'I know.' She would reply.

'I still love you. And I don't say
that to hear you say it back.'

'I know.'

I would then kiss her little breasts.
Run my hands from the side of her face,
across her neck, down her side, to her
waistline and then pull myself up to her to
kiss her. We would kiss and touch. It was
nice. Not sexy. Maybe sexy. Just full. Full
of everything I needed. We would whisper
meaningless expressions of a love fading
away, and we would make love. Not our usual
acrobatics, but a very slow, meaningful,
and savory motion. A dance that was painted
in pastel, making love as if it may be the
last time. Saying goodbye. In sadness that
it was over, in joy that it had happened.

We would hold each other all night. It
felt right. Right because we knew this was
right. The moment was right. The past was
right. The future would be right.

39

It was the end of January and my surgery to have the metal removed from leg was finally about to take place. I was nervous, all the doctors recommended against it. However, they also said that this was the last chance to do it before it would be too late, too consolidated with the bone to be removed later. I had never been too good at a permanent consolidation. So despite their wishes, I went through with the procedure.

I was back to being lame again as I had to wait for my leg to heal. At least a week of nothing but bedtime. And then three months of hobbling around on crutches again. I was used to being broken, so the idea didn't bother me too much.

Claudia found a place during that time. She took her time, but I really didn't mind. It was heartbreaking to live with a woman who was leaving you, but she finally found a place for the start of February.

I was in my week of laying on the couch, unable to move my leg as I watched her walk out the door. My friend, Petru, helped her carry everything. He couldn't say no to any woman that talked to him.

It was a lonesome feeling watching it all happen. I wanted it to be over so quickly, and then I wanted it to last forever.

She finally closed the door for the

last time and then it all hit me.

What a sight I was for such a long time. I didn't let go with grace; I wanted to know all the ugly details about how she really felt, a timeline of the ending from her perspective, always sending one more email with regret about it the next day.

She played me along for my feelings or hers for a few months. The first few were back and forth of deciding to speak to her or not. I always eventually did, but I'd go a week or two or maybe three in between and then go right back to my emotionally tormented state as soon as our friendly affair was over, be it coffee, text, or sex. Sometimes ice cream.

The first few months, I couldn't imagine being with anybody else, and even though I didn't want to hook up with anybody else, I did. I found out she had hooked up with a guy while I was in India, named George. This George was also the same fella we were supposed to be meeting New Year's Eve night. Now she had a plant in her new apartment from him she named after him. I wanted to piss on it when I saw it, or throw it out the window, or both.

Most of the time, I didn't care, I kind of laughed, I mean, she was starting something new with him and still calling me over to rub ice cream on her. I knew she didn't leave me for the sex. I was just shit at everything else.

It was a confusing and blurry spring.

40

The spring seemed to end with a letter.

I was still in my back and forth pains of the soul over Claudia. Still occasionally sleeping with her for what she would always say was the last time.

'So are you seeing him tonight?' I said.

'Why would you ask that?' Claudia said.

'Cause I love the pain, baby.'

'No, I usually only seem him on Wednesdays.'

'Ha, you have him down to a schedule?'

'Yeah, I don't want to get him too attached so quickly. It was only with you I broke that rule.'

'So he comes over Wednesday night, a bit of hanky panky, and then he's back out the door?'

'Pretty much. He tried to stay the first few times, but now he knows.'

'I bet he's already told you he loves you.'

'He has.'

'So why are you sleeping with me?'

She moved a little. But it felt like a lot since we were basically on top of each other on the un-pulled-out futon.

'I know,' I said, 'last time, right?'

'Yes, that was the last time.' She said, 'Did you ever read that letter?'

'Letter? You wrote an actual letter?

Or do you mean the email? I read the one
from last month or whenever.'
        'No,' she said, 'I wrote you a letter.
I put it in your book.'
        'Which book? When?'
        'A long time ago, just before your
trip to India,' she paused. 'I think it's
in that big black book you got from your
South African friend.'
        'Easterhouse?'
        'No...' She still hated him.
        'Ah,' I said, 'The other Slater.'
        'You should read it.' She said.
        We weren't as sweaty anymore, and the
breathing had slowed down. My penis was
getting hard again from being pressed up
against the side of her leg and ass. I
grabbed her. I loved to manhandle her since
she was so thin, and I'm not so big I can
do that with any woman.
        I threw her on her side, biting and
sucking her neck just below her right ear,
firmly pressing my hand down her chest, up
to her hip, and then down to her clit. I
rubbed it as I positioned myself in a way
that my now hard penis found its way
between her legs, right in the crosshairs
of bottom ass and upper thighs. I reached
my hand down further to grab the tip and
push it up inside of her. Her back arched
and her head pushed just below mine, with
our cheeks touching and the corners of our
lips making desperate attempts to taste
each other.
        She turned, and we kissed. Kissed hard
and with meaning. The meaning of passion

and no other. She was extremely wet and I could feel it running down the side of my penis and then down my waistline.

I rolled her to her stomach and sat up. Penetration was the key now. I slid my thumb off the bottom of her vagina and rubbed her asshole with her own juices. I did it again until it was ready and then slipped my whole thumb in. Sometimes rotating it, sometimes in and out, but mostly just rubbing that thin piece of skin, that fleshy wall between her ass and her vagina, my thumb and my penis, feeling it all.

We were animals now, and I felt like the lion king. I picked her up from her waist into a doggie position and stuck my nose and tongue into the center of the world. She danced around moving herself so she could grasp the back part of the futon with her hands and push herself onto my face.

Once I decided I should come up for air, I grabbed her by the waist and put myself back inside her. One hand reaching around to the front; to grab, to caress, to press, to possess.

I pushed harder and had her pushed full body against the back of the futon with her knees in the bend and her feet hanging off the front side.

We were dripping, drinking each other. We became a waterfall of bodily fluids.

Then the lion king started to become less of the animal and more the lullaby, feeling her body pressed against mine. My

face in her neck, my hand on her waist.
Gentler this time, exploring the side of
the boob and the curve that defined it from
the rest of her body, down to her waist.

Smelling her, tasting her, feeling her
- inside and out.

We laid there for another fifteen
minutes afterwards. Then I got up and left
looking back at her naked body still
sweating on the futon. God existed.

'Last time, right?'

41

I went home to find and read the letter.

It was in the book she had said, written on a small notebook sheet of paper, dogeared into the front page:

04.09.2012 (That's september 4th for my American readers) -Marseille-
Hey kiki …
I try to understand all… what happened in the last days…
I loved you! Diferent like i did before,
But it was notre love!
You are a very good person, with so much desire and ambition. That one of the reason that maked me stay so long true next to you.
Malheureusement, it is people who don't correspond to you. To your dreams, believes or your level.
You need to be around about the good and beautiful peopel. Like u are!
For that sometimes I was angree to you : because you let the otherse to take decision for you. The persons who haven't the same level lick yours.
Maybe I put a very small piece in your soul?! Maybe I will not be that 'mad and mechante fille' in your life!! I hop not!
I don't tryed to change you!
I just see how you can be in this world and how many things you could do!

*Be careful and don't let les autres
t'effacer de la surface 'terrestre.'*
   *I would lick to meet you after somes
years and see what your life is!*
   You have so much to say around!
   *Do what you must to do and what you
feel!*
   Love… ta petite amie…
                              Claudia.
   Biz

   I read the letter over and over again.
Laughing at the English, sad knowing she
had written it months before the actual
break-up. The whole relationship I
questioned whether she really loved me, and
there it was, in writing. She even spelled
out her name rather than her usual, 'CT'.
   I put the letter back where she had
put it and wondered if things could have
been different, if only we had communicated
the way we did after the break-up.

42

The letter was the closure I needed, but it didn't mean the ghost would stop haunting me.

I reread some of my journal from India and Nepal and thought about how I was right about her in my worries then. How I was worse than her in some ways and kinder in others. If only she had told me it was the ending, I could have used that time more effectively to get over her. But I didn't. It was the back-and-forth game she played with me from the beginning. The game I volunteered for. We were always honest with each other, but never completely honest. I could trace the blame game back to where? That we met in the first place? That we were who we were.

My friends got me plenty drunk though and out chasing strange. But none of it filled what was missing. Never more than a few hours. Women were magic. They were the curse that only they could remove. It was a fucked up world and I loved it.

Claudia was the first woman to really break my heart. I had been in one serious relationship before. Marriage even. Heartbroken even. But I broke my heart there. This was different. I had been possessed and then discarded like a used condom. A condom that had been to the center of the world and back. The things I learned from her changed my entire perspective on love. She took a boy and

made him a man in ways much more intimate
than sex ever could.

Claudia and I were made for each other
in that time and space. We never thought we
were, because when I loved her, she was
never there. Then I would tire of that and
fade away and she'd love me, and when I
finally realized and started coming back,
she'd be looking away again. We were never
on the same page. Ever. She was 30, and I
was 24. She was 32, and I was 26. She told
me I was like her at her age. I hated that.
She always called me 'boy.' I hated that
too, unless we role played.

But she was right, because I grew more
into her ways as time went on, but she grew
too, in a different way, more into my ways.
The last meaningful words she ever said to
me were how I made her feel something, how
I made her open up in ways that made her
want to feel and be felt like she never had
before. Lucky for the next guy I had told
her. We were never meant to be together
forever. But we were perfect for each other
for that time. Perfect.

43

My legionnaire boys and I still got drunk on a regular basis, and I usually ended up with a different girl every night. Some stuck around for a couple of weeks or more. Some were interesting. Some were intellectual. Some were caring. But I'd never let it last longer than that. It was good to be back out there and to not have to worry about coming home and waking up to a pissed-off woman. I missed that pissed-off woman though, and no matter how beautiful the naked body was laying next to me the next morning was, it was just that, a naked body. Flesh. There was no love. Only the starry-eyed romance that I felt in the pretense before the nakedness. I loved the chase more than the catch. I knew this, but I'd forget it the next night when I was back out again.

I started to get bored with it all after the first few months after the break-up, so I started regaining a friendship with Kay. I thanked him for ditching me on our India/Nepal trip as it had been better for me that way. There was that, and he had also recently had enough of Easterhouse. We were back to being mates.

So when drinking with the guys started to become routine, I would go up and hang out with him in his apartment. He was always doing coke. Cocaine was still not my thing, but I started to get into until I realized I could get MDMA from his dealer.

I still had some money left from my payout from the French Foreign Legion and didn't feel too self-conscious about spending eighty euros on a gram of it two or three times a week.

Before Claudia, I never did it because of the military career. With Claudia, I had only done it a few times with my Dutch friend. Now I had a supply and a desire to feel happiness whatever the cost.

The first few times made me want to commit suicide the next day. But then I eventually got used to that feeling, and I realized after the first attempt it was embarrassing to be seen as somebody that tried to kill himself. I learned to lie in a temporary state of death and ride it out. Plus, it was hard to cook when your neighbors took all your knives.

Kay and I were about to head to another outing. We didn't know where yet but we went with plenty of gear. We were pros, or thought we were about doing drugs in normally sane places. We always ended up in the seediest of bars until the sun came up, then we'd make the rounds of getting kicked out of nicer establishments until evening came around again. We could go out for three days straight without food or sleep.

We would roam the entire town, and I visited every bar in that city over the following months and almost never went to my regular. Almost never meaning only twice a week. I drank there for free most of the time, so I couldn't really lose that.

One night we were running low on the Peruvian flake and headed to our headquarters, the bar where we bought our drugs. Hollande was the cheap stuff at fifty euros a gram, and Obama was the good stuff at eighty euros a gram. The French loved their Obama, ate that chocolate right up. Hollande was a weak man, weak even for the French socialist.

We came beep-bopping in, still high, still drunk. It was always a laugh, creating stories in the moment while laughing about the ones we just had. Never thinking about the next morning, it was a beautiful time.

We walked into La Monde. It was a bar you probably wouldn't find unless you knew it was there, hidden in an alley hidden behind Galeries Lafayette on the main shopping street in Marseille, rue Saint-Ferréol. It always had the same customers, and we all hollered and kissed each other's scruffy or soft, smelly or sweet cheeks each time we saw each other.

As I walked in this time though, I met a new person. Not a person, but an angel, or demon, I wasn't too sure, but I heard nothing but the bells of lust and saw nothing but the aura that surrounded her as she looked to see who was walking in.

44

She had her hair up in a ponytail. I loved that. She was blonde. I rarely went for that. She was the perfect height. I had no idea how tall she was, but she seemed to be the perfect height. She wore a loose, delicate shirt. I think it was blue, but it was dark, and had a brown jacket that was barely enough material to be called a jacket. It too looked mesmerizing. She was wearing jeans with holes in them. Something I found both irritating and arousing. And dark boot-shoes. Not really boots or shoes. She was perfectly made, exactly the woman of my dreams.

I was in love, but I wasn't sure if that was just the molly enhanced with CC talking or not.

Then she smiled at me and I didn't care.

I had no idea where my partner in crime was, but he was probably still making the rounds of kissing everybody. I didn't see him or anybody else. It was only her, and I walked right up to her smiling like a damn idiot.

I stopped in front of her and our eyes never lost each other. I was still smiling like an idiot and she started smiling more in a way that showed she was curious who the hell I was and wondering if I would say something or just keep staring at her.

I just kept staring and smiling.

'Bonsoir.' She said.

'Bonsoir.' I said.

Breaking the smile made me go into one of those weird ecstasy twitches were you move your jaw around in a circle.

Damn, I felt that too. I knew I was fucked up then. I was aware enough in my drug experience to know how stupid that looked, but I was also experienced enough to prevent it even when high. Unfortunately, I was too distracted and just kept smiling.

She was experienced in the drug-induced world too, but she wasn't high or drunk. She kept smiling though, to keep from laughing.

'Ça va?' she said.

'Oui.' I said. How fucking clever. 'Ça va. Et toi?'

'Bien.' she said.

She was still laughing at me through her smile, but it seemed like an amusing and inviting laugh. Not a malicious one.

'Comment tu t'appelles?' she said.

'Will.' I said. 'Et toi?'

Full of fucking dialogue I was.

I just kept falling deeper and deeper into her beauty. Her essence. Here was this goddess. On Earth. And speaking to me.

'Aurora.' she said. 'I've never seen you here before.'

'Yeah.' I said. 'I come here sometimes. But not a lot before until now.'

I was tripping over my words in French. She gave me a strange look and then smiled again.

'Where are you from?' She said.

'American.' I said. 'And you?'
I was as interesting as a brick wall.
She laughed out loud this time.
'Me?' she said. Still laughing. 'I'm
French. Corsican really, but spent most of
my life here in Marseille.'
Then in English she said, 'I only
speak little English.'
That was the only thing every French
person knew how to say in English besides,
'Fuck,' and 'Oh, my God.' Fuck was
something casually thrown around on the
public radio here and apparently 'Oh, my
God,' came from the tv show called
'Friends' that the French were watching
about ten years too late.
A French woman could melt the world
with her words when she spoke. It sounded
sexy, infatuating, and sensual when a
French woman spoke the feminine language of
French, and when she spoke English, it
sounded cute and endearing. It was like
talking to two different people. Their
voice just sounded different. It was a
strange phenomenon that I enjoyed from my
experience with French women that tried to
speak with me in English. Apparently the
effect goes both ways, because after
speaking French for so long with one
person, saying something in English always
threw them off for a moment as it sounded
as if they were talking to a different
person. As if changing languages also
changed your voice. Changed who you were.
If it was possible to smile any
harder, I was.

If it was possible to be any creeper, I was.

I started rubbing her arm.

'Your jacket is so soft.' I said.

She just stared down at my hand and kept that smile as if holding back a laugh. She knew where she was, and like most girls in these sorts of bars, they were used to dealing with people on drugs and she knew what I was on. Ecstasy and MDMA had such a powerful effect that they not only made the person taking it happy, the people they were in contact with, usually literally, were also given a surge of happiness. It just rubbed off that way. Or it didn't. For those that didn't understand, it just creeped them out to have some stranger so loving nearby, possibly trying to touch them.

'Merci.' She said and started laughing.

I just kept rubbing and staring at her, and my hand started drifting all over her. She was so soft. She was so beautiful.

I wasn't sure if she was getting freaked out or not. She didn't stop me, but she didn't really respond either.

I don't think this went on long, but it felt like an eternity I could get lost in.

'Everything okay here, mate?' Kay said, coming up and putting his arm around me and looking at both of us for a response. It wasn't the first time that I had gotten touchy-feely with girls when out on the happy stuff. If they were on it too,

then a world of pleasure commenced, if they
weren't, it was a gamble of getting harshly
turned away or embraced. Occasionally there
would be a boyfriend around that would get
pissy for me touching and dancing with his
lady. Kay would sometimes watch me handle
it or step in if he thought he needed to.
We got kicked out of a lot of bars and some
clubs. We would always be back a week later
and talk our way in. Most of the time. Some
places we were 86'd for life.

I realized then that the rest of the
room existed. Kind of.

She smiled and then Kay drug me away
to talk to others.

Kay got happy off MD, but never quite
the way I did. Sometimes he wouldn't even
bother; he'd just save it for me. He was an
asshole to everybody but me. I was never
sure why he chose me as his sidekick. He
found something amusing about me. He would
just always go on and on about how everyone
else were just 'boring cunts.' Though he
would harass me and say, 'Ah, don't be
boring,' whenever I ever wanted a night
alone. I think I was the only one that
could keep up with him, or tolerate him.
Like most unloved people, he was kind, just
misunderstood.

It didn't take long for me to break
away and get back to the bar to find
Aurora. But she had disappeared. Out for a
smoke.

The bartender and drug dealer grabbed
me. He was a friend at this point.

'Faire attention avec cela.' He said.

I ignored him.

Aurora came back in and sat back in her seat.

We started talking again.

I started touching again.

I started kissing her.

She let me kiss her.

I was with her the rest of the night. She had me.

Kay was upset and came over to steal me away a few times, but eventually he gave up and called me a 'cunt.' We would usually take over a bar and play the music, usually Queen, I guess that just wasn't as much fun when your wingman left you to go on the make.

I did this to him often. Finding a lady friend and then ditching him. I had a reputation already in this town, mostly in this bar and my pub in Vieux Port with my Legion buddies, as a man who enjoyed the affection of women. La Monde called me the 'American Gigolo', but I never got paid for it, at least not in direct cash.

Kissing Aurora was more miraculous than I thought possible. We hit it off, and we spent the rest of the night mostly locked together.

The guy she came with eventually left without too much fuss. Kay and the bartender helped with that.

We kissed. And we kissed.

Her lips, her tongue, her smell, her feel. Fuck, this was heaven if there ever was one.

#

We eventually left to head back to my
place. I lived in Le Panier, so it was
closer than hers.

'I need to stop to grab my purse.' She
said.

'Okay…' I said, 'Where is it?'

'At a friend's.' She said.

We went to an apartment building not
far away and on the way to mine. She called
and buzzed. Looked up at the window, then
called and buzzed again.

Eventually we got in and there were
two Arab guys up there smoking hashish.

It started off pleasant, but then I
started coming down off my high and she
seemed to get more agitated.

I couldn't tell if the guys were being
difficult or if she was. I was just sitting
down, chilling, and smoking what they gave
me and letting them talk, not trying to
understand the conversation in French.

Then she started getting upset, and I
heard her threaten them I was a legionnaire
and could whoop their asses.

The guys tried to calm her it seemed,
but they seemed to do it in a mocking way.
I couldn't tell if I was high and
misinterpreting or if they were, but I was
in no mood or state to be taking on two
guys twice my size.

I got a little worried and a little
scared we were both about to get raped as
we were nowhere near the door and she just
escalated things further and further. I

just couldn't understand how grabbing a
purse could turn into such an ordeal and I
was barely feeling alive enough to make the
walk home, much less get into it
physically.

Shit, I thought.

I sat quietly and looked at both of
them but said nothing.

She kept reaching back to grab my hand
or sit next to me and lay her body against
mine before breaking out into her next
tirade.

I could feel them weighing me up with
their eyes. I'm not a big boy, but her
feistiness along with my calm quietness
must have worked because we eventually got
her purse and walked out with no harm done.

We got outside and walked around the
corner from the building when I stopped
her.

'What the fuck was that about?' I
said.

'They were fucking with me.' She said.
'They didn't want to give me my bag because
they were jealous I was with you.'

'Is that an ex or something?' I said.

'No.' she said. 'Just friends, but
he's always wanted to and I never have.'

'So how did your purse end up there?'

'I left it there so it wouldn't get
stolen at the bar.'

That was smart, but I didn't say that.
I just grabbed her hand and started walking
towards mine.

We walked back to mine, kissing and
undressing in the street along the way,

then redressing, then stopping again and doing it over and over. A seven-minute walk took near thirty-five minutes. But we made it. And went straight to bed.

She undressed completely and fell backwards into the middle of the bed.

I mounted and we must have caressed and teased each other for half an hour before penetration.

I heard Kay come in around four so I ran upstairs to grab more coke off of him to keep from falling asleep.

Aurora and I continued our night repeatedly until my alarm clock for work went off and she got up to take a shower.

I followed behind her and took her from behind, her back against my chest, my face in her neck, her face against the shower wall.

I finished and said, 'Thank you,' and then walked out of the shower.

She laughed out loud and then yelled out, 'You don't have to thank me. I enjoyed it, too.'

That was actually a first to have a woman say that, I wondered why no other woman had that humor until now.

45

Aurora and I continued to see each other.

Claudia and I still spoke and occasionally slept together, but it was not quite the hangup it used to be.

One day Claudia came over to print out her thesis for one of her classes in 'audiovisual'. She was an actress and model, but was looking to get into the movie making side of things and had started her masters while we were together and now nearly finished it. I admired her courage to write such a paper in a language that wasn't her first. But she had studied French longer than I had English and had plenty of men that volunteered to proofread for her so I imagined it would be okay.

Claudia was supposed to be out by lunch or so, but when I started getting antsy, she seemed surprised and asked why. Normally, I'd be kissing her and convincing her to say 'one last time,' but here I was eager to have her gone.

She knew me too well and picked up on that and started teasing me.

'So what's going on?' She said.

'Oh, you know me.' I said.

'I wish you would take better care of yourself.' She said.

'How much longer do you think?' I said. It was almost 13h now and Aurora was coming over at 15h.

'Sorry,' she said, 'I didn't think it

would take this long.'
      'Well, if you hadn't spent two hours
hanging out before you started printing,
you would have been done by now.' I
thought. Her computer was still connected
to the printer from when we lived together,
and she knew it wasn't the greatest machine
to translate digital data into ink on
paper. And why did she have to come here to
print it? I bet that other guy she was
seeing would buy her a printer if she
asked.
      'And I wanted to see Maverick.' She
said. That was always her excuse for
texting me or coming over. He was kind of
our child.
      'Well, you know that printer isn't for
books.' I said as the machine kept pumping
out one page at a time, a time of about a
minute each. 'I just got it for lesson
plans.'
      'Yeah, sorry,' she said, 'I didn't
mean to take up your day. You can leave. I
will close up behind me if you have to be
somewhere.'
      It's a strange feeling when an ex is
back in your old apartment: her same voice,
her same clothes, her same look, and her
same demeanor. It's as if she never left. I
would usually come to see her at her new
place so it was like sleeping with a new
person who already felt comfortable. This
was the opposite feeling.
      'It's okay.' I said. 'I'm sorry. I
just started dating somebody new, and she's
coming over at 15h, and I would rather not

have my ex in the apartment alone with me
when she gets here.'

She smiled.

'I'll be gone by then.' She said.

I got a text from Aurora. She'd be
here an hour early.

'Is that her?' Claudia asked.

'Yeah.' I said.

Claudia and I hung out for a bit more.
It was strange to just hang out again
without being naked. It was as if there was
still a string that tied us together,
something beyond the intimacy of sharing
your skin and fluids with one another. A
string that could never be broken. I was
still paranoid about her being here when
Aurora would arrive, but it looked like
there would be an hour gap between the two.
Juggling women I thought. My god, what a
circus.

'J'arrive.' Aurora texted.

Shit.

'How much longer do you think,
Claudia?' I said.

'I don't know, Will.' She said.

'Okay,' I said, 'Well, she's on her
way.'

She started to stand by the printer as
if her presence could make the machine go
any faster.

'Well, this is happening.' I thought.

'I won't be in your way if I'm still
here, you know.' She said.

She was doing this on purpose. She
wanted to see who I would be nervous about
her seeing. Normally, I would tell her

about all my little adventures whenever we would meet up, but I hadn't told her about this one and that got her interest.

'I'm sure she'll understand, and you don't have to tell her I'm your ex if you don't want to.' She said.

That thought had already crossed my mind. But I had already told Aurora about Claudia and so that wouldn't work. Not sure I could do that to an ex anyway, pretend she didn't exist for the comfort of another.

Aurora arrived and Claudia was still there.

Well, damn. I suppose having both of them at the same time would be a fantasy. But these two, I could barely focus on one at a time. I would explode, die from the attempt. They were each a force alone to overwhelm me; I knew I could never manage both at the same time. Any fantasy that wanted to exist didn't.

Aurora came in as stunning as ever in her casual clothes. I swear she could walk into a ballroom with jeans and be the most spectacular sight there.

She came in and kissed me at the door. I immediately looked over at Claudia who Aurora hadn't seen yet since the open door blocked her view. Claudia smiled in a mocking way.

'Ça va?' I said.

'Ça va.' Aurora said.

She walked in. I closed the door.

'Aurora, Claudia.' I said.

I had warned Aurora by a text that my

ex might still be here so she wasn't
surprised.

'Salut.' Aurora said.

'Enchanté.' Claudia said.

They didn't do the bisous.

I didn't know what to do with myself.
I was so nervous about Aurora already, and
now here I was in my apartment with both
her and my ex who meant more to me than I
ever could have admitted publicly.

It was awkward, but we all played our
roles correctly. Aurora and I hung out
around the kitchen table while Claudia
finished up the last of her pages. It was
fifteen minutes that felt like hours as we
all talked together.

I wanted to shoot myself.

Forever finally ended. Then the
bisous, 'au revoir', smiles, and Claudia
left.

'She's beautiful.' Aurora said.

'Yeah,' I said.

'She's beautiful.' Claudia texted.

What the fuck.

'I like her.' Aurora said.

'I like her.' Claudia texted.

Jesus Christ.

They were no doubt the two most
beautiful women I had ever seen, including
the fake screen. And two of the most
interesting women I had ever met after 26
years of life experience. The fact they
were overlapping was insane.

'How old is she?' Claudia texted.

'My age.' I texted.

'Ah,' She texted, 'I thought she was

maybe 30 or something.'

Aurora and I continued our day as expected without too much more talk about Claudia. Though I imagine there were thoughts on both sides. She wanted to know why we had ended even though I had already explained that to her before. She had met her now though. She was real. And she wanted to know everything.

Luckily, our sober beach time together gave us some time together.

'Will?'

It was Louise. An ex of an English friend of mine who was also a parachutist from the 2°REP and was part of my 'anglophone mafia' before. He had gone back home to England, but he and Murphy and our misuses and I at the time were all very close. Along with a South African friend of ours who had died in Afghanistan and a Welshman who was in and out of psychiatric help for PTSD.

But I was no longer with Claudia. Murphy was no longer with Niz. And English Bailey was no longer with Louise. And Johnson was dead. And Buell was in Paris in a hospital. Broken we all were, some more than others. Some gone forever. We still drank to the names and our former glory though.

Louise and I had had a romantic evening together a few times by drunken accident. We never slept together, not in a penis in vagina way, but we would get drunk and naked and lay in bed together and I would tell her stories and read her books and we would lay next to each other. Yet, we would never commit to the full act. She wanted to, but I couldn't. Out of some invisible contract I signed with my legionnaire brethren. She understood but didn't. She even asked for approval from Bailey and he gave it. Bailey said he always saw us together and had no intention of returning to France. But I was never one to fuck the lady of my friend, ex or not. Even on drugs or alcohol, I have certain walls built. Yet, Louise and I were close and like best friends of the opposite sex who openly talked about sex like most people talked about the weather.

So when she showed up on the beach with Aurora and I, it was strange but comforting.

Aurora was topless, and I was sitting behind her.

So when Louise showed up and said hello, I got up to introduce them.

Aurora and Louise got along amazingly.

We all talked about sex and love. It wasn't taboo. It was real and on the table. They were both in physical contact with me and Louise whispered that she really approved of my new girlfriend.

Aurora really liked Louise too.

What the fuck was going on?

We hung out for a few hours until the sun set enough that it started to become cool when the wind blew across.

Louise understood people and situations better than anybody I knew and took her leave at exactly the right time.

Aurora and I went back to our cuddling
position and lasted another half hour
before we went home ourselves.

We got back to our side of town.

Drank.

Went out for two more at a bar nearby
and pissed off a few people.

Then made a few more rounds of
drinking and talking.

We were the most beautiful people
around and we wanted the world to know it
in a violent way.

We made it home and made the gods
jealous.

46

Aurora and I had confessed our love to one another after about two weeks. It made little sense, but it was something I had always felt but never said out of obligation to the rules of love.

I was good at sensing the right time to say such things and she fell apart for me as soon as I did for her.

Confusing times.

Romantic times.

After about a month she was half way moved in.

We were laying in bed and I was running my fingers along her. I had noticed a scar on her stomach on our first night but figured it was something to ask later.

'What's the scar here on your belly?' I said.

'You don't remember?' She said.

'You already told me?' I said. 'Shit. I'm sorry. I forgot. Tell me now, I'll remember in both states.'

'You're an asshole.'

'I know.'

'I've never told anybody about this but you and my dad.'

Her dad was a legionnaire and became a French citizen after serving and marrying Aurora's mom. He was Czech.

'I want to know.' I said.

She rolled over.

Damn, she was beautiful in every position.

I ran my hand along her. Teased her for five minutes that felt like forever as I took my time from her toes to her neck.

She rolled over and looked at me.

'I shot myself.' She said.

I remembered the conversation now but didn't respond.

'I was young,' she said, 'depressed, and I took a gun and just shot myself in the belly.'

I didn't let her finish the rest of the story. I had remembered the rest.

'I love you.' I said.

She smiled.

I kissed her.

We made love.

Slow and sweet, very different from our normal rampage. Worlds parted in a symphony.

We made love.

She was no longer my object of affection. She was still beautiful. Sexy. Erotic. But she was human, and I loved every inch of her and she held onto me as if to never let go. Her claws dug into my skin as I penetrated her, as I kissed her, as I made us one.

47

La fête du panier was coming up and rather than just getting hammered and roaming around the neighborhood, I decided I would get hammered and make a profit from this annual festival. That opportunity ended up being Easterhouse who I still didn't speak to as a friend anymore. Nothing more than casual courtesies, it had been a year. I would never trust the man again, but he was still kind to me.

Easterhouse had bought a restaurant on la rue du panier a thirty-second walk from my apartment with the money he had won after suing the French Foreign Legion for his injury, a bad knee from a march in basic training. He never even finished la ferme or La Marche Kepi Blanc, but still ended up with the cap, 100 thousand euros, and three years of a full salary paid vacation.

I invited Aurora to come along. Well, I didn't really invite her so much as told her about it and she came along.

It was the south of France and meetings were very casual. We sat outside the restaurant and discussed our place at their place and their cut of the profits.

I ended up playing diplomacy half way through between Aurora and Easterhouse. They had never met before.

All went well though, and we even got half the storefront for my Dutch friend, Ackerman, to make drinks. He would make a

barrel of Mojito to sell Mojitos at €2 a
plastic cup. It was a good deal and a win
for all. Plus his new lady friend from
Holland was the typical tall, blonde,
attractive type to bring in customers. Her
along with Aurora and we would own the
panier for the weekend.
'Aurora is hot, boet.' Easterhouse
texted.
I ignored the message. He sent it for
two reasons. He sees the money she can
bring, and he's trying to get back in my
good graces. I didn't respond to him.
'Comment il s'appelle?' Aurora said.
'Easterhouse.' I said. I knew who she
was referring to. She already knew the
restaurant manager, his daughter, and wife,
and my Dutch friend and his missus, Jenny.
'He's crazy.' She said.
I didn't respond.
'I could see it in his eyes.' She
said.
I kissed her.
'I like her.' Easterhouse texted.
Fucking bastard.
I squeezed her hand then pulled her
off to the side and made out with her. She
was surprised but didn't refuse.
It turned her on though and she wanted
me. We made love twice in full force and it
exhausted me. I wouldn't be able to pick
her up and travel with her across the
apartment again.
She didn't like that.
She called Kay. She had his number
now. Though he had stopped talking to us

since we went reclusive in our sexual
state.

He responded to her though, but rather
than giving drugs to us for free he wanted
to charge us. I agreed. We payed. I took it
up the nose and took her until she finally
had enough. My muscles ached once the drugs
wore off.

A few hours later, the party started.
We could hear the people in the street and
the bbqs being set up out my window. We
rolled out of bed. I never knew how much
time we spent together in bed, but it was
never time lost by my count.

We got dressed. I was wearing my green
kilt that I got when officially adopted
into Murphy's family. His father took me in
has his own. I didn't even know the Irish
wore kilts until then; I had always thought
it was a Scottish thing. Apparently it's a
Celtic thing, and I was officially part of
the tribe now by recommendation and by my
alcoholism and ability to tell stories.

It was still daylight. It was the late
afternoon, and I told Aurora she could head
up whenever she wanted. I figured she'd get
bored too quickly if she came now when it
was mostly just old people and tourists
there. The fun crowd and the money didn't
really start flowing until it got dark.

I walked up the street and started to
help set up the restaurant and the tables
outside. Then I started drinking.

At first Easterhouse wanted to charge
us by drink, then I said I would help him
sell drinks, so he countered that only I

could drink for free and Aurora or anybody
else I knew had to pay. I didn't like that,
mostly because I was negotiating with that
guy, but it was fair and I agreed.

The evening started, and we made a
little money off people passing by. Most
were just there to look around, but when we
grabbed somebody, they would get something
for the whole family. The conversion rate
wasn't high, but the average sale was.

By the time the sky started to look
orange, I started to feel good from the
drink.

Aurora showed up right before dark.
She came and hung out behind the table for
a while. I got her a glass of wine and we
had a laugh talking up people that passed
by and trying to sell them a sandwich and
beer.

The night carried on and I had a laugh
with anybody within talking distance.
People enjoyed it, and Easterhouse came out
to pat me on the back while people were
laughing and standing around.

Aurora wandered off with Ackerman's
girlfriend to reel in more customers. I
wasn't sure how they would do that, but I
imagined it would be their smiles and legs
aimed at the more masculine sex.

And they did. They'd both come over
with a group full of guys, giggling and
talking. And sometimes it worked, sometimes
the guys would realize they had just been
played when Aurora would grab my hand or
I'd peck her on the cheek and Ackerman
would do the same with Jenny.

Aurora started to get drunk herself and started to take the job a little too seriously. It was meant to be playful, causal, but she wanted to seduce men at this point. As things got later, Ackerman's lady stayed with him and Aurora ventured off on her own. Coming back each time with a group of men, but being a little more familiar with them. Laughing a little more, touches on the arm or back. I got kind of jealous but figured it was all just a game and I was drunk and so was she.

I tried to kiss her, and she refused.

If I hadn't been pissed off before, I could feel I was about to be.

And I got pissed off with her, but not out of jealousy. She was beyond drunk at this point and causing a scene at the restaurant and in the street. She became oblivious to her own actions. I had been there many times before myself and been there with her. But I was calm drunk tonight, putting my energy and passion into the sale.

Ackerman and Easterhouse grabbed me and told me I had to take her home. I talked them down and then grabbed Aurora.

She was reluctant at first, thinking I was being jealous and pulling her away for that reason. But then I get her alone in an apartment stairwell and she started crying and apologizing.

'You need to go home.' I said.

She fought it at first, but then agreed.

I waited until she calmed down from

the crying, we hugged, and then held hands as we left the building.

Back at the table, she grabbed her purse, we kissed, I gave her my keys, and then she walked around the corner and down the street to my apartment.

All was well again, and I felt bad sending her home like that.

#

I wasn't sure if it had been a half hour, an hour, or more, but I saw Aurora coming around the corner. Perhaps she had calmed down and was going to just hang out behind the table with me like before.

She looked calmer, but it was just the eye of the hurricane. She walked right past me and gave me a dirty look. Then marched right into the restaurant and started another scene, yelling at Easterhouse. Calling him a piece of shit and using some information I had told her about him against him. I had my issues with the guy, but he didn't deserve that.

I grabbed her and started pulling her out of the restaurant.

'Why do you let him take advantage of you like that?' she said, yelling at Easterhouse about Easterhouse for me.

Easterhouse started calling her a cunt and then I didn't feel sorry for the misogynistic bastard anymore as I got a flash of all the shitty things he's said and done towards the fairer sex.

I walked her all the way to the

apartment building and called Pierre down.

She was crying again.

'What's wrong, Aurora?' I said. 'What the fuck is going on?'

'I love you.' She said. 'But I just let that get in the way sometimes. I just want to protect you.'

'Protect me?' I said. 'From what? Don't worry about me. I can take care of myself.'

'I know.' She said. 'But you're too nice.'

I just sat there with her. My street was quieter, but there were still people walking by and she had just stopped on the stairs up to the apartment building crying and speaking loudly.

Pierre came down.

'Can you please hang out with her tonight until I get home?' I said.

'Yeah, sure.' He said.

'Just call me if you need anything.' I said.

I left and worked the rest of the night.

'You need to get your woman under control, mate.' Ackerman said.

'She's fucking nuts.' Easterhouse said.

'Fuck you.' I said.

This went off and on the rest of the night until I called it a night.

I went home exhausted. Grabbed Aurora who had passed out on the couch. Walked her down in a state barely alive and leaning on me for support. Laid her down. Undressed her. And kissed her good night.

I went back up to have a beer and a cigarette with Pierre who was in the same place he always was, the far corner of the room, at his desk, playing World of Warcraft.

'Thanks for looking, homie.' I said.

'Yeah, no worries.' He said. 'She talked a lot when she first came up. She really loves you, man. You better hang on to that.'

'Yeah,' I said, 'if I can. She may be crazier than I am.'

'You're fucking lucky, mate.' He said.

'Yeah,' I said, 'I guess with women I have been.'

'You know she went up to Kay's place earlier?'

'What? When?'

'I don't know.' He said. 'Like 21h30, 22h'

'Huh.' I said.

'She said they were doing lines.'

'Mother fucker.'

I sat quietly for a while, finished my beer, and headed down.

Got undressed and laid beside Aurora. I pushed my naked body up against hers and just put my arm around her. I kissed her cheek, and she turned slightly as if to kiss my lips but she was so out of it she only managed half the turn and so I just kissed the right corner of her mouth, she kissed me back, but kind of kissed the air too.

I figured making love would wake her

up, and I was exhausted anyway. So one last
kiss to the corner of her eye and eyebrow
and then I rolled onto my back and fell
asleep.

#

        The fête du panier lasted the next two
nights, and I made a few hundred euros off
of it.
        Aurora didn't share the rest of the
weekend with me. On top of her scene and
her doing coke with Kay, I found out that
she still lived with her ex in her old
apartment. We argued more than anything. I
didn't care she still lived with her ex
since she spent most nights with me or a
girlfriend, but it seemed like she wasn't
trying to move out that got under my skin.
It was too much, and I wasn't sure I could
handle it all.
        I also confronted Kay about feeding
her coke when I wasn't around. On the
defensive, he became an asshole.
        'I could've fucked her if I wanted
to,' he said, 'she was so fucked up.'
        In one weekend, I had found that a
woman had yet again put me under a bridge.

48

The week after the fête du panier I had a South African friend from the REP and his fiancée come stay with me.

They had called the week before to ask and I told them sure. Aurora knew and didn't care when I mentioned it. But after the weekend, she soon found it to be a problem. She didn't feel comfortable staying with me with my friends occupying the living room all week. She stayed one night, and then ignored me the rest of the week.

I didn't really care. I enjoyed entertaining my company in Marseille. So, what REPmen that were left in Marseille, we all got together and stayed drunk all week at the pub.

One night I came home and drunkenly wrote an email to Aurora, telling her how I felt. Told her my feelings, but also how I wasn't so sure about things working out. I shouldn't be allowed near electronic devices when drinking.

She responded (*versione originale*):

'*Je comprends ce que tu ressens. Jusqu'à ce que je t'ai rencontré, je ne veux pas être avec quelqu'un d'autre. Une partie de moi est encore fragile aussi. Mais j'ai l'impression que nous pouvons réparer les uns les autres, se donner mutuellement la force. J'aimerais que tu restes avec moi, mais a tout le moins, tu dois sortie de ton appartement. Ce n'est pas un environnement sain pour toi et a causé la plupart des problems jusqu ici. En ce qui concerne mes amis et ces grand nuits de partager, qui sera bientôt ralentie. Un, parce que je suis fatigué de boire autant et deux, je n'ont tout simplement pas l'argent pour cela. C'est l'été aujourd'hui, et il y aura de BBQs et apéros, mais les gens qui viennent sans y être invité sur s'arrêtera, mes amis vont à la maison samedi, et si tu veux continuer a me voir, il sera just toi et moi toute la semaine prochaine. Je te le promets. J'ai peur d'être blesser à nouveau aussi, mais l'idée de te retrouver cet amour me donne de la force. Have a nice weekend and know that I am always here for you.'*

In English:
'I understand how you feel. Until I met you, I did not want to be with anyone else. Part of me is still fragile too. But I have the impression that we can repair each other, give each other strength. I would like you to stay with me, but at the very least, you have to leave your apartment. It's not a healthy environment for you and has caused most problems so far. As for my friends and those great nights to share, that will soon be slowed down. One, because I'm tired of drinking so much and two, I just do not have the money for that. It's summer now, and there will be BBQs and aperitifs, but people who come uninvited will stop, my friends go home on Saturday, and if you want to continue to

see me, it'll just be you and me all next
week. I promise you. I'm afraid of being
hurt again too, but the idea of finding
you, that love gives me strength. Have a
nice weekend and know that I am always here
for you. '

I thought it was ridiculous how upset
she was I had friends stay over and even
spoke to Claudia about it. She agreed with
me and told me to be careful with these
women I get so attached to.

Things got rocky for a while and
Aurora and I went off and on for the next
month. We were kindred spirits, but being
together was a perfect storm that neither
one of us could survive.

49

Kay and I had made up. A heart to heart about what happened. He still thought he could have had his way with Aurora, but wouldn't do that to me no matter how jealous he was that I was spending time with her rather than him. Drugs and alcohol really bring people together as much as they tear them apart.

Whenever I wasn't on with Aurora, I'd be with Kay. It started to become a running joke.

'Hazards on or hazards off?' Kay said.

'What do you mean?' I said.

'Are you fucking Aurora right now or not?' He said.

'What the fuck?'

'Hazards on, hazards off, mate?' He said.

'So wait,' I said, 'if the hazards are on, does that mean we aren't together or are together?'

'On means on, mate.' He said.

'Yeah,' I said, 'but they're hazards, so it could mean like caution, stay away, right?'

'No, mate,' he said, 'Hazards on means you're on, you're fucking.'

'Ah, gotcha.' I said. 'Then hazards off.'

'Here, take this.' he said. 'She is hot. And you have had that for a while.'

'Yeah,' I said. She was more than hot though, but how can you explain that to

some people. They understood I thought,
just didn't like to admit it.

'You know I could have fucked her,
right?' Kay said.

'Yeah, Kay.' I said.

We stayed up all night drinking and
doing drugs.

We roamed the town as we had done so
many times before. Some places remembered
us; some didn't. Some places loved us; some
didn't. We got to La Monde when the sun was
up again and bought more drugs to continue
the day.

It was about nine in the morning when
we saw a large group of people walking down
rue Paradis. I walked over to see what was
going on and Kay started yelling at me.
Then he just walked over behind me.

We stood there smiling like idiots at
what we saw. Making jokes at all the people
out loud.

They were all colorful and loud and
happy.

I looked at Kay and he understood that
I wanted to play too.

We jumped in the group and started the
march with these random people. There were
hundreds, thousands of people. As far as
the eye could see in both directions. There
were floats and trucks with speakers
playing loud music.

People were drinking. People were
high. It was great. We fitted right in. And
it was still morning.

I was high and dancing like a champion
down the street. Sometimes we would just

walk, sometimes we would stop at a store
and buy more beer, sometimes we would duck
into an alley to do more coke.

People were so happy and enthusiastic
that it made me happy and enthusiastic.

Then a pretty, young girl tapped me on
the shoulder. She had been walking in our
general vicinity for the past few minutes.

'My friend wants to kiss you.' She
said. She pointed to her guy friend.

'I'm not gay.' I said.

'Then why are you in the gay pride
parade?' She said.

'Morale support.' I said.

She smiled. 'Can I kiss you?'

I grabbed the side of her face and
kissed her.

We stayed together and made out off
and on until we got to the Avenue du Prado
where we eventually turned right to head
towards the beach.

Kay wanted another stop to do another
line, and I thought he was jealous again.

So I did and kissed the girl one last
time for goodbye.

Her gay friend gave me an ugly look as
if I had just used her, but she seemed okay
with it.

When we found our way back out into
the parade, I met an ex of a friend. She
saw me too and was with a few girlfriends.
She was also another girl that had
confessed her attraction to me. I had
turned down for the invisible contract.
French girls like to mix inside the circle.
It was unnatural for us anglophones despite

our many temptations.

I had my shirt off at this point and was already covered in the paint bombs of powder. Quite the sight I was, but we all looked like ecstatic warriors in our current state.

I kissed Clementine, and we danced together as we walked and I held her in front of me with my arms around her waist and her ass pushing into my crotch. Kay tried talking up her friends as we walked and Kay was a talker, he could sell anybody anything. He could get any woman he wanted, but he'd eventually fuck it up by being an asshole and saying too much.

Clementine and I stayed locked together for some time until Kay and I disappeared again for another line. Clementine understood and causally said she'd be up for it.

Kay told her to fuck off, we didn't have enough.

So, Kay and I wondered off down another alley avoiding the police.

We got back to the parade and marched the rest of the way, explosively interacting with other people and just as quickly moving on to the next victims.

When we got to the statue of David, there was already a massive crowd on the beach and looking back showed an even larger crowd yet to come. We were fairly early and looked for an open spot near the water.

We found two beautiful, dark-complected women and sat next to them.

They were Italian and spoke English
better than French, so that's what we went
with.
　　We sat with them and started chatting.
Then Kay pulled out the coke and tried to
set up a way to do lines, but the wind was
strong on the coast.
　　We folded a piece of paper in half and
did the lines from the crease of the folded
paper. There were probably better ways, but
that's what we came up with in our state.
　　The girls partook and Kay and I felt
like we had just made friends for the day.
　　We talked and talked. It was only
lunch by the time we arrived and still a
full summer afternoon and evening to get to
know each other.
　　We went swimming together, and I
started to become more attracted to one
girl over the other, so I made it known in
a casual sense. I would have been happy
with either girl, but one seemed more
feminine than the other and I went with
her. I didn't come out and kiss her, but I
just started to make contact with her more,
a hand on the waist or a kiss on the cheek
when she said something funny.
　　It wasn't enough to define anything,
but enough to show my interest and she
accepted it.
　　By the time the sun started to come
down, we started to divide off. We were
still four in a group talking, but at this
point I had my head in the girl's lap I
liked and she was petting me. Kay was
sitting next to the other girl, shoulder to

shoulder and things were going well.

Kay always just said I was lucky with women to get away with my forwardness, but I always thought he never tried. He knew I got rejected all the time, but he only ever remembered the times I got lucky.

The girl Kay was getting close to went for another swim.

'You fuck head, look at you just laying there being petted.' He said.

Mariella just laughed and leaned down to kiss me.

'Thank you, Kay.' I thought, but I just smiled.

'You know she's gay, right?' Mariella said.

'Of course.' Kay said.

'No, you didn't.' I said.

'The fuck you did.' he said.

I really hadn't either.

'Yeah, it seems pretty obvious,' Mariella said, 'but yeah, she's the reason we came here.'

'I thought you Italians just came to Marseille for vacation and shopping.' I said.

'We do.' She said. 'But she knew about this parade, so we chose this weekend to do both.'

Angie started to come back from her swim. She sat next to Kay and the feeling of the group had changed on the inside but not on the outside. I could tell by looking at Kay that he was debating whether he still had a chance.

Once it started to get dark, Mariella,

and I had already established our
attraction to one another and Angie told us
to go for a walk since we were being
disgusting.

So we did.

It was more evident to me than ever
that this girl was 6 inches taller than me.

We walked holding hands and talking
and I could barely concentrate on her story
because I was so mixed up about the awkward
swinging of our hands because of the size
difference.

I took her hand and pulled her down
into the sand.

There were too many people around and
she needed more privacy so we got up and
walked further down the beach.

We walked until the beach ended and
turned into a concrete barrier that
protected the park. We walked along that
until it turned inwards.

We weren't the only ones. We walked
past people, some gay, some not, laying
with each other until we got to the end.
Then we started our own exploration of each
other.

She went down on me. Then asked for a
condom.

I didn't have one.

She did. I didn't understand why women
asked when they had one.

We went at it for a while, but between
the 48 hours of booze and the 48 hours of
coke to go along with it, there was not a
chance of cumming with a rubber taking away
the feeling that was supposed to be felt

between two humans.

She was adamant about protection so we just played with each other and went down on each other for half an hour on that concrete slab.

We laid there for another half hour looking up at the stars, touching each other before she went down on me again and then we got dressed and walked back towards the beach.

Kay and Angie were still there but looked like they had exhausted pleasantries and were tired of waiting on us.

Mariella gave me her number and said she had to go. I told her I would come to see her in Italy. We texted for two weeks, but she was too far for a train ride, and I never attempted to fly.

She had smiled that night, and that made never seeing each other again tolerable, even if I regretted it.

50

Aurora and I were still off and on, but mostly off. I wasn't sure anymore if she was still broken up with her ex or not. I didn't doubt her feelings for me, but I doubted her honesty in everything else. I got to where I could think of more places where we had fought than kissed.

Kay and I were tighter than ever though, and my despair with love was comforted in brotherhood and drugs and alcohol.

Then I got a call from Aurora.

Kay and I had been up all night again. Another round of sleepless days, I believe it was day three.

'What's wrong?' I said.

'My ex hit me.' Aurora said.

'What the fuck?' I said. 'Where is he?'

'Don't do anything.' She said.

'Why the fuck would you tell me something like that if you didn't want me to react?'

Kay looked at me.

'Can I come over?' She said.

'Of course.' I said. 'What's your apartment number again?'

'No.' she said.

'I just want to talk to him.'

She hung up.

I told Kay about what happened. He was

ready to fuck somebody up too. We'd usually
pick fights for no reason. But hitting a
woman would enrage any man into action.

I called Pierre and told him that
Aurora was on her way, and that I would
explain later, but to keep her company
until I was back.

He said, 'Okay,' as always.

Kay and I went to her apartment
building. It was the tall tower at the
rond-point du Prado. We walked in as
somebody walked out and took the elevator
up to her floor.

We knocked on the door. Silence most
of the way, just letting the tension build.

I beat on the door.

A man opened up.

Kay was a big boy and grabbed him by
the throat as soon as he opened the door
and started cussing him out in French.
French I didn't know. We beat him down and
he just kept saying he didn't understand.

We left and made it back home.

Aurora knew what we had done and
therefore Pierre did. They both were
standing up and waiting to hear what had
happened.

Aurora was crying. Pierre looked
horrified. Kay and I just got even more
pissed off.

We yelled. Aurora tried to explain.

Something about her ex not wanting her
to move out and then getting jealous about
her being with me when he was trying to
work things out with her.

The worst part was, there were two

sides to the tower and I think we went up
the wrong side. The room numbers were the
same. It was just a matter of south side
and north side towers.

She told us about the cameras
throughout the building and then cried
more.

Kay and I considered our lives forfeit
at this point and ran off to Montpellier
for the weekend.

#

We had one hell of a weekend in
Montpellier but decided at the end of it we
should face the music and see what was to
become of us. Surely, the judge would
understand our actions. We agreed in this
world, that would be the case. We would go
down as noble heroes rather than cowards.

I had been texting Aurora and Pierre.
Pierre didn't respond much and Aurora was
staying with Pierre and said she was okay
and that nobody was looking for us.

If it was the wrong guy, maybe he
deserved it and didn't dare call it in.

It didn't matter. It was worse than
going to jail. Aurora now looked at me like
an animal.

She wouldn't forgive me.

She stayed with Pierre for a while,
strutting around in her pajamas. She won
him over with a smile, so he was against me
too.

She must have stayed there for two
weeks on his couch. Occasionally she would

come down to sleep with me, but mostly she just harassed me from afar.

I didn't care. I didn't regret what I had done. But what love I felt for her was now a love on a back-burner. The last month had been hell trying to understand where we were and when she called for help, I came, and I got crucified for it. Now she was turning one of my best friends against me without even sleeping with him. Just teasing him like a stripper with a client and he was too dumb to realize it.

My closest friend who consoled me after Claudia had just become my closest enemy, harboring my former lover right above me.

The whole situation caused another divide in the friendship of the apartment building, and Kay at least took my side this time.

I said goodbye to Aurora in my mind, but never in speech. After a few weeks of her realizing she wouldn't control me that way, she left.

Pierre never got laid and felt like an asshole for betraying us.

We forgave him, because we knew who he was and it wasn't the first time.

Kay, Pierre, and I were back to our normal roles again.

51

The next couple of months went in a blur of more drugs and alcohol. However, in comparison, I really started weaning off the drugs. They left me feeling so physically exhausted the next day. My muscles would ache from the torture of strenuous dancing and fucking the night before and countless miles I would roam the streets alone singing the 'tambourine man' in my head.

Booze was more honest, and because of that I started to spend more time with my legion friends again back at the bar and not so much with Kay doing lines and singing Queen.

I had met a few women since Aurora. Some I sang Dave Matthews, some I slept with and left before they woke up.

Once I even woke up in a parking garage, covered in piss, bloody knuckles, and one shoe missing. I couldn't remember a fucking thing, but I remembered the walk home with one shoe and still wet of my piss.

But there was always one woman to rescue you from the other as she sets her claws in you to destroy you. I met her. Another her. Nothing to brag about, but she had it. Her strength may have just been an accident that came from my weakness, but she had it.

I couldn't help but think it was a coincidence that the night before I met

her, I watched a movie where the lead
actress looked like her. The same lips as
one of my first lovers. The body, a
beautiful average of my last two lovers.

A ring on her finger, she was
invisible to me at first. For three nights
she tried talking to me. I was so
oblivious, and she was so obvious. She
thought I was married, gay even. Her third
attempt I proved both to be untrue.

Here I went again. I was falling for
one that confused me rather than one I
could so easily read. Was it the challenge?
Was it the chase? She showed interest, but
I did not feel the same control with her as
I did with the others. Was that what
grabbed me? If she submitted to me like the
others did, would I lose interest?

I wrote poetry about her to better
understand her, and I walked away with no
answers but a stronger desire to find them.
This was a woman I would write poetry
about, and that scared the shit out of me.

She was something incredible. So sweet
and gentle. We went home that third night
and the next day she told me we made love
four times.

She was cute and younger than me. This
was new to me and I wasn't sure if I liked
it or not.

#

As much as I liked her though, I was
somewhat entangled with another. She was
very much my type aesthetically, but not

the right psychotic. When she kissed, her tongue was everywhere. Which was nice unless we kissed. But her body was perfect. She did anything I asked, and she loved camping and took very good care of herself.

So I already had plans with her to go camping on a small island off of Brest, and I followed through with those plans despite my new infatuation.

Alice and I continued to talk during my train ride up to my camping trip. I was already looking forward to coming back just to see her again, but she wasn't intending on staying in the area since she was going to school in Corsica and would return soon. I was apparently her first one-night stand.

The girl I camped with was just as awkward and conservative has she always had been since we had met. We still had a pleasant time bicycling the whole island and visiting all the lighthouses there. I also met her parents who came to my surprise. They rented a cabin rather than camping so we didn't stay the night together, but we spent some dinners together, and French dinners can last a lifetime when you didn't want them to.

The weekend finally ended though, and I told her I just didn't see things working out. She was much more heartbroken than I expected considering our short time together, but she seemed to understand.

I got back on the train and started texting Alice again. I wanted to see her before she left for Corsica.

52

Alice was waking up. We had been together for a few months now. She never left for Corsica and stayed in Marseille. I'm not sure if it was for me.

I was calmer now and had calmed down since I started seeing Alice. I can't say it was for her, but it worked out that way, as if I meant it to be.

I was running late, which was normal, but now I could blame it on Alice, in my mind at least. She was still getting ready, and we weren't to the point yet where I would let her lock up behind me.

Teaching wasn't a dream job, but it wasn't bad either. Unless it was a new class. You couldn't help but wonder if they liked you or not. If they respected you or not as a teacher. I always worried that they knew I did not understand what I was doing. I always counted on that first class going well to give me momentum for the rest of the day.

It seemed like no matter how well you did though; you were always being judged. The new prof d'anglais. Look how young he is, is he really going to speak English the whole time, this isn't how I learned English before, I want a human dictionary. Most of them didn't want to be there, and I didn't want to be there with them. I'd be happier laying in bed next to a beautiful woman and having a glass of wine to start my day. I didn't want to have to get up,

shit, shower, and shave to entertain these
people to help them find a job or help them
keep their job.

You would find a few who were there to
learn though, and almost all the private
classes went well. Yet most of the students
were adult children that needed constant
attention and positive reinforcement to
convince them to better themselves.

I couldn't seem to make myself a
better adult, the more I tried, the more I
seemed to fail. How was I supposed to help
others do what I couldn't?

Alice gave me a hug from behind, and I
knew she was ready to go. She really was a
sweet girl. I really hoped that I wouldn't
hurt her. I was sure she loved me.

I was missing my blurry summer as I
was waking up into a world of overdue taxes
and bureaucratic shit that killed me inside
more than the pack of cigarettes I smoked
every day.

Just waking up every day into this
world is the most painful part of my day. I
didn't think falling asleep took me as long
as it used to. Alcohol and sex always
helped with that, but damn I really wish I
never had to wake up. I wasn't sure if it
was because of laziness or a lack of
motivation or both.

There was a part of me that wanted to
get my life together. A positive change. I
even didn't drink as much. I knew how much
money I had in the bank account and there
was a small part of me that could see
myself growing into a man that could

support a family. To love and take care of
them like a good man would. I wanted to
know if I could be that person.

53

It was Friday, and I had my psyche appointment in the afternoon. I had been going since the end of summer, not long after Aurora and just before Alice. It was the end of November and I felt like I was doing pretty well and started to question if I was really as unstable as I had been convinced I was.

She was an American woman providing services to mostly anglophone expats and students in the Aix-en-Provence area. She was a kind of hippie and I liked that about her. She understood all that Eastern philosophy that I used to understand the world. We got along well and had some intense talks about my relationships with women and love. It was mostly all we talked about besides perhaps my creativity. She said I had something that needed to be said and so every week I'd bring something I had written. She enjoyed it and would then talk about it with me the next week.

The appointments weren't covered by the universal healthcare system though and cost me €80 a pop. I was wondering if it was worth it. Besides that money, it would take up my afternoon with the bus ride there and back, but she was the only English-speaking psychiatrist I could find.

It also didn't help I wasn't working as much as I could have been. Working for yourself was never easy unless you truly believed in what you were doing. And as much as I enjoyed entertaining my students, I hated preparing for them.

After cleaning up from the summer and realizing my financial situation, the sessions were looking like an exuberant check-in. A luxury I couldn't afford. I would have a talk with Lisa about it.

One thing for sure, I could never understand was that no matter how much I slept, be it four hours or ten, I always woke up just as tired and unwilling to face the day. I knew I needed the time to get things done in the morning. Mostly just walking the dog, but I would fight it with everything to stay in bed; my nice warm bed with a naked girl in it.

Shit. My life wasn't so bad.

I mean I found out I gave Alice chlamydia, but she wasn't that upset. Her friends had warned her when we met that I was dangerous for women to get close to, and to her friend's surprise, we were still together months later. I felt bad about the chlamydia thing though. We were supposed to avoid sex for a week while we took the medication, but that didn't happen. I guess we'll go back next week to see if we kept the bacteria or not. At least I wasn't sleeping around with anybody else.

Alice and I were an undeclared item. We were becoming more infatuated with each other as time went on. I drew her naked one night, and it reminded of me when I had done the same thing with Claudia. I wasn't sure if that was fucked up or not, so I didn't mention that detail to Alice. I also

shared with her one of my favorite things I
started when dating Claudia. Double-blind
folds, losing sight and each fumbling,
discovering each other purely by touch.
That always led to a night of passion.
Sharing these things with Alice made me
worried that I was falling in love with
her. I didn't think that would ever be
possible again.

And though, Alice had yet to say she
loved me, I loved the way her face looked
when I would pull away from kissing her and
would open my eyes before she did. I could
see her still feeling the kiss. It made a
man wonder, can love be as temporary as a
kiss? Can a man love a woman in just a
moment, in just a night. Did love have to
mean tolerating each other for eternity or
could it be as powerful and as temporary as
having a moment of nirvana? A small moment
in time where everybody around you was
happy at exactly the same time. One moment
that was shared collectively, unknowingly
by most, but felt by all.

If love could exist that way, I had
loved many.

And then my thoughts faded from
Alice's face, of her sweetness tasting what
love I had left to give her and back into
the real world. I was still being harassed
by taxes and was succumbing to the
pressure. My carte vitale still wasn't
working. As an immigrant, I didn't get all
the benefits of this country, but they
still wanted my money.

I also thought about what I would

teach for the next week. It was
Thanksgiving next week. The least
commercialized holiday of them all. I
wouldn't get the days off being that it
wasn't a French holiday, but I thought I
might still do a dinner even if it would
only be Pierre and Alice that would show
up. Something small for the ones that still
wanted to spend time with me.

54

I slept in until 15h the next day. It was a Saturday, and I had stayed up all night until 09h watching movies and eating. I was doing my best to avoid alcohol and the pub and though it felt good to be alone and sober, I'm not sure if it was any healthier than being drunk.

It gave me time to think about stupid shit that I never cared about before. Like how long my hair was getting. I liked it long when I combed it back, but that took a couple of days before it would train to stay back and then it was time to wash it again and go back to a fluffy mess that came from the 70s.

Taking care of my dog became more irritating. Drunk, I just didn't really care when he tore things up. But sober, I am forced to find some Zen moment of detachment. Of letting go of these material possessions I treasured. That damn dog was a handful and a pain in the ass, but I loved the bastard and he was definitely my best friend and probably the closest thing I would ever have to creating a family.

I really had no intention of leaving the house. I was loving the time alone. I would close the shutters and make the place dark. Open the windows for fresh air, and only close them when the 20-year-old kids would be back outside sitting on my stoop, drinking their juice boxes, smoking their hashish, and listening to shitty French-

Arab rap music. I got to where I started
pouring bleach on the steps so they would
fuck off onto somebody else's porch for a
week.

Those same kids had stolen my laptop
through the window once. I had just bought
a new one because Maverick had spilt water
on the one before. Besides losing my work,
I didn't mind too much; I convinced myself
I needed a new one. And can you blame a
dog? They only knock the dominoes over;
they don't line them up.

But my new computer I had only just
gotten two months after Maverick's spill
and got it back to where my old one was
just before I left the shutters and window
open. It being summer; I thought it would
be okay in daylight and with bars on the
window. I was wrong, and they took a long
pizza pan for the oven and slid it through
the window bars, scooped up my computer on
my kitchen table 3 feet from the window,
then brought it back to themselves. Clever
bastards.

Well, that's the way I imagined things
went. I sent word amongst the kids I would
pay €200 to get it back, but after 3 days,
they came back saying it was already gone.

#

Alice was gone for the weekend to
spend time with family. She was texting me.
She missed me. I missed her, but I enjoyed
the solitude so much more in this moment.
After a few days alone, I would be ready

for her and the world again. Until then, I would reply from time to time to her messages to let her know how much I would be ready to see her after the weekend was over. And I would be.

But this was my first opportunity to be alone in a long time. The first this year I felt I needed it. Without a woman or work. Just take out food and cigarettes. A day like Pierre's every day, but he never wanted it. He wanted what I had most of the time. I would have given it to him if I could have, but life didn't work that way.

I suppose I could have done it before. Quiet weekends alone. But I was too busy drinking and chasing women to not think about one woman. To not think about myself. An ironic and fucked up way of being outwardly selfish to avoid being full of myself. If my trip to India and Nepal had been my crest, the following summer would have been the crash and trough.

I wasn't sure where I was now. I felt old and used up. As if I had lived too many lives in one. I needed this weekend alone. To rest. To close the blinds and die for a little while.

It would be a great weekend.

#

I slept in again on Sunday. I took Maverick for his morning walk. It was a beautiful day. I was thinking to grab a coffee and read a book at Manelo's later, a little café/bar across the street from me.

A bohemian pair owned it. She was French, and he was Spanish. We had become good friends, and I brought them a lot of business over my active summer that I would drag home with me from Vieux Port. We would hang out after hours and smoke and drink once the customers were all gone. There was something nice about going to a little café and the owners knew you by name and habit.

I was in a good mood. Motivated even. It was strange.

I took Maverick home and gave him his breakfast. While he ate, I made my lesson plans for the week. It didn't take long since I had already written it in my head, just needed to put it on paper and look up the words I didn't know in French that the French would expect me to translate rather than use their own dictionary or god forbid an English dictionary.

The quiet weekend, or doing nothing, had really done me good. It almost felt nostalgic, but I couldn't think of when I had had such a pleasurable weekend alone in the house; no going out, no alcohol, and no drugs. Not even sex. I almost felt like a kid again. An innocent. That must have been the sweet taste in my mouth.

#

Alice would come back over to stay the night. I was ready to squeeze her again. I was a squeezer and with Alice I started saying 'squeeze' in my text rather than 'bisous' or other things. She liked it and

started saying it back. Alice was a doll.
Her body was perfect in its own way. She
wasn't long-legged or had striking
jawlines. She would never be a model. But
she was young and voluptuous without being
fat. She just had the perfect amount of
everything and I could never get enough of
her. I always had to be careful not to
squeeze her too hard.

I had more classes in the coming week
and it was enough to balance me out. It
wasn't a full load, but enough to cover my
way of life. I had already cut down my
psyche sessions to every other week, so
that opened up some time to find more work.
I just needed to find it and then maybe I
could save up some money to do something
more with life. Shit, working and having a
lady changed a man. How long would this
last? Was I finally doing good for myself?
I at least felt like I was out of the deep
dark hole I had been in before.

#

My classes for Monday involved one
class of 4 at a business for importing and
exporting. One private class with two, and
then a private one to one at 18h30. I would
teach Thanksgiving all week except to my
beginners or faux debutants.

When I walked the dog, I used it as a
time to wake up and think about my day. I
still had my taxes. Mother fuckers. But
mostly, I was thinking about work. Could I
handle doing as many classes as I thought I

should do? I made €20 an hour, but I didn't get paid for the time it took me to travel to these different businesses or the time I prepared the lessons. Then I remembered my English teaching course. For a month, we learned during the day, taught in the evening, and I still went out every night. Fuck it. I was a goddamn champion. A badass legionnaire. An American war veteran. A douchebag apparently. But I could do it.

I was also taking care of an apartment for an old legion buddy. A Swedish guy we called Svensson, whose real name sounded like 'Swanlove', but was spelled 'Svanlöf' or something like that. We had joined when identities were still protected so none of us called each other by our real names.

Swanlove sent me a message to ask about mail. He was expecting something. I was also taking care of the tobacco plants he had in his window. They were growing tall and sticky. You could almost see the growth every day. Swanlove was a big pipe smoker.

I walked back inside with Maverick, and Alice was still downstairs getting gussied up for the day. While I waited for her, I thought about whether to cook a Thanksgiving dinner. I was teaching all week and Thursday was a busy day, but I could probably find the time. I had time on Wednesday to do the shopping and Friday to invite people over.

Despite my walk, I still came home to a dark hole. It made me want to go back to sleep while I waited for Alice.

I tried to focus on my day and what
needed to be done. There was a school I
could probably find work at, Wall Street
Institute. But it would be hard to accept
lower pay than what I was making now. I
would have to check it out to be sure.

55

I woke up aggravated. My momentary bliss had ended.

I had another dream I wanted to remember but had forgotten due to falling back asleep. The snooze button is a curse to this society only because the alarm clock is.

More than that though, Alice slept over, but she built more pressure than released. I made the mistake of trying to encourage her to take more initiative. To be more aggressive in bed. To take charge. To seduce me with more than just having a beautiful body. I tried to explain. I tried to tell her I don't mind being the 'man' and her being the 'woman' in the relationship. But it all just pushed her further away, and I was making things worse.

She eventually opened up and proved to be a much more timid girl than I had thought. Within in the first two weeks of really being together she had told me I could fuck her in the ass, seemed proud of all the things she had done. Laid it on the table. Now it seemed those things were off the table. The story had changed, and these things took her months to build courage for and only happened a handful of times rather than the big talk at the beginning of our relationship where she led me to believe that she was some porn star. I wasn't sure what kind of pissed off I should have been.

So last night ended with a cold shower and a sleepless night filled with disappointment and guilty pressure.

Now I would carry that into my day. I had never left a girl for being bad in bed, but that seemed as good a reason as any.

Fuck it.

The world was here.

Back at it.

#

I started my Wednesday off not much better, tired and frustrated. So keeping the torture going, I decided I would go knock out my taxes. Being half asleep made the process more tolerable.

I could remember my dreams, at least one of them, better than I had on my previous nights. I started thinking about it as I was waiting for my turn at the Centre des Finances Publiques.

In my dream, I was back in Norfolk and moving back into my old apartment in West Ghent. It wasn't identical to the actual apartment, but like the dream version. When I got there, nobody was there, so I figured no problem. Later I saw Leslie, the girl I used to live with when I had been there before. She wasn't in the same apartment but in the one just below now. When I passed her, I started to say, 'Hi,' but she looked at me as if she didn't even recognize me.

'Leslie,' I said. 'How's things?'

'Will?' she said. 'I mean, where have

you been?'
  'Afghanistan.' I said.
  I wasn't sure why I had said
Afghanistan. I guess that dream version of
me had just gotten back. Maybe it was a
parallel universe I was peering into. The
rest of the dream just involved me walking
up and down the stairs. I wasn't sure what
the point of that was, but rather than
trying to figure that out the rest of my
wait, I just thought about Leslie. Tall,
skinny, blonde Leslie wrapped in a white
bath towel.

#

  I decided Thanksgiving would happen
and invited Kay, Ackerman, Jenny, and
Swanlove. Then Louise texted me and was
curious if I was doing anything, so invited
her too. Then Alice and Pierre (and
possibly his mother) would be there too. I
figured I would invite Murphy and Rose too.
  Despite my laziness and poor planning,
it looked like there might be a French
Thanksgiving. I figured being in the
holiday spirit, I should write a
Thanksgiving message. My writing activities
with Lisa must have been playing their
role.
  But I wasn't that jolly just yet, and
the few posts that I had written had caused
a bit of tension between Alice and I. I had
gotten back on Facebook to work my way back
into becoming a normal citizen of the
world.

The last time I had written something, I thought it was a clever post about pain and detail. I never considered myself an artist, but I had always enjoyed writing even before Lisa encouraged me to do so. Sometimes you just needed to bleed your words out into the world and Facebook was a convenient medium for that.

So I wrote something:

'It may seem like my writing, my posts, are a lot about pain. I never knew why that was until I started looking back. Pain made me focus on every aspect of what happened. The curve of a lost lover's neck. The reasons why my dreams have never been fully realized. Broad strokes have never done much good for me. I can plan, but I'm coming to learn the futility in such a concept. It is that still image that haunts me, all those fine details that stay with me.

'At first, I thought I was torturing myself, and so did those closest to me. But it in fact allowed me to heal. To get out the hidden anger from my failed goals. I learned this a lot by accident, as I have learned most things. I just needed to write my life out, at first for perspective, to see as Rilke put it that we are all 'unutterably alone.' ('Letters to a Young Poet' helped me a lot.) But later it became more.

'This may be different for you. But it was this pain that I learned to pay attention to the details in life. The details of now, rather than the anxiety of

*tomorrow and the disappointment of
yesterday. Each moment is always
manageable. By focusing on the moment,
everything would be all right. Breathing in
and out. I knew, for all my waiting, I may
never get the phone call I want, but it
didn't mean there wasn't beauty in what I
already had.'*

It was all cheesy and pretentious for
me and I regretted it just after I put it
up as I did most things I shared with
people. But Claudia liked it almost
immediately and sent me a private message
saying she particularly liked the part
about 'the curve of the neck'.

Within 30 seconds of Claudia liking
the post, Alice sent me a text saying 'Je
vais la tuer.' I wondered if they both had
notifications on for when I posted
something or if they were just both always
on Facebook. Neither would have surprised
me.

I ignored them both and went shopping
for Thanksgiving. Pumpkin purée for a pie.
The works for the stuffing and some
cranberry sauce. Potatoes for mashing. Some
green beans and corn. I was going to have
to buy a lot of small miscellaneous things
since I rarely got this exuberant with my
food.

56

Happy Fucking Thanksgiving. I was actually happy about it. It would be my first Thanksgiving since my move to France. And so far there would be 8 of us. I felt like a thankful man.

Though not so much about my morning. Another night of bad sleep and disturbing dreams. I was so late getting up that I had to leave Alice to walk the dog. She didn't seem to mind. I think she liked that I trusted her to leave my keys with her.

I made it to my first class on time, but wouldn't have time to relax and catch up mentally. It would be a busy day. I had to buy cigarettes. Teach more classes. Get my carte vitale sorted out now that I had paid my taxes. I had to cancel my TV, which I had never used to avoid paying the extra €180 in taxe audiovisual. The French will tax any and all. This one came attached to the taxe d'habitation, basically a tax just for having shelter, not the same thing as property tax, which is also a thing. All this along with all the taxes they normally take out of your paycheck, anyway. And if the taxes weren't enough, they had another name they used to draw more money out of you every year: les impôts. No such thing as a refund in France. They take, then take again.

I would not let that ruin my favorite feast of the year though. There would be Turkey, sweet potato pie, pumpkin pie, stuffing, cranberry sauce, mashed potatoes, gravy (from the turkey), green beans, corn, and biscuits American style. Plus a bit of drink, I was planning on making du vin chaud - I bought six bottles of red wine for that, plus brandy and cider.

It would be an international Thanksgiving: 2 French girls, an Englishman, an Irishman, a Swede, 2 Romanians, possibly 2 Dutch, et moi - l'americain - at the head of the table.

#

The cooking took a day and a half to put together and was still being finished when people started to show up. I had a new respect for my family that took the time to prepare this meal.

Pierre and Alice were there first and helped where I needed it. Alice looked beautiful in her dress, and Pierre looked like he just rolled out of bed as he usually did wearing sweatpants and a t-shirt.

Then Ackerman and Jenny showed up.

Then Murphy and Rose, bringing plenty of alcohol as always.

Swanlove arrived bringing a bottle of whiskey and some dried meat he had just made.

The table was full now, and I was a little glad Kay texted saying he would not make it. Louise texted to say she would be late and to start without her.

Then I had a last-minute guest show up

with her signature bottle of Maker's Mark,
Katie. She was a Tennessee girl also living
in Marseille. We teased each other about
being from the south and always got along
well. We had had a few nights staying up
all night drinking together. There was
something there, but we never went past
kissing. She was always timid about that.
And now, she knew I was with Alice, but I
couldn't not invite her once I heard she
had no plans.

I was putting the last dishes on the
table as people started to grab their
places and sat down. The table took up the
entire kitchen and half the living room,
but we managed. Luckily, Pierre had plenty
of tables and chairs to share.

I sat at the head of the table with
Alice to my left and waited for people to
finish taking their food pictures.

'So thanks for coming and whatnot.' I
said.

There were mixed languages of saying,
'Thanks,' in return.

'So what we do here is go around the
table and say something we're thankful
for,' I said, 'but that seems awkward as
shit, so unless you just want to say
something, let's eat.'

Everybody looked around and nobody
said anything.

Shit. I did that wrong.

'We're all thankful for each other,
right? Friends, lovers, good food, and a
place to sleep.' I said.

Alice squeezed my hand that she had

pulled into her lap under the table.

Another mix of languages each saying their own affirmation.

Then I raised my glass and said, 'Cheers, Santé, Proost, Noroc.'

We all raised our glasses and touched them as best we could with the best eye contact we could. Another French thing. If you failed to make eye contact during the 'ching' of glasses, it was seven years of bad sex.

Then we dug in and I continued to explain all the different foods. Most of it was new to them.

'C'est bien, cherie?' I said

Alice smiled, 'Oui.'

And everybody started talking amongst themselves.

I talked to Swanlove about his latest adventures in finding work in the private security world. He wanted me to join him as an intelligence analyst and driver.

Jenny and Ackerman mostly talked to each other.

Alice talked mostly with Rose and me and then Louise when she showed up, Alice was still uncomfortable with English.

Murphy, Swanlove, and I spoke mostly in English and told our same old war stories from the Legion and our drinking days.

All was jolly and merry. Everybody was smiling, talking, eating, drinking, and then Kay came in.

'Oh, am I late?' Kay said.

'A little.' I said.

Most people had finished eating by this point, and there was plenty left. We made room for him and he took off his jacket and sat down. His face was red, and he kept smiling.

'What the fuck are y'all looking at?' He said.

Everybody started to quietly return to talking while Kay fixed himself a plate.

'Oh, Will,' Kay said from across the table, 'so this is fucking Thanksgiving?'

'Yeah, bud,' I said. 'Give some thanks and eat up.'

He ate his plate in two or three bites. Then started harassing everybody at the table. Most people knew him by now and most weren't a fan. I could feel they were getting ready to leave.

'Thanks for inviting us, Will' Ackerman said. Then we gave a hug and Jenny and I did bisous as they left.

'Je dois partir aussi,' Rose said, 'Je travaille ce soir.' More bisous and another person gone.

'What the fuck's going on?' Kay said. 'Everybody's leaving? Don't be boring.'

Another hour went by and Kay was only getting more excited.

'Merci, Will,' Louise said, 'pour le dîner. C'était très sympa.' More bisous.

'My mom is probably waiting on me.' Pierre said. I gave him some food for her and he left.

'This is shit.' Kay said. 'Worst party ever.'

'You want me to kick his ass.'

Swanlove said.

I laughed.

'So leave, Kay.' I said.

'You're a bunch of cunts.' He said. And he left grabbing another biscuit for the road.

Alice and I were snuggling at this point while Swanlove, Katie, Murphy, and I spoke in English.

Alice knew we were all heavy drinkers, but she still left frustrated once it got late. She wanted to call it a night and go to bed, and I didn't want to kick them out.

So she went downstairs to bed alone.

Swanlove staggered home not much later, and that left Katie, Murphy, and myself as the last ones standing.

We must have stayed up for hours later. Alice was sending me texts from downstairs. She couldn't sleep because we were being too loud. That and she was jealous at how well Katie and I got along. She had nothing to worry about, but I understood, though I didn't react as if I did.

Eventually Katie and I decided it was late, and Murphy was in his repetitive state, so I offered them a place to crash, but he felt well enough to walk home.

The last of the hugs and bisous for the night and I started to clean up. I stopped halfway done though, and went downstairs to lie down and call it a day myself.

Alice was awake but said nothing to me.

\#

Thanksgiving had ended, and I spent the entire next day recovering from the hangover. The dinner itself went well enough. The most embarrassing thing had been calling my dad and putting him on speakerphone so the others could hear an Arkansas accent.

The apartment was still in a state. Alice had done the dishes, but after that we spent the rest of the day having sex and watching '30 Rock.' It seemed everybody left in a rough state and spent the next day recovering.

Today though, people would come over to get the things they had left behind. Swanlove was on his way to grab his pipe, and a few others left without their jackets.

I was still recovering and felt another shit coming on. It would do me good, along with a shower, and then I'd have to attack the kitchen and do my best to catch back up to the digital world; emails, texts, etc.

As I was sitting there though, I felt happy in my extended hangover. Alice on one side, my puppy on the other. I felt so comfortable, so damn loved. I was thankful.

57

It was officially the first day of the last month of the year. My laundry list of things to do seemed to never end; haircut, ship off Christmas presents, pay rent, laundry, chase after that fucking carte vitale more, prepare my lesson plans, and send in my facture to get paid. The shit never ended. Fuck I was looking forward to the upcoming Christmas break, so I could just sit down and read a book in peace without thoughts creeping in of all the things that needed to be done tomorrow.

I was supposed to be going to see a movie with Alice, but I had thought about canceling since the night we made the plans. I felt like I needed more alone time, plus movies just felt like a waste of money and I was just starting to break even financially.

But money wasn't really the issue or Alice. It was this desire to be alone. I couldn't tell if it was a healthy feeling, a healthy desire or another sort of depression trying to find its way out. I figured even if it was another round of the black dog, it would still be better to stay home alone and face him head on. I had gotten better at talking to this beast that had become a part of my life.

I also considered having Alice over so she could see this side of me and judge how she reacted to it all. She would be here but without my attention. She would just be a body in the room while I was off in my dark world. I figured it could be good for us for two reasons. To show her how I needed my alone time and to give her a chance to get comfortable with that. And if this was the black dog coming for me again, it might be good to have her around. She could help me out of it, more than I could usually help myself in those states.

I started to think about drinking. I had really cut back and losing a whole day to a hangover over the weekend reminded me of that. I thought I should either cut back even more to avoid losing days like that, or go back to drinking everyday so the hangovers weren't as bad. My bank account balance liked the sober me better, and I even got excited at the prospect of being back in the black within a few months. Shit, the black dog was creeping in and reminding me that a lot could happen in a few months.

#

Alice and I ended up watching the new Coen brothers film. It was as good as all the rest of them. But I wasn't in the best of moods and the black dog slept with me that night along with my happy black dog, Maverick. Unfortunately, neither he nor Alice could protect me in my dreams. I didn't have to wake until 10h, but it was 10h40 by the time I got up and out the door. I felt bad rushing Maverick's walk in the morning when I slept in like that or asking Alice to take care of him for me.

But sleeping was still a struggle, and when I slept it was always to the strangest of dreams that left me feeling frustrated. I would wake up, remember them, get frustrated and go back to sleep to try again and then repeat this cycle 2 or 3 times before giving up and just getting up, remembering only bits of each dream. I knew the first one was about Maju, my Argentinian ex-wife back in America. We were on some metro system, traveling from one place to another, but never arriving at where we wanted to be. Something bad happened to her, but I couldn't remember what, just that half of her face was always covered. I couldn't really remember much more than that, other than the feeling of being in more control of the dream than I normally was, but also more frustrated at the things I couldn't control. It all gave me a headache and another shit mood to start my day.

I told Alice about my shit mood because of the dream and asked if I could be alone for some time. She took it okay. She got a bit stressed and took her medicine for her panic attacks, but said she would stay at her place. I told myself it was for the best. I loved having her around, but this wasn't fair to her.

So I tried to fight the spell. A new day. A new week. A new to-do list. Another chance to get ahead in this world or fall further behind.

I just had to make it to Christmas

break I kept telling myself. I hoped that
my plans with Pierre to go to his hometown
in central Romania for a week long of
skiing would go through.

I also got an email from Aviva, Cathy,
Friedrich, and the Dutch couple from my
Nepal trip, wishing me a one-year
anniversary of our trip. Damn. It should
make me smile, but it just made me feel
worse. What was I going to say to them?
They seemed to have all been traveling the
entire time I had been gone. Should I tell
them about the drama with Claudia whom they
knew by picture and stories? Or all the
bullshit that ensued afterwards? The crazy,
blurry summer and how I achieved nothing of
substance, only consuming many substances.
Or how my life was finally starting to
settle with work and a girlfriend and being
responsible. Fuck, I was a wreck or boring.
I would have to come up with something and
respond later.

Then that reminded me I had other
emails to respond to that I had postponed
waiting for a better mood, particularly my
sister, one person I had always kept in
touch with. The black dog was laughing at
me now through a scowl.

#

I woke up in a sweat at 5h30 and
couldn't go back to sleep, but remembered
two of my dreams. One involved skydiving
with Robin, a Swedish guy that I was with
in 2°REP. I kept jumping, and my parachute

kept closing just before landing and
breaking my leg all over again. The pain
was intense and left me laying on the
ground until I got back up to do it again.
And I did, multiple times. I would jump,
the parachute would close, and I would end
in a lot of pain each time. Every jump, I
would be scared but excited. I would adore
the fall and then end with the same
horrifying result.

That dream didn't end until I went
into the next dream where my brother died.
I went to his house and started collecting
his stuff, which was a lot of baseball
memorabilia. And while I was collecting his
stuff, I had flashbacks of the times I had
spent with him. Not real-life events, but
things that happened in my dreams before
with him. Most of it just involved sitting
in the kitchen together, cooking, talking,
and drinking Nesquik.

I got my Christmas gifts wrapped and
shipped off and then bought and wrapped
Alice's gifts; a toy set of cleaning stuff,
a toy set of cooking stuff, a book on how
to draw cats, a pair of house shoes, and an
art drawing kit with an easel, paper,
charcoal, pastels, etc. I also bought a
book for drawing nudes for myself and drew
one of them when I got home. I suppose if
there was anything that would save me in
this world, it would be a woman. There
would be no existence without them. I even
thought about going back to get a starter
paint set for myself. It was something I
had always wanted to learn how to do and my

art teacher back when I took random courses at Old Dominion University told me I would have a knack for it after he saw me work with charcoal and pastels. I enjoyed art, but I just didn't see it as a real pastime or profession. Maybe I just didn't have the discipline for it.

The mornings were getting colder now and all I could think about was getting back into my nice warm bed under the covers.

Then Alice called. She wanted to come over, but I told her it would be best to maintain the space. She didn't like the idea, but said okay. I came off telling her I needed to learn not to be needy of her or her attention. And a large part of that was true, as when I came home without her already there, it felt strangely empty. I had already become too accustomed to her presence in my life and in my space. It had been moving fast. Well, but fast. I needed to breathe and catch up mentally. The feeling of losing someone was still lingering in my thoughts. I couldn't rush into this too quickly with this one. No more than I had already done.

I could tell it was hard on her too as she sent me messages in the middle of the night saying she couldn't sleep without me. I had the same problem. I had tried everything; writing, soft music, incense, meditation. Nothing was happening, other than a sleepless night. I never slept well, but at least I slept some when she was around. So we stayed up talking for an hour

until she dozed off and not long after, I
did too. My thoughts that night ended with
hoping the space would bring us closer
together rather than further apart.

One thing she said echoed through my
mind like a lullaby that could put a baby
to sleep, 'You are perfect in somebody's
world.'

58

I was supposed to wake up this morning
to go do that carte vitale waiting in line
and paperwork nonsense, but no. I slept.
Woke. Rolled over. Slept. Dreamt. Woke.
Rolled over. Slept and repeated that
process at least half a dozen times until
just after lunch. Did I feel like a dirty,
lazy good-for-nothing? Yeah, I did, a
little, but then not so much. After a
'morning' walk with Maverick that feeling
faded away like the clouds across the sky.

No doubt there was the feeling I
should do something productive with my time
now that I was up. But not today. Not
today. I paid rent. Got a new class with a
girl named Juliane for this Friday and
picked up my check from the language
academy I worked at. Which then made me
wonder where my check from GMPA was.
Fucking government.

I was walking above the ground. I just
didn't care anymore. I guess I bound it to
happen, pushing myself to be productive
these past few weeks, making every minute
count for something.

Sleeping in was a nice, fat middle
finger to my ambitious side. A good side to
have, but a side that was driving me crazy.
I would keep the day in the same tone. I
would have Alice come over, order some
takeout, and have the day off.

Sing with me:

♪ *Je Ne Veux Pas Travailler* ♪
Ma chambre a la forme d'une cage
Le soleil passe son bras par la
fenêtre
Les chasseurs à ma porte
Comme des petits soldats
Qui veulent me prendre

{Refrain:}
Je ne veux pas travailler
Je ne veux pas déjeuner
Je veux seulement oublier
Et puis je fume

Déjà j'ai connu le parfum de l'amour
Un millions de roses
N'embaumerait pas autant
Maintenant une seule fleur
Dans mes entourages
Me rend malade

{au Refrain}

Je ne suis pas fière de ça
Vie qui veut me tuer
C'est magnifique
Être sympathique
Mais je ne le connais jamais

{au Refrain}

Je ne suis pas fière de ça
Vie qui veut me tuer
C'est magnifique
Être sympathique
Mais je ne le connais jamais

{au Refrain}

59

The next morning I got up by 08h. At my first few attempts of getting out of bed, I retracted back under the sheets like a snail in sunlight. It was cold in the sous-sol of my apartment and both my conscious and subconscious agreed that rubbing up against Alice's warm naked body was more enticing than the daily routine of the cold and groggy world.

But Maverick got up, and laid his head on the pillow and stared at me, so I asked him if he was sure, and he lifted his head and then plopped it back down on the pillow. I said okay, and we went for a nice long stroll in the cool morning air to start our day.

The good thing about my Thursdays was the fact they ended by the early afternoon. I could get back home, prepare for the lesson plan for my new student the next day, and write something up real quick for my psyche visit with Lisa. I hated going there with nothing.

Today was also my brother's birthday. I had a dream about him he had a girlfriend and he was happy. It made me happy to see him that way. I thought about calling him, but I didn't have his number.

I also thought again about buying myself some painting supplies and just trying it out. I gave the nude drawing book to Alice, and she liked it. Being the clever girl she was, I think she got a hint

of what I got her for her Christmas gift.
Hopefully, what I got would still be
enough. I told her not to spend too much on
me, because I didn't for her. Considering
she didn't have much money, I doubted that
would be a problem.
      Then I thought about gifts for the
guys. Pierre would no doubt like something
that had to do with computer games. Then
there was Murphy, Kay, Ackerman, and
Swanlove. Swanlove had already bought me a
carton of cigarettes and gave them to me.
This Christmas was getting expensive. I
told myself I wouldn't force it, but if I
found something by chance, I'd grab it. If
money hadn't been an issue, I probably
would have enjoyed giving them some shit,
but money was an issue and so was my way of
just giving it away.
      I needed to talk to Murphy about
getting the business up and running.

      So, I met up with Murphy to go over
the business. He was still supposed to be
getting it up and running with paperwork
and planning, calling me when he needed me
to help, but he never called. I would
always call him and the night would end the
same way, he'd mumble something about
waiting on something, and by the end of the
meeting, we would be three or four pints in
and back to just hanging out.
      I got pissed off with him this last
time and walked off in a drunken state to
roam the streets of Marseille.
      I got kicked out of a few bars.

Then a woman was trying to take me
home. I laughed it off at first. Then she
kissed me and stuck her hand down my pants.
    I stepped away and pulled her hand
out. I was hammered, but loyal.
    I went home after that and woke up the
next day feeling like shit for even
allowing that to happen. Then I turned into
a positive. Something I should be proud of.
I turned down a woman with her hand on my
penis and lips on my mouth while drunk in a
gut reaction to stay faithful to a woman I
had been dating for a few months. There had
to be some reward for that.
    It played on my mind in a mostly
negative way though and rather than taking
advantage of my bi-weekly psyche
appointment, I just didn't even go. I
didn't even call.
    I went shopping in that time instead
for some basics: Maverick's food, toilet
paper, socks, toothpaste, paper towels, and
a gamer's keyboard for Pierre for
Christmas.
    I lugged it all home ready to settle
for a quiet evening.
    'Happy 4 months!' Alice said.
    Shit. I guess it has been that long.
    'Crazy.' I said.
    Shit. That was probably the wrong
thing to say. I still felt like I was
leaving a relationship. Maybe that was the
way it was always supposed to feel. To
feel. To feel something for someone always,
and transfer that feeling over from one to
another over a process. I didn't know, and

I wasn't sure I wanted to know.
    Cigarettes.
    Oblivion.
    Sex.
    This is what I knew.
    This is what I thought.
    'Stop drinking so much. No. Fuck it.
Drink to death, get it over with, give up.
Quit.
    'My tattoo: Om
    'Peace.
    'Love.
    'Give up - Give in. Release control.
    'Humility.
    'Courage.
    'You can do this.
    'Do what?
    'Stop the spiritual bullshit. You are
nobody special. You are a piece of shit.
Lower than or just as low as the other scum
out there. Stop walking so tall. Crawl your
way back home, broken and defeated, and
cry. Cry in your bed. Where even your dog
won't feel sorry for you. He's just as
tired of your shit as you are.
    'Stop your whining. Look at your
anger. Get angry, but don't get sad.
    'Paralyzed.
    'Get angry and make a change.
    'Alice is writing her bilan. Maybe
I'll do one too. It's like a journal entry
describing your evolution over the past
year. Not a bad idea. I'm sure I've done
something similar before. I'll wait and do
one closer to the end of the year.
    'Cliché!

'That's it. Get angry. At least do something when you get angry. Go running. Remember that painting kit. Go do that. Maybe it's a new outlet for you. A new hobby. A new passion.

'Alice is tearing up her bilan.

'Fuck this shit.

'I need to trim my beard.' I thought

60

The ass fucking at 16 issue came up again.

During our first weeks together, Alice had told me about a lot of the things she had done sexually, and one that caught my attention was her getting fucked in the ass at 16.

The first time it came up, it was a fairly short conversation.

'I didn't see why it's such a big deal.' She said.

'I didn't see how you could be so bored with sex at 16, you need to take it up the ass.' I said.

'You're just jealous because you didn't do it.'

'Maybe,' I said, 'maybe if I had just been having sex at 16, I would have been happy enough with that.'

This time it went on a little further.

We piled all this onto the recurring issue of her bragging about the things she had done before, but then refusing to do them with me. And when I drank, I liked to pick fights, and this was an easy one to start.

'You're so immature.' She said.

'Yeah,' I said, 'Well, maybe there's more to it than just taking it up the ass as a kid.'

'I wasn't a kid.' She said.

'You were where I come from.' I said.

'It's normal here.' She said.

'That's normal here?' I said. 'Jesus Christ. So if I went around and asked French women if they got fucked in the ass at 16, they would say, 'Yes.''

'Normal in Marseille.' She said.

'And you're proud of this shithole mentality?' I said. 'I still think you're full of shit about it being normal even in the asshole of France.'

She just rolled her eyes and made a loud huffing noise.

It started to worry me, that maybe there were some deep underlying differences in us that would last forever, if we lasted forever, if we had kids, would we teach them it's okay to get fucked in the ass at 16 or to maybe wait until they were at least an adult before taking it that far. Shit, I'd be happy if my kids waited as long as possible. Well, not too long, life is short. But the brain isn't even fully mature until 25, and sex fucked things up in life just as much as it made it great. I wanted any offspring of mine to have some shot at making it in life. Was this my Arkansas bible-belt coming out?

I couldn't help it. I didn't want them to grow up using sex for popularity, or just to get somebody's attention, or any other fucked up reason. Especially if I had a girl, a double standard or not, I wouldn't want her being judged. I knew it sounded heroic to not care what people thought, to do what you wanted, but I didn't know many people that were actually happy that way. Hell, maybe nobody was happy.

I was thinking like a parent. My parents even. I guess you can never really escape them. But I understood why so many parents were like that. You didn't want to point them or allowing them in the wrong direction, at least not until they were an adult and out on their own and making their own decisions.

Then I realized it was something more than just sexual experimentation - which I would have been okay with. I could tell she was almost ashamed of it and was just defending herself because I was attacking. And I knew it wasn't just a culture thing.

Alice was actually a lot more of a saint than myself with sex. Yes, she started younger, probably normal by most standards, and I started late by most standards. But that was always the case with any girl I dated and it never bothered me. Alice was a good girl and had nothing but a few long-term relationships before me. I was the whore of this relationship and here I was giving her shit about her sex life.

But more than anything, I wanted to understand why she did what she did. For someone so timid and from a good family, why was she attracted to that so young. Was she just doing it in a desperate attempt to be loved, to be accepted and appreciated?

I looked at her and I knew I would never get my answer out of her.

We were both quiet.

I just looked at her and she looked at

me with those eyes. Eyes that were angry, but mostly sad.

I was falling in love with this girl. That's why I wanted to pick apart her life and understand every part of her, to understand why she made every decision she made. I didn't give a shit if I was being unfair or going overboard with my gestapo. I was vetting her like some CEO taking on a new partner. I wanted her to be more than just a friend I spent time with.

Shit.

I hugged her and she let me.

We talked things out a little, and we seemed to be good.

Then we played the Sims together. Well, she played, and I watched with amusement. It was nice. We cuddled and pretended to be a little family. She made me a writer and let me pick the names of the books I wrote.

'The Kepi Blanc with Shoe Polish'

'Simba the Kiki King'

'Found in Translation'

There were a few others and then my favorite, 'Sex, Farts, and Skydiving.'

I figured if I ever wrote a book, I would call it 'Found in Translation' with the prequel being 'Sex, Farts, and Skydiving.'

Then I stayed up all night wondering if this would work out.

#

The next morning was another Monday

morning. I was still unresolved with myself about what I wanted, but I was tired of thinking about it and tired of feeling that way. Moving forward always seemed erratic, two steps forward, one step back, but the thought of going forward this way though, a day job, one day at a time, did not seem like the reason for living, the modus operandi.

I needed to go for a run to clear my head. It had been almost two weeks since my last one. I wasn't quite the runner I used to be with my leg, mostly in distance; it didn't slow me down too much. It just left me more sore the next day. An internal pang rather than just a tired muscle. Shit, it was that time of year though, between Thanksgiving and New Year, gaining a few pounds would keep me on the modus operandi.

I would trudge through my classes and days.

61

Claudia was still on my mind from time to time. I wondered how she was doing. If she was happy. How I would react if I saw her. I got a nervous feeling thinking about it. It had been so long since I had seen her. I figured that was why it would be weird. The last few times I had seen her I was okay, no strong feelings either way. Whatever I felt, I doubted I would see her again soon. We had avoided each other this long. That was once again her decision, as we had slept together a few more times after Aurora, until she told me she was having feelings for the other guy she had been seeing and wanted to make things work with him. Then I met Alice a few days later.

I still didn't know how to feel about her. We were well beyond closure. It had been 10 months since she moved out and 4 months since we last slept together, yet I was still feeling something inside of me for her that seemed to set up its own private room inside me, refusing to leave.

I wasn't sure if it was love, but maybe a reminder of another disappointment and failure in my life. A rocky past that would stick with me forever like shell shock. It made me feel sorry for her she got that part of me, but the truth remained that Claudia was the past and Alice was the present and possible future.

Just as I finished that thought, Alice

texted me. Funny how those things happened,
it made you believe in a Jungian collective
unconscious.

'I just want to say,' She said. 'To
add on to our conversation last weekend
that I thought a lot about what you said
about values. I didn't have any before. But
I do now. And I want to develop them. I
appreciate your values and the fact you
have them, and I hope in the future, as we
grow, our values will mesh together.'

'Nice idea.' I thought. But I doubted
I had any real values. I had imaginary ones
passed down onto me I yelled without
thought, but they weren't mine. They
belonged to others, and I was now enforcing
them on those I cared about. It was an ugly
thought, and I hated myself for it as I
reread the text.

I talked to Pierre a little about it.
I talked to him about everything with
emotional conflicts. Most of the time, I
didn't agree with his way of thinking being
as Christian Orthodox as he was, but he was
a good guy for unloading on.

'Alice's good for you, mate.' He said.

'I am happy with her.' I said.

'You look happier.' He said. 'I
thought you would not make it through the
summer.'

'Yeah,' I said.

'I never want to see you in your own
blood again.' He said.

'Okay, Pierre.' I said.

'Seriously, mate, that scared the shit
out of me.'

'Well, all good now.' I said.

'You're still seeing the psychologist?'

'Mostly.'

'Keep going.' He said. 'I'll pay for it if I have to.'

'You don't have the money for that, Pierre.' I said.

He didn't respond.

'So I just don't know what my future is with her.'

'What are you talking about?' He said.

'Alice.' I said, 'I mean I care for her, but I can care for a friend. Would I enjoy her as a partner? The aspirations and standards raise when you talk about that possibility.'

Pierre just gave me a look like I was an idiot.

'It's not fair to put that kind of pressure on her so early,' I said, 'but it's also not fair to find out in six months that she's not the one and break her heart.'

'Don't fuck this up, Will.' Pierre said.

'I'll stick it out then.' I said. 'And leave the question in the back of my head.' I thought.

62

Alice let me come in her mouth, which was an achievement for me, to overcome the thought of doing something like that. I couldn't figure out why I could never do it before, why it was such a mental block for me. How it seemed so normal for the rest of the world and yet more disgusting to me than to her, or any of them. But she was patient with me. Worked at it. And worked at it until I came. It was amazing. A victory of some sort I couldn't describe, but a victory. But only for about five minutes, until it bombarded me with guilt. Why would I do that to her or any other woman? I just became another guy on her list of guys that had done the same thing to her, except they were before me. And not only did they come before me, they had many times before. Well, I played it in my mind as many times, truthfully it probably wasn't as often as I made myself believe.

If I found it disgusting myself, how can I truly accept it as a victory, especially when I was supposed to casually accept all the other's she has taken? Her soft lips on so many other cocks. Not that many cocks I guess, but the amount of times I still tortured myself imagining. Imagining her at 15 or 16, so much younger than she was now, wrapping her lips around a penis.

I felt so immature by a girl younger than me, by the world. I was too far

behind. If I thought of her doing these
things as an adult, it wouldn't bother me,
but she did more as a teenager than an
adult and I could only see this young,
innocent version of the girl I know cared
about as some manipulated porn star.

I could talk about this shit with
Claudia or Maju or anybody else, but
Claudia waited until 20 and Maju waited
until she was 18. Alice started fucking at
15, taking it in the ass at 16, and
swallowing come ever since. And not just
for one lover, but many. Men she thought
she loved, but admitted she wasn't happy
with.

There wasn't anything I could do about
this, but the thoughts always came back
like cockroaches. The more I tried to swat
them, kill them, the more they would come
out of other corners of my mind. It was my
mind that was the problem. Not her or her
exes. It was my mind, and I knew it, but I
would continue to take it out on her
whenever drunk and given the opportunity.

My logical side was one side, and it
worked out okay. Most of the time, I was
okay with the cockroaches. The lights were
on; they were in their dark corners, out of
sight and I wouldn't even think about them.
But then once a month, that one hour of
every month where it crept in and haunted
me ruined any chance of me being happy with
her.

I wasn't sure if trying to find a new
love would be the answer, at least not in
France if my issue was about my

insecurities with sex and this country and
its women were half as sexually mature as
Alice claimed they were. I figured I would
keep my eyes open, but then again, maybe
that's what the issue was all together, an
escape route. A way to run from this girl.

She was a good girl, and that scared
me that things might work out between us if
I stopped fighting it. But I wasn't ready
to stop fighting. I wasn't ready to settle.

What shit.

I was having a hard time swallowing.

#

I had the day off and I woke up with a
sore stomach and a headache that had been
with me for a few days. I was supposed to
go to Cassis today, then a show at work. I
just wanted to stay at home and relax, but
I did my best to convince myself to make
the most of it. I knew it would make Alice
happy.

Lisa texted me saying we wouldn't be
able to meet up this week and that our next
appointment would be in January. All the
better. I couldn't be bothered sitting on
the couch. It wasn't her or the hour we
spent together. It was the idea that I had
to be there at all that bothered me.

I had a dream about a hotel,
skydiving, and fishing. I wished the shit
made sense to me afterwards. It was like I
had the keys, but couldn't find the car.

Besides waking up sick to confusing
dreams, I had more dreams about Claudia.

She was dating an old sergeant of mine from the Air Force. It wasn't as weird as I thought it should be, especially since in the dream we had just broken up. The weird part was an old legionnaire buddy of mine, Buell, was having a training camp in my apartment with a bunch of shirtless men. It seemed kind of gay and I didn't bother asking what the hell was going on.

My headache was still there as the day progressed and my throat became sore. I was sure I was sick.

I talked to Alice about the shit in my mind.

She understood but found it unattractive. She was right. But then she said she got jealous all the time too. I wanted to correct her I wasn't jealous, but envious, but I let her go on. She got jealous whenever Claudia would post something on my Facebook wall.

'It makes me want to vomit.' She said, 'But I control my feelings. I do my breathing exercises.'

It made me feel a little better that she got that way too. She controlled it better than I did though. I just got drunk and yelled about it.

She impressed me. Younger than me, no great trips to India or Nepal to find calmness, she found it in a fucking breathing exercise here in her own country. A breathing exercise and she was as calm as a Hindu cow. Voila. Maybe this woman would be good for me. Maybe she just might be the one to save me.

\#

It wasn't quite the weekend or the holidays yet, and I had another class to teach. I hadn't prepared for it and was struggling to come up with something new with my mind elsewhere. The conversation with Alice seemed to put me through the five stages of grief, and I was finding any random ideas I had for the lesson plan to be boring. A news article. No. Friday the 13th folklore. Fuck no. I'd just wing it.

63

I was sick all weekend and kept mostly to myself.

Kay had come in at five in the morning coked up, and I talked to him for a couple of hours until he passed out and snored the morning away, keeping me up. When I finally fell asleep, I must've been woken up about 15 times from my phone.

Pierre.

Voicemail.

Claudia.

Alice.

Repeat.

Pierre didn't answer when I called him back.

Claudia was next.

'Coucou,' she said, 'ça va?'

'Yeah, Claudia,' I said. 'What's up?'

'Just wanted to know what the name of that show was that we watched together that one time.' She said.

'What show Claudia?' I said.

'That show we watched together.'

'We watched a lot of shows together.'

'That funny show you made me watch.'

'When you say show,' I said, 'do you mean TV show or movie?'

'TV show.' She said. 'But I think it was a movie too.'

'Okay,' I said. 'And how many movies have we seen together?'

'Uff,' she said, 'I think it was Swedish or something. They had funny voices, remember?'

'Klovn?' I said.

'I think that's it.' She said.

'That's Danish.' I said. 'Look it up and let me know.'

I heard her tapping away on her keyboard.

'Klovn with a 'k' and a 'v'.' I said.

'That's it!' She said.

'Okay,' I said, 'enjoy watching it with him.'

'Oh, Will,' she said.

'Bye Claudia.'

Then I called Alice. Best for last, I thought. Or worst, I still wasn't sure where we stood with each other.

'Bonjour, mon cherie,' she said, 'Ça va? Tu te sens mieux?'

'Better now.' I said.

'Tant mieux,' she said, 'Il est toujours bon si je viens ce soir?'

'I think so.' I said.

'Did you just wake up?' She said.

'I guess so.' I said.

She laughed.

'Okay,' she said, 'A tout a l'heure. Je t'appelle quand j'arrive, d'accord?'

'Okay.' I said. 'Bisous.'

'Bisous, mon cheri.'

Well, back to the real world. I needed to clean the place up a little. Clean myself up even more. I still needed to do a favor for Swanlove. And I should knock out the lesson plans for the week before Alice arrived.

Just as soon as I can roll out of bed.

Living the dream in the south of
France.

Made in the USA
Middletown, DE
08 March 2020